NEVER BE ANOTHA: *REPENTANT*

Book 2

Troii Devereaux

Never Be Anotha: Repentant Book 2
By Troii Devereaux

This is a work of fiction. Names, characters, places, and incidents are the product of the author's imagination or are used fictitiously. Any resemblance to actual persons, living or dead, events or locales is entirely coincidental.

First paperback edition September 2019
Book design by SheerGenius

ISBN 9781693292668 (paperback)

Contact us and leave feedback about the book at www.AKTPublishing.com.

ACKNOWLEDGEMENTS

Life is absolutely GREAT! This past couple of years has taken me through all types of emotions. Worry, stress, sadness, pain, tears, sleeplessness, brokenness, excitement, strength, gratefulness, thankfulness, impatience, humility, joy... the list could go on and on. I STILL give all honor and glory to the most High, my Lord and Savior, as always. And I know He will never place more on my shoulders than I can handle. I am ecstatic to experience what God has in store for not only me, but also everyone connected to me! 'My Cup Runneth Over', thanks to Him!

I would like to sincerely thank my husband, family and friends for the continued support. Without their support and encouragement to step out on faith and follow my dreams, I'm not sure that I would have had the confidence to do it. Special mentions include Tuloria Knight, Phillip Knight, Sharon Waters, Britney Harold, Shalethia Taylor, Adrianne Harley (my BOMB stylist), Terrakah Harold, Calvin Knight and Tiffney Steverson.

A few others that deserve special mention during this journey: my soulmate, Monique Ayala, if it wasn't for you, I'd still be at square one trying to figure out how to get my works published in the first place! Thank you for setting up the book signing and the news interview. I'm still in awe of you and all that we accomplished together this summer! My little protector and BIG piece of my heart, you are irreplaceable, and I pray for your heart's desires because you deserve everything that God has in store for you and so much more!

Christy Mair, thanks big sis, for always making yourself available to support everything that has to do with me in general, anytime I've needed you without fail. From the intimate book signing you set up to the content editing of my manuscript, your tremendous support does not go unnoticed and I thank you from the bottom of my heart. Ladies, I am indebted to you for your contributions to my projects, love you both forever!

I want to thank the rest of my tribe: James Walker, thank you for the assistance with the research needed to make my first book work, and I'll never forget that; Stephanie Glover, for the business assists and late night talks off the ledge; Lilliana Harris (aka Lilli~Ann), for translating and being there through the good bad and the ugly, with no judgment and also keeping me sane through all successes and challenges; Adrianne Johnson, friend, for being my personal counselor and prayer warrior; Takesha Anderson, for always keeping it real no matter what; Tamika Baker, for your direct support, feedback and love through it all; Ramona Miller, for the unending support and, love and friendship. I am thankful that God brought you back into my life last year, as a piece of my heart was truly missing; Rachel Faulkner, thank you for being my sounding board and temporary retreat from everything I was going through; Tomika Smith, Nikima Porter and Sherika Dyer for pushing me to do what I love! I appreciate you all and love you so much for believing in and sharing my art. Muah!

To everyone I haven't personally named, I didn't forget about you. Whether it was a share on social media, a purchase you made directly from me or via Amazon, kinds words and/or motivation you extended during my journey... I am truly grateful for the support. I couldn't have done any of this without YOU! So again, I thank you, and look forward to having a "drank" – on me – together! (I'm serious, I got you!)

Being completely retired now, after a twenty-year career with the United States Air Force has unquestionably encouraged me to step outside of my comfort zone and challenge myself to do something for the next 20 years and beyond (Lord-willing), that I enjoy. I will forever be thankful to this organization, for the values and foundation that have been instilled in me. I pray that I can continue to support the men and women who serve honorably and proudly.

Last but certainly not least, this book and every work that I produce is and will always be dedicated to my mother, Deleatrice A. Knight. Thank you for passing on your love of reading to me at such a young age. I know you are looking down from Heaven and saying, "well done." It is my life's goal to make you proud of me, by living out my dreams. I just wish you were here with me; that would be the only thing that would make this absolutely perfect. I will love you always. Rest in Heavenly peace, Mommie. Damn, I miss you. Part of me left when you did, but your memory will always be cherished. I believe that God doesn't make mistakes though.

I am also dedicating this book to my big brother, Alton D. Taylor. You've been in my corner for as long as I can remember. I appreciate your candid suggestions and feedback because you totally get me and how my mind works. You know how completely sensitive I am when it comes to anything dealing with life in general because I'm super sensitive. But you've never judged me. In addition to this journey, you've always been able to articulate what I needed to hear in the very best way. Love you always, and I cannot wait to link up and live out the rest of our lives together! I'm so proud- and I've always been proud of YOU! What you've endured, only the strongest survive. The best of us make the biggest mistakes and thrive after the storm. I am YOUR biggest fan!! Love you big Bruh, Bruh! Love, Goofball

As I said in the last book, FELLAS (and my ladies who love the ladies), buy this book for your woman/man and thank me later! From the feedback that I received thus far, all I can say is if you haven't purchased your copy of Resentment (Book 1) and this installment, you're missing out on all of this goodness and you better get on it!

Love and blessings to you all. Muah!

-Troii Dev ☺

Table of Contents

Chapter 1

Three Months Later

James

"Hey Princess, you hungry? Come on let daddy feed you, baby." I cooed to Tamia. She wasn't my daughter by blood, but just looking at her you wouldn't know. Tamia was born on June sixteenth, my thirty-first birthday, and I couldn't have received a greater present. She weighed six pounds, thirteen ounces and was nineteen inches long. A little thing that fit right in the crook of my arm like it was made just for her. She was a bright little thing, with these amazing big brown eyes that just penetrated your soul. She had so much hair, just a pretty ass baby!

I fixed her a bottle and changed her because I wanted to let Fresia rest. Tamia was only a few weeks old and I'm just in love times two. Free started school again, and she was so enamored with our daughter and being a new mom. It came so natural to her and although I know she's happy, I catch her crying sometimes. After the first few times that I witnessed her tears, I just would come over and hold her. I knew she was missing her mom. There was nothing I could do but support her during those times.

Fresia

It's a little after three in the morning and I hear James singing to the baby while he feeds her through the baby monitor. He is just the best daddy I could ever hope for; our little family is so blessed. You wouldn't know she wasn't biologically his by looking at them. He's not as light as me, but his pecan brown complexion could have produced her just the same. And Tamia's smile, it's big just like his.

After that one time Rob just showed up to my house, I never saw or heard from him again. I figured James took care of him. I didn't ask questions, I understood what he did while working for

Money. They had been a team for years, and Money always treated me with respect even if James' family did not due to my past as a stripper.

I'm so thankful to God that James is back in my life. We broke up a couple of years ago because James couldn't get used to the fact that his boys could see my naked body any time since I was working at the club they frequented. He met me there, but he couldn't handle it. Go figure! My daughter's biological father, on the other hand, was this piece of shit that I was thirsty over in recent years. I still to this day, can't figure out what was going through my mind and why I allowed him to use my body in whatever sexual way he chose.

Robert dated my ex-friend Aubrey from college. I would always flirt with him, but he would never bite. His reputation wasn't that great, but he was fine though. He had to be at least about six foot three, with his chocolate brown skin. Rob kept his hair cut low and he was slender, but his frame was muscular. After he and Aubrey got together, she hung out with me and our other friend Sanai less and less, until she was just no longer available. I saw her around, but Rob seemed to be the center of her world. I realize now, I was jealous because no man ever took me seriously. I also have since realized it was because I didn't take myself seriously either. If I could go back to that sunny day almost two years ago, I would probably do a few things differently.

Over a year ago

I had pulled over near the Target after I finished shopping because my car was pulling more to one side than the other. I hoped it wasn't anything more serious than me needing to get a new tire or something. Damn, I don't have time for this shit today! I am not prepared for car trouble because it is awfully hot for it to be early April. I got out of my car, and after surveying the damage I retrieved my phone from my purse in the front seat, with the intention of calling for car assistance. I then saw a familiar face pull up behind me.

I adjusted my perky triple D's, which made them a bit more visible in my low-cut blouse and checked my reflection in the passenger window. The man got out of his car and I stood there with my back to him while scrolling on my phone. I wanted him to have the best view of my sexy heart-shaped ass.

Nice Man

"Excuse me, Miss Lady, do you need some help?" he asked me. When I turned around, his demeanor changed quickly, as the recognition set in.

Free

"Rob is that you?" Of course, I knew it was him. "Hell yeah, you can help me! Boy come over here and give me a hug! How you been doing, boo?" I replied excitedly.

Rob

"Hey Fresia, how you been?" I replied with less enthusiasm than I'm sure she would have preferred. "I'm doing good, on my way to handle some biz before I check up on Aubrey."

Free

We hugged and I made sure to slightly grab his butt before letting him out of the embrace. I momentarily hit him with the stank face at the mention of Aubrey, but he didn't say anything. Then I decided I was gonna play with him a bit.

"Oh, y'all still together. I ain't heard from her in a minute, I didn't know what was going on with her. Why you don't come to the club anymore? I've been trying to get you in the Champagne room for a minute, you know for a private dance... or whatever you wanna do." I said as I shrugged my shoulders a bit.

Rob

"Yeah, *we* just been chilling, and I haven't had a reason to go to a strip club. *My girl* got all that covered."

Free

I guess he was trying to keep Aubrey in the conversation, but I know I was looking damn good. Smelling good too… my voluptuous body was on display in the liquid leggings that hugged the curve of my ass sitting just right. He was damn near salivating at the sight of me, and I couldn't blame him. I knew I had it going on and then some. I saw the way he kept trying to sneak a peek at my titties through my halter top as well. I never needed a bra. It was as if God spent a little more time sculpting me than most.

Rob

"Let me change this tire for you." He said as he shook his head. "You got a spare?" Rob asked.

Free

"Yeah, let me get it for you baby." I said as I sauntered past him. I purposely switched my ass and made it jiggle just a little bit, while reaching inside the trunk for the spare tire. "I'm not sure how to take it out though, do you mind getting it for me? I don't wanna break a nail." I asked seductively with my perfectly manicured finger in my mouth.

Rob

"Yeah, no doubt." He said as he proceeded to retrieve the spare.

Free

I laughed a little bit on the inside at the plan I had just come up with in my mind. As he was changing the tire, I bent over real close to him and started asking questions that I already knew the answers to. I made sure to bend over close enough to the side of his face, that he would easily gain the best view of the inside of my blouse.

I knew it would just be a matter of time before the thoughts of 'Miss Perfect' Aubrey would be out of his mind. I inched closer and closer to him as he finished up with the spare. He had to maneuver awkwardly around me as he stood to his feet. It was warm, but I think the sweat popping up on his forehead was due to the discomfort of me being so close to him. I knew he was trying to maintain control of the situation. But I have my wiles about me.

Rob

"Alright, I'm done Free. It was nice seeing you." He said as he started to bid me farewell.

Free

"Thank you so much Rob, but I'm a little nervous driving on it. Would you mind following me home?" I asked as I drew even more attention to my beautiful breasts by adjusting the halter I was wearing. "It's only about fifteen minutes from here, in Waldorf."

Rob

I paused for a bit before answering. "Yeah, no problem, just drive slower so you don't have an accident on the way."

Free

Rob agreed as I smirked while getting in my car. I had to get him out of his head before he could resist me. Luckily, I didn't live far. I drove just a little faster than he advised, to ensure we got there a bit faster. On the way to my house, I refreshed my perfume and put some gum in my mouth. Once I pulled into my driveway, I made sure to hurry up and park, so he couldn't just pull off without saying goodbye.

Rob

"It was nice seeing you. Take care, Free." Rob said hurriedly.

Free

"Oh Rob, would you mind helping me with my bags please? I have quite a bit of stuff in the back seat. I had to purchase a new microwave and I have no way of getting it inside by myself. Pretty please?" I sensed his hesitation, but he told me he would help me. After getting everything inside, I offered him something to eat and drink, but he declined.

Rob

"Could I use your bathroom though?" He asked me nervously while trying not to look anywhere but my face.

Free

"Yeah, but you'll have to use my upstairs bathroom because this one down here is under construction." I hoped he would believe me, because had he looked into the bathroom that was right behind him, he would've noticed that the bathroom had nothing at all wrong with it. I told him to follow me as I swayed my hips provocatively up the staircase. I led him into my very elaborately decorated master suite. The first thing that anyone lucky enough to make it into my bedroom saw, was this very gorgeous full body portrait of myself. Did I mention that the only thing I was wearing in the artwork was my beautiful curves? I saw his mouth drop briefly, and that's when I knew I had him.

"See something you like?" I giggled from behind him while he was seemingly frozen in place. I started to slowly undress after he went into the bathroom and closed the door behind him. I wouldn't doubt that he was hard as a brick behind that door. I spritzed my comforter with Bath and Body Works body spray in the scent 'Warm Vanilla Sugar' and proceeded to alluringly position myself on my king-sized bed to set the seductive ambiance. Once he emerged from the restroom, Rob had a clear view of my manicured garden, from the angle I granted him. He stood there long enough to internally battle with himself about what he would do next. Then, he turned as if he was about to walk out of the door.

Free

"Rob come on, I just need you to help me with one more little thing and then you can go. Please don't say no." I purred while caressing my thigh, which was as smooth as butter cream.

Rob

"Yo, but why are you naked? What is it you want me to help you with while you're naked? You know I got a girl and she used to be your friend at that." I swallowed hard. "This is real scandalous, Free."

Free

It seemed he was trying to talk himself out of what he knew he would and wanted do next. "Rob you know you won't let Aubrey be my friend or anyone else's, so please stop. I just need a little oil on my back where I can't reach." I made sure to roll over onto my stomach and arrange my body in a way I knew he wouldn't be able to resist. I then pointed at the back of my neck that I feigned not being able to reach.

I was definitely setting him up for the kill, by arching my back and allowing him to smell the tantalizing scent of my sex. Eventually, he relented and picked up the bottle of oil and warmed it between his hands. As he spread the oil from my neck and down to the small of my back, I then "encouraged" him to massage the oil onto my ass and then into each of my breasts, one by one. After I was fully facing him, I unbuckled his belt and unfastened his jeans while bent over and proceeded to twerk my ass for his viewing pleasure.

"You like what you see baby?" I asked him as I removed his large member from his boxers. I was pleasantly surprised, as I didn't expect it to be so impressive. I slowly took him into my mouth until I heard his shallow breaths. I could tell that he was completely awestruck at the skill of the disappearing act I performed with his shaft.

Rob

"Damn shawty, you doin that shit!"

Free

Got 'em! His eyes started to roll into the back of his head, and he was so into it that this felt like we were puzzle pieces. It was as if we had done this before. In that moment, I was thinking to myself, 'yeah nigga, you've been missing out on all of this running behind Aubrey's "picture perfect" ass.'

Rob

"Fuck yeah, deep throat that shit bitch."

Free

I don't know why that turned me on even more, but I started going in even harder once he referred to me as a bitch. I definitely get off on that shit.

Rob

"I'm about to nut all down your throat. Ahhhhhh sssshhhhhhiiiiittttttttttt!!! Damn baby, oooohhhh shit!"

Free

His nectar flowed into my mouth and down my throat while I watched his knees get weak. He had to grab onto my nightstand to maintain his balance. I chuckled a bit as I thought it was pretty funny. "Did you like that baby? Just know you can get that and more, any time you want it. I know Aubrey can't do you like that." He grabbed my face roughly and threatened me after mentioning "her" name. She couldn't be too special. Shit, he was here with me after all.

Rob

"Look hoe, you say anything about this to anyone and I'll beat the fuck outta you. You hear me bitch? My girl better not ever hear nothing about this." Rob threatened.

Free

"Mmmm, I gotchu daddy." I said as I guided his fingers into my mouth erotically. "You can have all of this anytime you want it." I know I turned him on because his sex was saluting me yet again, as he tried to act all hard.

He pushed me on the bed, bent me over and proceeded to knock the bottom out of my pussy as she purred right back to him. He placed me in all types of positions, all of which I thoroughly enjoyed. It had been a good minute since a man had shown me such pleasure. I lost count of how many orgasms I experienced and was already counting down the days until I would see him again!

When it was his turn, he directed me to get on my knees and painted my face with his seed. I was on such a high, that I just gave him my number and told him to come back whenever he wanted to. My body was in an instant pleasure zone that I enjoyed for the rest of that evening and I tried my best not to check my cell phone for his call every five minutes. I was hooked, off of one encounter that would haunt me for some time.

Present Day

I essentially became a prisoner in my own home when he was around after that. And I'm still not sure how he convinced me to allow his ass to have a spare key to the home that I paid all the bills for. How did I ever manage to consent to his use of my body as his personal playground, whenever and however he wanted? I'm not even the type of woman to make it that easy for a man that does absolutely nothing for me.

I did manage to receive a great blessing out of the entire disenchanting ordeal with Rob though. But enough of the history surrounding that fool, I was truly in a very positive space now. I am so thankful to God for James, and *our* daughter Tamia. She's an angel. I started to fall asleep to the beautiful thoughts of the present and started to dream of a better future than my past.

James

After getting the baby back down, I got back in the bed with Fresia and dozed off into a deep sleep. "This is what life is supposed to be like", I thought as I drifted off, still a bit uneasy about not knowing what happened with Rob. He didn't make the same mistake of owing Money anything like the last time he disappeared, but they hadn't seen him anywhere. Neither him, nor his bitch had made an appearance as of late.

Sam

Things have been going so well in both my personal and professional lives. My practice has broken ground and we should be fully operational some time later in the winter. My focus was choosing furnishings, hiring staff, and ensuring the contractors were on time according to the schedule. Personally, I was having the time of my life! Joseph is absolutely amazing and just brings out such a different side of me. We're together all of the time, and we have double dated with Aubrey and Monroe.

At first, things were a bit awkward with the double dating. I know Joseph and Aubrey were still working out the kinks in their friendship, but I just had a feeling there was a bit more to it. I do know that he was interested in Aubrey at one time, and I thought I saw him looking at her in a longing kind of way a few times. Lately, I haven't felt that way, and have since pushed it to the back of my mind.

Joe

I think I'm in love, I thought to myself. Samantha is the woman I never knew I needed. She's so loving, ambitious, beautiful... and as it turns out, my personal little porn star. She's willing to try anything, but I haven't worked up the nerve to ask about adding anyone to our sex games. Such a lady on the clock, but behind closed doors, she's my little freak. Damn, my dick jumps every time I think about her ass. And speaking of her ass, I think that thang is a little plumper since I've been hitting it. And the pussy, oooh, it fits my dick like a glove! I've written my name all in and over that gushy!!

Ever since that night months ago, when I got my wires crossed with Aubrey, Samantha and I have been together constantly. I originally went over to Sam's house with the plan to ask Aubrey out, after I thought she had taken enough time to get over her failed relationship with that dickhead, Rob. It wasn't until I got there that I realized she wanted Samantha and I to hook up. Even through all of the shit I did for her, walking her to and from her car every day just in case she ran into that bitch ass, Rob. Consoling her through all her tears and not once taking advantage of her. Listening to her go on and on about that nigga.... I felt she owed me *something*!

Well, whatever. I'm happy with Samantha now, but I do hold a bit of animosity towards Aubrey. She's still so damn fine to me. I could've treated her right; I would have done anything to make her happy. I could make that beautiful body feel good. I still dreamt of getting the chance to please that little pussy. Mmmmm, my dick is getting hard just thinking about it. I mean, what did her new dude have that I didn't? Monroe is cool and all, but he benefitted from what I was able to help her heal from. *I* did that. But my lady deserved better than that, so I would let it go… for now.

"Babe, the food is almost done, are you ready to eat?" I asked her. I heard her footsteps as she started walking towards me, and she let me know she's on the phone. She had on this little teddy, so I thought I'd play with her. She's so professional, so she had no choice but to go with it, and from the sound of it, she wasn't nearing the end of the conversation. That beautiful, smooth butterscotch skin with that sexy red hair.

I turned off the stove and removed the bacon. The eggs were already scrambled, fruit was cut, and I decided to wait until we were actually ready to eat to make the toast. She sat at the dining room table with papers spread in front of her and the phone was in her hand. She wasn't facing me, so it was perfect for me to be able to crawl underneath the table undetected.

Sam

"Greg, I did not order eggplant C20, I ordered eggplant in the shade C48. It's a difference. I do not want C20," Sam replied incredulously. It was all in the details for me when it came to my practice. Greg was trying to convince me that the other shade would be better. I was not interested in debating him on what I wanted. People already hated going to the dentist, so I did not want people to be uncomfortable when they entered my building because with dental surgery there's an extra nervousness associated with it. My specialty as an orthodontist, primarily deals with correcting the position of the jaws and/or teeth and occlusion.

Suddenly, I felt Joe gently separating my thighs underneath the table. "What are you doing?" I whispered as I pointed to the phone to let him know that I was indeed conducting business. He just put his finger to his lips, as if saying "shhhhh". Okay, so these are the type of games we're playing. He knew I couldn't resist him. I just hoped Greg couldn't hear my labored breathing. I was so turned on right now.

Joe

I pulled her body to the edge of the chair and grazed my lips across her center as I prepared her for what I was about to do. I knew that she loved when I paid special attention to her pussy, so I wanted to do it every chance I got. I blew onto her clit before diving in. I licked and sucked gently, as she tried not to make any noise during her phone call.

After thrusting my tongue in and out of her wetness, I locked in on her "love button", as she called it, and suckled her while licking at the same time. I spelled her name over and over with my tongue, until I felt her swell. I then inserted two fingers into her pussy and resumed the pleasurable assault on her g-spot and her clitoris simultaneously, until she orgasmed. She was a trooper, because she was able to put the phone on speaker and on mute so she would still be able to hear what her colleague was talking about and moan freely.

When she came down from that temporary high and I was sure that I savored every last drop, I emerged from under the table smiling. I'm sure all of my teeth were showing as she was completely beet red and looked like she needed a nap. I resumed my duties in the kitchen, fixing breakfast until my lady was ready to eat.

Aubrey

Work had been uneventful, but I was happy that Joe and I were able to rekindle our friendship. It's like we're besties again, and back to making fun of the "peanut gallery". Marie, our receptionist, still can't stand me for whatever reason and makes little comments like she's bragging about something. I don't pay her crazy ass no mind. But she does look better. Even though she won't let either of the practitioners fix the huge gap in her front teeth, her skin is glowing, she has a little bit more confidence about her, and she's been less chatty. She used to talk about everyone's business. She's given her two weeks' notice though. I heard her telling people she was moving out of state with her new man. Good for her!

Monroe and I have been doing very well. We managed to go on that trip to Mexico with my mother and my stepfather. It was the best week I'd had in such a long while. I had my two favorite people together, my man and my mommy. We spent a week there and I can't be sure who's more in love with Monroe, me or my mom. She's such a trip!! My phone started ringing as I recalled the love that was made during that getaway.

Monroe

"Hey Beautiful, I'm near your job. Wanna do lunch?" Monroe asked.

Aubrey

"Yes, babe. You got a taste for anything in particular?" I replied. Monroe was so fine. His mocha brown skin, muscular build with broad shoulders and curly black hair that he kept close cut made my heart flutter. I looked forward to seeing him any chance I got.

Monroe

"Other than you, not really." I said seductively. We both chuckled a little bit at that remark. She's been working so hard lately, and I've been absolutely craving her. She had this beautiful and soft mahogany skin, those mesmerizing hazel eyes and that plump ass and curvaceous body that I couldn't get enough of. She was just gorgeous. I stopped and picked up some tulips, her favorite, and I decided to make my lady feel special on her job today.

Aubrey

"Babe, you know I'm down with that. What you tryna do to me at work?" Now he knows it doesn't take much to get me wet for him. Shoot, forget lunch, we need to go park that car and get it in. But I know he won't do it. He told me that's behavior for side chicks. I'll convince him one day though.

Monroe

I pulled into the parking lot adjacent to Aubrey's job. As I was getting out of the car, I noticed Rob's girl, Marie, walking to what I presume was her vehicle. I ducked back into my car to see what she was doing. Looked like she was moving out of somewhere. She was driving an older model, burgundy Nissan. I was able to write down her license plate as she pulled away. Once she was out of sight, I walked into Aubrey's clinic to take her the flowers.

Aubrey

"Thank you, baby! My favorite, I love these!! Let me put these in my office so these chicken heads can be even more jealous!" I laughed. I noticed he was a little distracted. "What's going on babe? What has your attention?"

Monroe

"Did a young lady with a gap in her teeth come out of your building or the next one?"

Aubrey

"Oh, you talking about Marie? Yeah, she's our receptionist. This is her last week, she's moving out of town with her man soon, I guess. Good riddance though. Why, you know her?"

Monroe

"Nah, I know of her. You said this week is her last week here? Like Friday?"

Aubrey

"Yeah babe, you need me to call her for you?"

Monroe

"That's alright, Beautiful. I know someone that is looking for her. But she doesn't know me, so don't even mention it. You ready to go?"

Aubrey

“Yeah, let me put up these flowers and grab my purse.”

Monroe

Once Aubrey went to the back, I dialed James up.

<<<*ring, ring*>>>

James

“Boss, what’s going on? I thought you were taking the day off. You need something?” James questioned concerned.

Monroe

“Hey, man. You’ll never guess, so I’ll just tell you. Rob’s girl is the receptionist at Aubrey’s dental clinic. You have some paper and something to write with?”

James

“Yeah, Boss, go ahead.”

Monroe

“Her license plate is DMV nine one nine, Maryland tags. Find out what her address is, they are about to skip town.”

James

“Gotchu, Boss.” Finally, both Rob and his bitch were going to die! James thought to himself with satisfaction.

Chapter 2

James

I had been bugged enough by travel companies to practically remember their sales pitches to get unsuspecting folk like myself to purchase a vacation package. It happened back when I first met Fresia. When my cell phone rang with an unknown number from my hometown, I was just a bit rattled thinking something was off-center seeing that 'seven-five-seven' area code for the first time in years.

Three years ago

"Hello?"

Unknown caller

"Good afternoon, Mr. Casey?"

James

"Yes, this is Mr. Casey. Who is this?" I was a little irritated, because I got worried thinking something was going on with my mom or something. She had just gone down there for her high school reunion.

Unknown caller

"Mr. Casey, this is Demetrius Richards calling from Ellipsis Dream Vacation. It seems, you have qualified for a seven-day, six-night cruise aboard our well renowned ship, 'Destiny'. Now, I hope you have a few minutes to hear about this wonderful opportunity-…"

James

I heard him out, but I admit I was caught off guard at first. Come to find out, someone I knew referred me because he had had such a good time. I was excited! I had never been anywhere, and now that I knew this had nothing to do with my family back in Newport News, I was enthusiastic about going somewhere. And I knew just who I was going to go with.

This fine ass honey I had met in the club. She danced at Sugar's and went by the name Isis. She was so fine, and I just want to get her alone for a few days. About five foot five, coke bottle shape, phat booty on her with the prettiest titties I had ever seen. Maybe if I take her to the Bahamas, I can get to know her better. We had great conversations and she would just sit with me when I came in there. She wouldn't be dancing in that club and shit if she belonged to me. I know that. And she was way too fine to be single, so I hit her up to find out.

Isis

"Hey Jay, how are you today? You looking real good out here boo. You here by yourself tonight?"

James

"Yeah, I just came to holla at you real quick. You the one that is looking delicious." I scanned her from head to toe and she did a slow twirl for me. She looked at me with desire in her eyes and I knew I was making the right decision asking her to accompany me. She was feeling me too!

Isis

Jay doesn't usually come to the club on Thursday nights, but I was excited to see him. He was my favorite customer. And not because he tipped well, but because he treated me like I was someone's daughter. Like a real person.

His smile was genuine, we had real conversations. It wasn't just "ooh baby, turn around and clap that ass for me" or "bitch, open your legs wide so I can see them pretty ass lips" or "bend over and grab your ankles so I can blow in ya pussy". The dialogue we shared had much more depth. He was respectful, very interesting and oh so handsome. I invited him to the VIP room on a couple of occasions in the past, but he always told me we were good where we were. Maybe he just wasn't into me like that, but it's cool. I wasn't offended.

Had I known he was coming tonight I would have worn something a bit more special. All I had on was an open cup, black lace bustier, some pasties to cover my nipples and my matching black lace thong from Frederick's. I paired my lingerie with my six-inch Luscious brand clear heels with the two and a half-inch platforms. I didn't even wear any body glitter. Nothing was special about Mondays through Thursdays, but I made my debut every once in a while, depending on whether or not I had something to do, or if someone needed a favor.

"Jay, my set is about to start. Will you be here when I'm done? I would like to sit and talk with you for a bit."

James

"Of course, Isis. Do your thang." I said as I kissed her hand. She strutted her fine ass up to the DJ and requested a song. When she went to the back, he was staring at her walking away so long that I believe he got a little sidetracked. That was how she left you though. Mesmerized and mind fucked. Fine was an understatement to describe her.

The DJ started playing an older hit, "Love in this Club, Part II" by Usher, featuring Beyoncé. Once the first note played, she sauntered onto the stage with her eyes glued directly to me. There weren't very many people in the club this evening, but she still made me feel like it was just she and I.

As her set went on, she climbed up the pole and did this little move that I had mentioned to her that I loved, so I knew this dance was especially for me.

"Come a little closer, let Daddy put it on ya
Need you to know, what happens here stays here

Well I'm ready and willing, Mama's got to go
Gotcha standing at attention, keep it on the low

Ain't nobody watching, don't worry they can't see us
I know I got you hot, now let me in

You in the club or the car, wherever you are
Run and tell the DJ, run it back on replay..."

She spun down the pole deliberately, expending just the strength of her arms with her body upright clapping that ass just the way I liked while looking me in the eyes when she faced me. Once she touched down on the stage, she did this sexy little move that placed her on course, walking straight towards me. Once she got to the edge of the stage, she dropped down into a split with her back toward me, bent her body over and gyrated her ass in front of me. I had a clear view of how perfectly she groomed her pussy and I could see how wet she was, and I must say it was beckoning me forward. Before I knew it, I was so close that I could've tasted her right then and there. She definitely had me standing at attention and when the song finished, I had to force my mouth closed.

She didn't seem startled that I had made my way that close to her in the least bit and pecked me on the lips as she retreated from the stage. Once she made her rounds in the club and accepted her tips, she made her way back to me and told me she needed to freshen up a bit, but that she would be right back.

Isis

"Don't leave Jay, I won't be but a moment." How I got wet thinking of him while I was dancing was beyond me. I had pleasured myself with him in mind before, but I had never experienced anything like this. I went to the back and jumped in the shower briefly so that I could wash the light sheen of sweat off of me and to extinguish that fire between my legs before I did some things I would later regret with him.

After I was done changing into my leggings and crop top, I applied shea butter and rubbed the sweet pheromone oil onto my body. I grabbed my bag and headed out front to see James. To my dismay, he was no longer in the same seat he was sitting in when I left. I looked around, and no James.

James

I had to readjust myself… a few times, because I could have split bricks with the hard-on that I had. Isis' performance was one of a kind, and one I wouldn't soon forget. She would probably be in my dreams, literally, until whenever. And it was taking a bit longer than I would have liked to get myself together. I went into the restroom and splashed some water on my face. After a few minutes, I washed my hands and went back out into the club. Thankfully, there had been no one else inside the bathroom, or in the club for that matter, that would be paying any particular attention to me.

I then saw the gentleman with the roses that was usually in the club on weekends when I frequented and decided to purchase all of the flowers he had on him. He looked at me disbelievingly and then told me they don't allow him to stay in the club if he's not selling anything. Who knew, that this unsuspecting, older Eastern European man was in here enjoying and watching ass like the rest of us?

I offered to buy all but one, and he seemed content with that. I peeped his wedding ring and I wondered where his wife thought he was working most nights. I chuckled a bit to myself and then she walked out looking for me. I couldn't read the look on her face initially, but I knew she was searching for me. She seemed to be disappointed that I wasn't in the same spot she left me in. I walked up behind her and said, "You didn't think I was going to leave without telling you, did you?". The smile on her face was absolutely lovely. I inhaled her captivating scent that seemed to envelop me. I'm sure I was entranced in that moment.

Isis

I felt such relief that he was still here and when I turned around and he had flowers in his hands, I couldn't help but blush like a schoolgirl! "Thank you, Jay! This is so sweet!" I made sure to hug him tight, while also kissing him on the cheek. He then led me to a booth that was away from everyone and I was super curious about what he wanted to talk to me about.

James

She smelled so good, and looked as good as she always did, even with her clothes on. There was truly something special about her and I looked forward to getting to know her better. I told her about the trip, and she seemed as excited about it as I did. "But Isis, I have just one more question for you."

Isis

"Yes Jay, ask me anything." I cooed.

James

"What is your name?"

James

The dude on the phone offered me a deal I couldn't refuse! I purchased the seven-day, six-night cruise which sailed to Amber Cove, Dominican Republic; Nassau, Bahamas and then back. I was in Heaven with Isis, also known as her given name, Fresia. I would never admit to a woman turning me out but, she came as close to it as anyone probably ever would. And not just sexually, she had my mind intrigued like never before. She encouraged continuous deep conversation and once we got through the initial phase of getting to know one another my life seemed so tranquil.

Present Day

I was able to reach out to my contact from the police department to get Marie's address using the license plate combination that Monroe just relayed to me. I'd been watching and waiting to see if the lil nigga Rob is with her, but she always seemed to be by herself whenever she came and went. I know she lives on the second floor in apartment 202, but there's no way for me to confirm right now whether he's in there with her. So, I decided to get a little creative. I left for the evening and came back the next day, around the time that she arrived home the day before. I had also retrieved her phone number and decided to block mine and call her up. Hopefully, she didn't recognize my voice from that day at the warehouse.

<<<*ring, ring*>>>

Marie

"Hello?"

James

I cleared my throat before speaking and did my best impersonation of the white I guy worked for at the last company and position as an Information Technology Specialist. "Hello, and good evening ma'am." said James, in disguise.

"My name is Reginald Talley and I am calling on behalf of Halton Vacation Rewards. Are you familiar with our company and what we offer? I would only require about eight minutes of your time." I was hoping she would agree to take the call, because I am not cut out for the pushy telemarketer flow. I had my fingers crossed though.

Marie

“Well, I just walked into the house, but if you could hold for just one second while I get situated, I can give you my undivided attention.” I replied.

I went into my bedroom to put eyes on Robert since he had just started refusing to eat or drink anything again. I gave him the choice of me killing him slowly or being with me the way he needed to be. That was three months ago, and he made the right choice starting out. But here recently, I guess he was trying to wean himself off of my mixtures or something since he knows that WE are moving. And I was serious about it being ‘WE’. He better get his shit together. I don’t want to, but I will kill his ass. He also doesn’t know I have a new trick up my sleeve. After checking his restraints, I went back into the living room to resume my phone call. “I’m back, thank you for holding sir.”

James

“Yes ma’am, as I said before, my name is Reginald and I’m calling on behalf of Halton Vacation Rewards.” I spelled out that the company was offering a five-day, four-night stay. All she had to do was pay one hundred and twelve dollars, sit through a ninety-minute timeshare presentation while there and that I would need both person’s names to place on the reservation. And what do you know? She agreed to it all. “So how does all of that sound ma’am? This offer will only be good for the duration of this call.”

Marie

I think this will give Robert a renewed sense of being with me, Marie thought to herself before answering. This trip could be something that could jumpstart our relationship officially. For some reason, I really didn’t want to kill him. The dick is absolutely A-1 and his oral skills are also second to none. I also think I love him; I might even be even in love with him. I just want Robert to love me in return. “Yes sir, all of this sounds amazing!! What would I need to do?”

James

"Oh, you can just call me Reggie ma'am." At this point I'm almost laughing. "What I will need you to do right now is to just choose your location: the choices are between Las Vegas, Miami or New York and please verify that you are between the ages of eighteen and sixty-five years old."

Marie

"Oh, I like to be totally locked in with my man, so New York it is. And yes, we both are in our twenties. I'm so excited and I'm sure he will be too!" His ass better be. I'm tired of the ungratefulness, honestly.

James

"That sounds great, ma'am. Now, for the names on the reservation...", I encouraged.

Marie

"Ok, let me get my wallet... Okay, I'm back. So, my name is Marie Bijoux."

James

"Yes ma'am, and the second individual please?" I was sweating by this point. I couldn't believe how easy this shit was!

Marie

"Do I really need to put two names? I mean, I'm ready to pay the money." Marie questioned.

James

Fuck! I hope she goes for this. "Well ma'am, the promotion is based on two people attending the offer. I would have to check with my manager about recording just one person's name and unfortunately, my manager isn't here at the moment. As I said before ma'am, the promotion expires at the conclusion of this call."

Marie

I thought about it for a hot second and thought 'what the hell?!' "Ok Reggie, let me get my boyfriend's wallet for his last name. Don't judge me sir, it's a new relationship." I said embarrassed that after all this time, I didn't know Robert's last name nor his birthdate.

James

"No problem ma'am, do you need some time to speak with him about it? Would you like me to go over this with the both of you? Is he available right now to go over the details with as well?"

Marie

"No thanks, I'll tell him when I get off the phone. He's currently all tied up. His name is Robert Williams." Marie relayed. I then gave him my credit card information. "Would you like for me to repeat that for you sir?"

James

"I got it. Thank you, ma'am, and I will send you an email confirmation." And with that I hung up the phone. So now I know Rob's punk ass in there with her.

Marie

"Hello sir… sir?" Marie exclaimed excitedly. "But I didn't get a chance to give him my email address. Well since he had my number, maybe he has my email address too!! I'll just await the confirmation, I'm so excited! Robert better get his act together before I leave him in this apartment for someone to find what's left of him. Long after I vacate the premises."

Monroe

I'm back in the office with four of my henchmen hashing out the details on how we're going to kidnap these two and kill them once and for all. I'm just waiting for James with the confirmation of whether or not Rob is in there with her.

<<<ring, ring>>>

James

"Boss, it's a go." James told Money. "He's in there with her. She usually turns her lights off in the apartment around nine-thirty pm."

Monroe

"Great work, Jay. Stay there and I'm sending the goons over to meet you after I'm confident there will be no mistakes." We hung up and I resumed issuing my orders. "James is there now keeping an eye on the targets. You have to be very careful as this woman is armed and should be considered very dangerous. Do not underestimate her! Get in, grab both of them, and get the hell out. Put them in separate cars, blindfold them and then bring them to the rendezvous point. Inject them both with these solutions. No fuck ups, got me."

Echos of "Got you, Boss", were received in response to my orders. I would meet them at the rendezvous point because I never had my hands directly tied to the fire. That's what I pay all of them for. James was just there to oversee, but if any of them fucked up, it was his duty to clean it up. And that's what I pay him for.

Aubrey

It was Friday night and Joe and I are hanging out over Sam's house tonight because Monroe is working late. I'm trying not to be a big ass baby, but I hadn't heard from him since this morning. I was trying not to pout, but I missed him so much! This relationship with him was like no other that I'd ever experienced. He just makes me so damn happy.

Sam

"Stop pouting over there, sis!" Sam said teasingly. She and Joe giggled while making googly eyes at each other.

Aubrey

"That's easy for you to say, you all hugged up over there with your boo. Y'all get on my nerves!" I threw my pillow at them and they laughed harder. My phone rang, and unbelievably, it was Rob! Seeing his name and number some across my phone's screen irritated me even more! But why hadn't I blocked and deleted him completely in the first damn place? Ugghhh!!! I'm not sure why, but I decided to answer it this time. I mean, what else was I doing but being a third wheel? Shit, I was already annoyed anyway, I might as well take it out on him. "What the fuck do you want, dude? Stop calling me! Didn't you get the hint before, dummy? I don't want you anymore!" Sam and Joe stopped their flirting and were now looking at me curiously and trying to figure out just who it was on my line. I'm sure they surmised by my tone that it couldn't have been Monroe.

Rob

"Aubrey, please baby. Help me! Marie has me trapped in her apartment and she won't let me out. Please!" Rob whispered nervously.

Aubrey

"What the hell are you talking about, Rob?" He sounded like he may have even been crying. I really didn't know what to think. Is this some sort of a joke? Is he talking about Marie from my job?

How did he even know her? I had all these questions swirling through my head until he spoke again. He sounded so scared!

Rob

"Aubrey please," he whispered. "I know I did you wrong, but I don't know anyone else's number by heart. Please help me. I'll never bother you again if you help me get out of this situation. Please, please help me Aubrey! I'm sorry for everything I have ever done to hurt you. Please."

Aubrey

"Yeah, you more than did me wrong. Why do you feel so comfortable calling me? If Marie does have your ass tied up somewhere, good for her! Maybe you need to experience that type of treatment. Since your ass could never appreciate what you had with me, nor love me the way I deserved." At this point, I was on the verge of tears! Not because I missed him or anything like that, but because I was so enraged that he was calling me like he deserved my help! I was able to escape from an abusive relationship after being with Rob for three years. My momma didn't like him, Sam didn't either and he ended up getting my former 'friend', Free, pregnant while he and I were still together. He was definitely a piece of work, but apparently, I still had a soft spot for him. But why?

Suddenly, I heard a woman's voice in the background and then the phone call was disconnected. "Hello? Hello, Rob?" I couldn't just ignore it, what if he's in serious trouble? But I still couldn't understand why he would even be at Marie's house in the first place? I quickly wiped my tears and asked, "Joe, do you still know where Marie lives?" I asked as I put my shoes back on. "Can you give me the address? I need to check something out real quick."

Chapter 3

Joe

I looked at her like she had two heads or something. “Are you fuckin crazy, Aubrey? That nigga could be setting you up and you tryna run to his damn rescue?” I asked disapprovingly. She had just finished cussing this lame nigga out, and now she wants to ‘go see something’? What in the entire fuck could be going through this girl’s head? “What’s wrong with you?”

Sam

“Joseph! Language please!” Sam chastised Joe with a sharp look, then turned her attention to Aubrey. Her manner softened to try and reason with her. “Aubrey, he’s right honey regardless of his approach to the situation. You don’t need to go over there; you don’t know what you’re going to walk into. Didn’t you say that Marie already doesn’t like you? This just isn’t making any sense, sis.”

Aubrey

I explained to the both of them what Rob told me was going on. I know it seemed far-fetched, but I couldn’t just sit here and not do anything at all. Or attempt to, at least. “Alright y’all, I know this man did me so very wrong, but I did love him at one time. And I would never forgive myself if something happened to him because I didn’t at least try to see what was going on.” I exclaimed worriedly. What *was* wrong with me?

Sam

“Aubrey, think about it. How was he calling you if he was trapped somewhere? Do you think he would be given access to his cell phone? Think about it. Didn’t he just call you from his number?” Sam asked her.

Aubrey

She did have a point. But I know that he has a smart watch he could call me from also. And he never cried unless it was serious. Never. I can count on one hand how many times I've seen him cry. Something just doesn't feel right to me, and I just have to check it out. "He didn't call me from his phone, Sam. He told me my number was the only one he could remember." Before I psyched myself out, I had to get out of there. "I really have to go. I promise I'll be careful and will keep you both up to date with everything going on." I started to head for the door, when Joe jumped in front of me all crazy.

Joe

"Aubrey, I'm not letting you go out there by yourself. I'm coming with you." Joe proclaimed with his arms folded across his chest.

Sam

"Me too." I said with just a twinge of uncertainty and hoped neither of them noticed. I wouldn't know what to do if I ever had to be in Rob's presence ever again. But I knew I wasn't ready. "I'm coming too." I tried to say a bit stronger. Thankfully, Joe tried to convince me to stay behind to avoid a situation with Rob in case things went awry. That way I would be able to alert the authorities to their location, if needed. I didn't agree to anything though. But I doggone sure didn't put up a fight either.

Monroe

It's almost time for the young boys to retrieve the 'packages'. I just need for this to go as smoothly as possible. I decided to hit James up to see exactly what was going on. I was trying my best not to grow impatient with everybody.

<<calling James>>

James

"Hey Boss, the team is in position. Just waiting a little while after the apartment light goes off, then we'll cut the electricity to the floor and move in on them."

Monroe

"Sounds good. Keep me posted." I replied and then ended the call.

Sam

I don't know what has gotten into Aubrey. Why is she trying to see about this man? This… this thug! I'm so nervous about all of this. Why would Joe let her go to him that easily? Sam questioned. "I really think I'd be of some use guys." I tried to sound convincing to Joe to let me tag along. I wanted to sound supportive to Aubrey.

Joe

"Sam please, babe, I need you to stay here. I don't want you to end up in any craziness, if this goes left." I knew she wanted to go, but I would never forgive myself, or Aubrey, if anything happened to her because we're about to try and save a dude that don't care about nobody but his damn self.

Aubrey and I left Sam's house moments later. "I can't believe you got me out here tryna save this bum ass nigga. Why the fuck do you even still care about him though?" Joe looked over at Aubrey and had never seen her look so worried. After noticing her current state, he tried looking less disgusted. Joe sighed loudly, while rubbing his face. "Aubrey, I know you're a good person who cares about people and all but write this dude off already!" I'm purposely taking the long route to see if I can change her mind.

Aubrey

I kept hearing his scared voice whispering on the other end of that phone line in this scared little voice over and over in my mind. There's no way he was faking any of that. Hold up, where is Joe going? "Joe, where are you going? I thought you said Marie lived near my old spot? You passed the exit a while ago. Did you forget where her apartment is?"

Joe

"Hell nah, I ain't forget! You still haven't answered my question. Why do you care so much about this dude? You couldn't see when I had feelings for you, but you out here running to *his* rescue? I mean, what the fuck Aubrey? You think he would drop everything and do that shit for you? Damn!" I turned my attention back to the road and away from her and kept driving in silence. Why did I say just that? Why did I still even care though? Oh, I know, because this dude was bottom of the barrel! He wasn't shit! And I knew that I was THE shit! Fuck wrong with her crazy ass?

Aubrey

"Joe, what are you talking about? You choose now to tell me you "had" feelings for me? I can't believe you!" Now it all makes sense! So, he really was angry with me that night I tried to set him and Sam up. Because he wanted *me*! Oh my goodness! I am pissed!!! Why would he choose right now to tell me this bullshit? I couldn't even look at him right now! I was livid!

Joe

I just shut up at this point after Aubrey said that. I've already said way too much, and I didn't want it getting back to Marie that I may still be hooked on Aubrey's big sexy hazel eyes… that plump ass and those mesmerizing hips. Those titties that I just wanted in my mouth constantly- I'm trippin'! I need to focus on the task at hand. I couldn't believe I was helping her rescue this fuck nigga. That's if his shiesty ass wasn't lying just to get close to her. It all makes perfect sense that Rob would be fucking Marie. He prolly stuck his lil dick through that hole in the front of her mouth where that tooth was missing. He'll fuck anything! But Marie ain't crazy like that to have his ass tied up, is she?

Aubrey

We finally arrived. I've never seen these apartments even though I passed by when I went to work in the mornings. Now this, is the hood! Seems like some shit Marie would live in. And she always acted like she was better than everyone else. Aubrey thought incredulously.

"Are you gonna walk up there with me? Or you just gonna keep scolding me for not choosing you before?" Aubrey asked Joe while rolling her eyes at him. After about thirty seconds of no response, Aubrey opened the car door as if she was exiting the car. Finally, Joe spoke up.

Joe

"Man, let's go. FUCK!" He said while exiting the car and slamming the driver's door.

James

"Alright Boss; the lights are out. The young boys are about to head up there." James informed Monroe.

Monroe

"Do not let them fuck this up, Jay. This is on you, whatever happens." Monroe ordered.

James

"I got it, Boss. I want them dead, even more than you." Trust and believe I was ready to get rid of this muthafucka. My trigger finger has been itching ever since he popped up at my woman's house, threatening to take Tamia from her.

Monroe

"Alright, see y'all at the spot soon."

James

"Move in...", James ordered through the walkie talkie. I was just gonna sit out here and wait, but I didn't trust that this shit was going to go well without me being up in there with the young boys. We headed up the stairs and the door was already open. What the fuck? Did they know we were coming? "Be clean, in and out... y'all know what to do."

Marie

"Who could be knocking at my door at this hour?" Marie asked no one in particular. I left Robert in the room so that I could check out who was here. Why are the lights not coming on? Maybe the neighbors are experiencing the same electricity issue. I looked through the peephole, and to my dismay, it was Aubrey.

"What business do you have knocking at my door at this hour? How did you even know where I lived?" Marie asked with venom.

Aubrey

"I was just stopping by to check on you. I didn't get to say goodbye when you left work the other day, and I just wanted to stop by to bid you a proper farewell." Aubrey had to think quickly if she expected Marie to open the door. She didn't have a plan on how she would get inside or how she was gonna try to rescue Robert. "I apologize for the late hour. Could you please just open the door so we can talk?

Marie

Something is askew. She knows I don't like her in the least. But, I have just the trick! "Come on in, my electricity seems to be out right now, but let me light some candles." Marie let Aubrey in the apartment and noticed she didn't close the door.

Aubrey

Aubrey saw in Marie's eyes that she was questioning why she left the apartment door open. She had to think of something and quickly. "I left the door open for the moonlight", Aubrey said nervously. "I hope you don't mind."

Marie

"Yeah okay", Marie replied unbothered. I don't need the door closed for what I'm about to do to you. I reached into my basket to remove some of the concoction I was looking for and sprinkled some herbs into my hand. When I went back into the living room, she wasn't there. I walked upstairs and out of the corner of my eye, someone moved around in the living room. I crept back down the stairs trying to get to the kitchen, when I was grabbed from behind. I managed to wriggle free and blow my herbs into his face. He went down. Then someone else grabbed me and had me wrapped me in a bear hug so tight, I started to pass out from not being able to breathe. He took me outside, put a needle in my throat and that was all she wrote.

Aubrey

"Rob…. where are you? Hello?" Aubrey was tiptoeing in the dark and whispering trying to find Rob quietly, when suddenly she heard all of this commotion coming from downstairs. She saw someone grab Marie from behind, and as quietly as she could, Aubrey hid underneath a bed in the closest room she got to. She could hear something moving in the closet, but just laid dormant and didn't move until she thought the coast was clear. After a while, she heard the front door downstairs shut. After waiting what seemed like forever, Aubrey walked over to the closet, opened the door slowly while using the light from her cellular phone and found Rob tied up with tears coming from his eyes. She almost broke down crying herself, upon seeing him like that and started untying his restraints to get him out of there.

"What did she do to you? How long have you been here? Why are you here?" Then she realized that she needed to remove whatever it was that was stuffed in his mouth.

Rob

"Aubrey, you came!" Rob cried. "Thank you so much baby, I love you so much! I've been here for months! She just keeps me in this apartment and makes me do all these nasty things to her. Please baby, I'll never cheat on you again. I'll never hit you again. Please baby, take me back!"

Aubrey

"Rob, what are you talking about? First of all, how did she make you do anything? You're like so much bigger than her. Shit I'm bigger than her and you used to whoop my ass with absolutely no problem!" Aubrey retorted, unconvinced that he was being truthful. She finally got him free from the various bindings Marie had on him. She had him in there good too! That's what his ass gets!

I chuckled to myself a bit, now that I'm sure he's no longer in danger.

Rob

"Baby, she snuck up on me one night outside of our apartment and injected me with something from a needle. She was feeding me shit that made me do things against my will. I just wanna get outta this muthafucka. Please can we just go?"

Aubrey

"Yeah, but we gotta find Joe first. He snuck in right behind me, but I lost him once all of that noise started going on." Why is it so dark in here? I tried turning on the lights so that we could make our exit and look for Joe. "Joe! Joe, where are you?" I called his phone and I heard it ringing inside the apartment. I picked up one of the candles Marie lit and carried it with me as I searched for him. Joe wasn't there though. But why would he leave me here and with his phone?

Rob

"Aubrey, why are we still here? We need to go before that crazy bitch comes back and hems us both up!" He said frantically as his eyes darted back and forth throughout the apartment.

Aubrey

"Rob, I saw someone take her. She's not coming back anytime soon I'm sure, so relax." But where's Joe? It's not in his character to just leave me in here like this. Aubrey thought. Especially with Rob.

Rob

Maybe they took Joe's ass with them too thinking it was me! Good, I'm taking Aubrey home with me. If she doesn't come willingly, I'll force her ass. "Maybe they took him too. I need to go home so I can have access to my gun. Can you take me over there? We gotta be careful, those people might still be out here."

Aubrey

I sighed heavily, because I was becoming frustrated that Joe was nowhere to be found. "Alright, let's go to the car, Joe left the keys inside in the event we had to make an exit quickly, so we wouldn't have to fumble too much. He didn't have any pockets, and I'm glad or we would be stranded here." We got in the car and I pulled off heading to his apartment. Once we arrived, the door had an eviction notice on it which warned of his belongings being removed soon. I guess because he's been gone for as long as he said he has. He broke the padlock on the door, and we went inside. He started gathering some things to put in a bag.

Rob

"Can you hide me at your house for a few days?" Rob asked as he hurriedly gathered some of his things.

Aubrey

"I don't think that's such a good idea Rob. I can take you to get your car and maybe you can go to a hotel or something."

Rob

"Oh, I bet if I was Monroe, you'd let me come over though, huh?" Rob said as he started to walk toward Aubrey with a menacing stare. His fists were balled up and flashbacks of what happened between them in the past as instances started to replay in her mind.

Aubrey's heart started to thump loudly in her chest. How does he know about Monroe? Oh God, his eyes are getting dark and I know that look. What did I get myself into? How will I get away from him now? I should have listened to Sam and Joe. I may never get away from this man again, I feared.

Chapter 4

Monroe

The crew was finally en route to the spot and I was already there awaiting their arrival. I have the tarps ready for the quick disposal of both of the 'packages' and I'm hoping this goes quickly because I'm trying to see Aubrey tonight. I see one set of headlights turn onto the dirt road and then two more sets. Everything must have gone well because James didn't hit my phone. They all dimmed the lights as they got closer to the entrance and parked off to the side as I instructed them to do earlier. In the first car, I see two men exit the vehicle and then both come around to the rear passenger side. As they start to remove the person they had in the backseat. I could tell that was the young lady. Now, I want to see them pull that lil nigga out of the car.

"Go ahead and take her inside and chain her to one of those chairs. Aye, where that lil nigga at, Jay?" Monroe demanded.

James

"Right here boss." I said as the young boys roughly removed his body from the vehicle. "You want him inside with her, too?" I asked.

Monroe

"Where's Demetrius? I thought he was with y'all on the job?" Monroe inquired peculiarly.

James

"Oh, when he tried grabbing the bitch, she blew something in his face. He's been passed out ever since. If he doesn't wake up soon, we prolly gonna need to take him to the hospital." I answered.

Monroe

"What the fuck could she have blown in his face to make him pass out like that though?" I was truly annoyed with this situation. This nigga was in the back of the Expedition laid out with his mouth wide the fuck open. Damn, this bitch is dangerous. Now I gotta wait until she wakes up to see what she did to him to try and reverse the effects. We didn't need that kind of attention by taking him to the hospital. I stepped inside of the spot and instructed them to remove the bags from their heads.

James

"Yo, who the fuck is this nigga? That ain't Rob!" James yelled at no one in particular.

Monroe

"That's Aubrey's friend Joe from her job. A better question would be is how he got here instead?" Monroe responded calmly. Everyone is looking at each other waiting for someone else to speak. "Well don't all fuckin' speak at once! Wake his ass up and unchain him from that damn chair!" Monroe ordered.

I was hot! I didn't want this nosy nigga knowing anything about my business, but my priority at the moment is to find that lil nigga Rob immediately. "Aye, on second thought, take him back to the warehouse and wake him up there. I can't have Aubrey's friend knowing my business. And don't take the Expedition, leave Demetrius' silly ass here."

James

"Boss I got you, but once he wakes up, what's the story?" James asked.

Monroe

"It's gotta be something that I can explain to my lady that will make sense. How would we have ended up with Joe and how did he end up drugged and at my auto parts warehouse?" replied Monroe. I did not need this shit right now. I needed Joe to wake up and tell me if he knew where Rob was.

Sam

It's getting late and I haven't heard from either of them. I've called Joe seven times to no avail. I've also called Aubrey three times and she hasn't answered either. Where could they be after all of this time? I don't know what to do, and I know that pacing this floor the way I am is eventually going to wear a hole into it. Uggghhhhh! Just as I was about to go out and comb the area near where Aubrey used to live with Robert, my phone rang.

"Aubrey, where are you all? Are you both ok? Who is that talking in the background?" But she didn't answer me. It sounded kind of muffled, but I could have sworn that the voice I heard in the background was Robert's. And it sounded like she was whimpering. Oh my God, what is happening right now?

Rob

"Oh, so you ain't got nothing to say to me? You just take all your shit and bounce without leaving a note or anything else? Like fuck me, huh?" I manhandled her ass til we got up in my apartment. If she kept fucking with me like this tonight, she was gonna make me hurt her ass.

Aubrey

"Rob, you said if I helped you, you would leave me alone. Can you please just let me go? I need to find out what happened to

Joe!" Aubrey cried. I'm so very scared in this moment, I know this look in his eyes. I've seen it too many times before.

Rob

"So you fuckin that nigga too? You just out here being a whole entire hoe, huh? Since you giving the pussy up to every muthafuckin body else out here, come here and get my dick wet too." She got me fucked up if she think I'm gonna let her go that easy. I knew she was fuckin that dude. While she up here crying for him, she should have been crying for me while that crazy ass bitch was holding me hostage. And if it wasn't for her ass not being at work that day, I would have never even paid attention to her ass! It was her fault that I got tangled up with that crazy bitch! "Aubrey, don't make me ask you twice, take them got damn clothes off, NOW!"

Aubrey

"Nooooooooo! You can't do this to me! I helped you get away from Marie! Please let me go, Rob. PLEEAAASSSEEE!"

Rob

"So, you wanna do this shit the hard way? Ok!" I punched her right in her eye and she fell to the floor. I then kicked her in her side and got down and started punching her some more.

"I don't give a fuck about how you look in public now! Since you out here giving this pussy up to them niggas, and you have a nerve to tell *me* no? You serving up this pussy tonight!"

Aubrey

I was numb at this point from all of the pain. I couldn't see straight, my eye was swelling shut and my ear felt like it was split open. I prayed that I didn't have any broken ribs from him kicking me so hard. I felt him tugging at my shoes and then my joggers. Then I felt the coldness from the floor below me. He ripped my panties off and made me turn on my stomach. I winced as he shoved himself roughly into my vagina.

Is this my karma for giving him so many chances to hurt me in the past? Is this what he did to Sam? Will he kill me when he's done? I heard him grunting in my ear and he had the nerve to ask me if I liked it. When I thought he was done, he turned me over and pushed himself inside me again, but this time he lubricated his dick with his saliva. Please hurry up! And please don't let my body betray me by getting wet. I can't believe that I used to absolutely live for this man less than a year ago and he's now raping me.

Rob

I knew she wanted me for real. I can feel her pussy gripping my dick from the inside. I missed this pussy, but why is she still laying there not saying nothing? "I know you miss me too baby, stop fighting me and just enjoy it. I'm sorry for hitting you. And this pussy feels way too tight for somebody else to be hittin' it. Damn girl, ooooohhh. You know I love you Aubrey and I know you still love me. This is where you are supposed to be. I'm glad you're back home. Mmmmmm..."

I was kissing on her neck and her back as I continued to pound in and out of her sweet pussy, and even though she didn't answer me, I know that I just heard her moan. I reached underneath her sports bra because I missed those titties, too. I guess she wasn't pregnant after all, because I could tell she had lost a few pounds. Why the fuck did I have to hit her in the face though? I'll just buy her something pretty tomorrow and everything will be okay. I felt myself about to nut, so I spread her legs open as wide as they would go, so I could be deeper inside of her.

"Damn, you feel so good baby. Uhhhhhhh ooooooohhhhh mmmmmhhhhhmmm, baby. I love you so much! I'm so sorry baby, please forgive me for hurting you again." I said as I felt my dick start to throb and release inside of her. I really meant it, I know my temper is ferocious. She didn't say anything, she just laid there and continued to look into nothingness. I took my time to regain my senses and pulled out of her slowly, then pulled my pants back up. I scooped her up off the floor and took her into the bedroom and laid her down on her side. I pulled the covers up over her and laid beside her and went to sleep with my arm draped over her.

James

Now, how in the fuck did we end up with this nigga? I know Rob was in that apartment, where the fuck did Aubrey's coworker come from? I pull into the warehouse parking lot and ran inside to get one of the rolling beds we keep in there for our overnight staff. I rolled it out and it looked like he was starting to come to. I hurried and got him out of the car so my story would stick.

"Aye, Joe. I'm here to help man. I saw you wandering the street a little while ago, do you remember where you were going? You hear me man, wake up."

Joe

I felt like a dump truck hit me at full speed. Where was I? And who is this big ass nigga in my face talking all loud and shit? "Yeah, yeah man, I hear you. Stop yelling in my fuckin' ear!! Who are you?"

James

"My name is Reggie man, and I found you wandering on the road. Then, you just passed out. Just stay calm. You want me to call you an ambulance."

Joe

"Nah man, I just need to shake this off. Where's my friend?"

James

"You were wandering by yourself man, was someone with you?" I know he wasn't talking about Marie. But I guess he worked with her too, since he was Aubrey's work friend.

Joe

"Nah, nah, nah man! Are you sure you found me alone? My friend Aubrey! Female, brown skin, she had on sweatpants and a light jacket. Where am I again?" I asked as I looked around. This did not look familiar in the least. Something is fishy.

James

"There was nobody with you man, just lay down for a few minutes, so you don't hurt yourself."

Joe

"I need to find Aubrey." Damn, I sat up too fast and had to lay back down. "Man, if Marie or Rob did something to her, I'm gonna kill them both!"

James

I rolled him into the building as I began to panic a bit at the mention of Aubrey's name again. "Aye man, I'll be right back. Sit tight real quick."

<<dialing Money>>

"Yo man, he's woke, but he's asking for Aubrey. Said she was with him and something about Rob or Marie doing something to her."

Monroe

It felt as if my blood was boiling at this point. What in the world was my lady doing at Marie's house tonight? Why would her and Joe go over there? I need to find her expeditiously and I know where to look first.

"I'm going to go check and see if she's at her friend's house. Did he say why they were there?" I'm trying my best not to panic.

James

"No, Boss, but let me ask him if he remembers what they were doing and where he thinks they were and I'll call you right back."

Monroe

I need to call Aubrey. I dialed her number and she didn't answer. I called four more times and I got the same result. I need to stop by Sam's after James finds out what they were doing tonight.

"Wake her ass up." I demanded from the young boys. I need some information from Marie before I ended her life. "You need to be very careful and watch her though. You do not wanna end up like Demetrius."

Free

I have been back in school for about a month now and Tamia's doing really well at daycare. James and I have settled on a date for our small wedding for some time in the fall. It feels weird not to be working, but I'm not hurting for any money. I've been really smart with my investments, as well as ensuring that I'm not spending the money my mother left me or the money I've saved from dancing. I have a little over a year and a half left in school, and

I'm very excited to be back. I know my mother would be proud of me, and I know she's keeping Tamia company because she's always smiling while looking at nothing.

"Are the angels talking to you again, Princess? Do you see my mommy? You look so much like her baby girl. You're so pretty, yes you are. Mommy's so happy to have you, my princess," I cooed as I kissed her all over her little face. I never knew that I could love anyone this much. She's everything I never thought I always needed. I thank God every day for her.

<<<ring, ring>>>

"Hello?" It was from an unknown number.

Unknown Caller

"You ready for me to come and get my daughter?"

Free

It was Rob. I had blocked his number after he showed up to my house unannounced months ago.

"What are you talking about? My daughter is not your baby! Don't call this fuckin' phone ever again!" I hung up on him and noticed Tamia was crying. I didn't realize that I was yelling, nor did I realize how much I was trembling. I must have startled her when I was talking to her sperm donor. I have to call James. But let that muthafucka come over here if he wants to. I'm gonna blow his damn head off!

Aubrey

I laid there all night while Rob held me hostage with that one arm pinning me underneath it. As the sun began to rise and get brighter, he woke up and noticed that I was still laying in the same position with my eyes wide open looking at nothing in particular.

He went to the bathroom but kept his eye on me to ensure I didn't try to run away. At this point, even if I tried, I don't think I would be successful. My side was aching, my right eye was swollen shut and my head felt like it was going to explode. I just wanted to give up on my life. I wanted to fall asleep and never wake up. But I was going to find a way out of this situation or die trying. He wasn't going to torment me for another three years.

Rob

"Aubrey, you gonna lay like that all day? You hungry? Don't you have to pee or something?" I knew she was upset with me, and I'm sorry or whatever. "Eventually you're gonna need to get up and take a shower and get cleaned up. I'll go make you something to eat while you get yourself together. I know you'll feel better after you do. Then we can put some ice on your eye. I don't know why you make me hurt you. If you just stop provoking me, everything would be perfect for us." She will get over it, she always does.

Aubrey

I didn't say anything, but I took my time getting myself up. I didn't want him to see me cry, so I waited until I got in the bathroom to do so.

Rob

"And don't lock that door either..."

Aubrey

I took my time and peeled off my bra that was stretched out and then removed my sweatshirt carefully. I observed my reflection in the bathroom mirror and the tears just started falling silently. He's never gone this far before, but after hearing what he did to Sam, and knowing that he got Free pregnant, I knew he was capable of anything. I used the bathroom and upon wiping myself, there was blood on the tissue. My vagina was in so much pain from the brutal rape from last night. I turned on the shower and got in, and I wish I could say that the water felt good. I was still so numb and in shock. And all I wanted was for Monroe to come and rescue me. How could I be so stupid? I should've listened to my friends and left this nigga where he was.

Rob

Free thinks that just cuz she blocked a nigga number that I couldn't get to her. I was gonna kill her just for being disrespectful. And know now that I have a daughter! Damn, I bet she looks just like my mama. I can't wait to see her. I just gotta figure out how to convince Aubrey to stay with me and not run away again. I couldn't take her with me over Free's house. I didn't want no witnesses. Matter of fact, lemme go check on Bree to see what's taking her so long. She's still so damn quiet.

"Are you almost finished?" She didn't answer. She jumped just a bit as I pulled the curtain back but continued to just stand there underneath the water. She didn't look back at me or nothing.

"I said, are you finished?" With that, she turned the water off and stepped out of the shower. I backed up to give her some room. The side of her rib cage was bruised, and her eye was swollen shut. She grabbed her towel and I saw her grimace at the pain from drying off her body. I took the towel from her and dried her off. She still wouldn't look at me or say anything. I know she was mad, but she should be mad at herself for being out here with these other niggas. Lemme stop, before I get mad and can't control myself again.

"I made you some breakfast. Get dressed and come eat." After I left the bathroom, I saw her starting to put on the clothes she just took off. I laid one of my tank tops and a pair of my shorts on the bed for her, but if she wanted to put that dirty shit back on, that's her choice. After she put her sweatshirt back on, I guess that's when she realized her underwear and her pants were still on the floor in the living room. She began walking over there slowly to retrieve them, but the way her ass jiggled as she walked just looked so good to me. I went up behind her, as she approached her clothes and bent over gingerly careful not to aggravate the pain she experienced last night. I couldn't help myself and hugged her from behind with my sex against her backside, careful of the pain in her side. My dick grew simply by me being next to her.

I bent her over the couch, being mindful of her injuries and started playing with her pussy from behind with my fingers. She still wasn't responding in the least to me. So, I crouched down and nudged her to open her legs wider apart, planting my face as I licked her pussy from behind. I knew she liked it like that. After a few minutes though, she still wasn't reacting. So, I flicked my tongue faster across her clit. She adjusted herself a little bit. I'm not sure if she was trying to balance herself or if she started to enjoy it. I continued dipping my tongue in and out of her pussy and I noticed she was getting more and more stimulated. I started flicking my tongue against her clit again and eventually she started trembling. But still she wouldn't moan for me. Once she was finished cumming, I inserted my dick into her pussy gently from the back.

"Moan for me, baby. I know you still love me just as much as I love you." I started kissing and nibbling on her upper back as I drilled in and out of her wetness. I felt myself about to bust super quick, so I guided her to the front of the couch and eased her onto her back because I wanted to see her face. She still wouldn't look at me, and she still didn't say nothing or moan for me. I lifted her legs so that her ankles were on my shoulders and pulled her down to the edge of our couch and gently entered her wetness once again. She was so wet for me that I know she had to be enjoying it. I felt the head of my dick starting to swell, so I pushed her legs back as far as they would go. I let loose all of my hot seed in her walls.

My newborn daughter could use a lil brother or sister anyway. It felt so good that I felt a little dizzy when I was finished. I kissed her lips and went into the bathroom to clean myself off and get a warm rag for her as well. When I came back into the living room, I noticed the front door was wide open and she was gone.

Aubrey

I fucking hated that I rescued him! As soon as he disappeared into the bedroom and I heard the water turn on, I grabbed my pants and ran out the door. I ran faster than I ever have before and I was never coming back. Luckily, the keys to the car were on the floor with my joggers and my torn panties. Once I got to the car, I looked back and saw him running down the stairs as he yelled my name loudly.

Rob

"Aubrey!! Don't get in that car! When I catch you, I'm gonna kill yo' ass. AUBREEEEY!!"

Aubrey

I was able to open the door quickly and as soon as I started the car, he was there trying to open the door. I had locked all the doors when I got in and I backed up so fast that I hit the car behind me. It also knocked his ass on the ground too. I tried running him over after putting the car in drive, but he swiftly rolled away from the vehicle. I saw him in my rear-view mirror getting smaller and smaller. I wanted to immediately go to the police, but I was naked from the waist down.

And how could my body deceive me in such a way? When he went down on me from behind, it wasn't supposed to feel that good. I wasn't supposed to cum. His dick wasn't supposed to feel so good inside of me. He was the enemy! I started crying so hard at what I was thinking that I didn't notice that the light had just changed to red. I also didn't see that SUV turning the corner and coming straight for me until it was too late.

Chapter 5

Saturday morning, 4 :17 am

Monroe

I pulled up to Sam's apartment and knocked softly so that I wouldn't startle her if she was sleeping. The door rushed open as if she was awaiting someone's arrival and she looked a mess. I could tell that she had been crying, but I couldn't be sure of what she knew, so I just acted like I didn't know anything

"Sam, what's the matter? Are you okay? What happened? I stopped by to see if you had heard from Aubrey. She's not answering her phone and she's not at her house. What is going on?" She tried telling me, but she was too worked up. I pulled her into my chest and just hugged her for a moment.

"Shhhhh, calm down. Let's sit you down while I get you a glass of water so you can tell me what's going on." I escorted her back into her apartment and handed her a tissue from her coffee table. She got herself together while I brought her a glass of water and then she told me what happened.

Sam

"Joe and Aubrey left earlier tonight to go find Rob because he called her crying about being held hostage by Marie. I tried waiting for them and then I went out looking for them earlier, but I don't know where she lives." Sam cried into her tissue. She blew and wiped her nose before continuing. "Joe isn't answering his phone and Aubrey called me from her phone but didn't say anything. I think I heard Rob in the background with a whole bunch of commotion and yelling. I was about to call the police but I hung up when you rang the doorbell, thinking it was one of them returning. I just know something bad is happening to both of them right now and I just feel helpless!"

I hugged her again and tried to reassure her that everything would be alright. She cried some more, and I told her that I would find them both and that I'm sure they were okay. Truth is, I didn't believe was coming out of my own mouth. I was worried. After getting her to agree to lie down, I headed back to the warehouse to find out what Joe said. I didn't want to be on the phone discussing any of this shit. I pulled up to the building and went in the side door because I didn't want Joe to see me. Once I got to the office, I saw that James was in there by himself. "What did you find out, Jay?"

James

"Joe said that he and Aubrey went over to Marie's apartment last night because Rob called her phone crying about being held hostage. Then he said, he doesn't remember anything else. He keeps asking me to take him to Rob's house, where Aubrey used to live with him. Did you know he used to be with your girl?"

Monroe

"Unfortunately, yes, I found out shortly before all of this went down. So not only was he in a relationship with Aubrey, he cheated on her with her old college friend, your girl Free. What the fuck is it about this clown? This world is getting smaller by the fucking minute and all of these issues this lil nigga has caused. I want his ass dead today! No more fuck ups!" Monroe demanded.

James

"Boss, so what's the next move? You think this nigga was dumb enough to take Aubrey to his apartment? I remember where he lives, you wanna sneak up on his ass?" James asked, pumped up to find Rob.

Monroe

"Yeah, but first I need you to take Joe home. I can't risk him seeing me, I don't want Aubrey knowing shit about what I do." Monroe ordered.

Joe

"I thought you were a mechanic." Joe said quizzically. "What is it that you do exactly Monroe, and why can't Aubrey know about it?" As Joe rounded the corner.

Club Owner, *Sugar's Strip Club*

"Yeah, twerk that phat ass baby. Make big Curt nut. Ssssssssss…"

Taisha

This is what I've been doing to ensure that I can keep this sorry ass job because Curt thinks I'm getting too old to work here. I have to 'sit on it' from time to time because his big ass ain't getting on top of me! It's always the same routine, I gotta dance for him so he can tell me what the young girls are doing better. And by dancing for him, it makes his dick hard. In my mind, if I'm not as good as the younger bitches, why you get so brick every time that I do? And I have to put on a fuckin show like I didn't just do this for hours on end for these cheap ass customers in the club. *Damn, I'm a dummy for not putting the money away that Monroe was gifting me all those years.*

So anyway, after I dance, he likes to apply oil all over my body and while he's doing it, he likes sticking his finger inside my ass. I hate that shit! I'm like, just fuck me and get this shit over with already. After that, I have to give him head, and not quick head, he wants me to make love to the dick. And his dick ain't no punk either! Gotta be at least eight to nine inches and it's thick. He likes for me to talk to it with the head resting against my lips, almost like a whisper. Then I have to lick him and suck him until he wants to put his nasty fingers in my weave and fuck my throat. I know I'm a stripper and sometimes fuck men (women too) for money, but that's some degrading shit. This here was not for me. I'm not sure how much longer I can do this.

The finale is me sitting on his dick, with my back to him while clapping my ass. You really have to have some strong legs for that shit. He doesn't assist by pumping me back until right at the end when he's about to cum. And if it wasn't already shameful enough by letting him force my head down on his dick over and over, he releases his nasty seed all over my face and I'm supposed to lick it off my lips real sexy. Like what in the entire fuck is sexy about that shit though? And, I still had a little while to go.

When we were done, he would let me feature three nights out of that week during the prime slots. That meant that at eleven pm and two am I had the stage to myself and I got to keep all of the money I made. He made sure that it was just a week at a time because he wanted me to keep coming back. I didn't do it as often as he would like, but when he got really fed up, he would give me the shitty slots, like one time I was on the stage at seven am, like anybody worth it is still at the club tryna throw some money. Yeah, that nigga was petty.

I had gone up to the prison in Jessup to see Big Don a couple of times, but he really wasn't tryna fuck with me like that. I thought that the arrangement I proposed was gonna be enough to have me set. I reminded him that Monroe and I were not together anymore. He told me that Monroe told him that too. Ain't that a bitch? So, this nigga is really tryna be done with me, but okay. I also told him that Money didn't need to know about anything that we did behind closed doors.

Last week during my visit, I was still trying to convince him. I know I looked desperate, but I was tired of being fucking broke! "Don, nobody has to know what we do? It's a win-win situation. I break you off, you break me off. And I'll come back whenever you want me to. I work at night, so I'll never use that excuse. And I don't have a man. So why not?"

Big Don

"Tai, now you know that Monroe is my mans. That kind of loyalty, you don't just throw that away. He manages my business, so he would be the first to know." Big Don said.

Taisha

"Come on Donnie, you know I'll set up a bank account under a fake name and do everything online. Besides, he's really not fucking with me like that anymore. I really need some help, boo." I know I looked a bit sad in that moment, but I got myself together as I leaned over the table so he could have a better view of my titties spilling out of my body suit. I even let my nipple slip a couple of times, while the guards weren't looking, of course.

Big Don

"Tai, I don't understand why you just don't ask me for help. Why you think the only way you can get money from me is to fuck? But you look good as always baby girl. Stand up for me and let me see that ass again real quick." He directed.

Taisha

I did as he requested. Even bent over and clapped it a little. I didn't give a fuck who was looking at me in that waiting room. I could tell that a few of the other inmates were trying to sneak peeks without alerting their girlfriends and baby mamas during their visits. I didn't care! I was truly on a mission.

"Donnie, because I know what your expectations are if I just asked you for help. You would want me to smuggle shit in here for you, and I can't risk my freedom like that. You know that. It's easier for me to just come in here and fuck and suck you real good. I already know these other bitches not doing it for you the way that I can. I promise I would make it worth your while." Tai expressed seductively. I let my nipple slip again and I saw him licking his lips and adjusting his dick underneath the table.

That all happened earlier today. I had been back at my house for about thirty minutes since I made that almost hour drive back. He still wasn't having it, even after my little show though. That's why I'm surprised to be getting a phone call from him this evening.

Automated Prison Operator

"You have a phone call from 'Donald Weathers', an inmate at a federal correctional facility. If you wish to block this call, press 'nine' now. If you wish to accept this call, press 'zero' now."

Taisha

You know I was accepting that call. "Hey Donnie, what's going on baby?" I asked with a bit of sex dripping from my tone.

Big Don

"When you coming to see me again? I need to feel you. Set that up for us, and I'll send you a lil something." He said.

Taisha

"Yes daddy..." I replied. He hung up and I set it up for the day after tomorrow.

Free

<<<ring, ring>>>

"Come on, pick up the phone! Pick up, pick up, pick up." I've been trying to call James but he hasn't been answering his phone. I know he won't answer his phone while conducting business with Monroe at the warehouse, but shit, it's only eight in the morning. They can't be meeting this late after pulling an all-nighter. He told me there was something he had to handle last night, but he said he would be here by now.

I've locked up the house, got all my security cameras going and I'm sitting here locked in the computer room with Tamia. And my nine millimeter. I'm not taking any chances, I know Rob is crazy. He's not coming anywhere near my daughter. As far as I'm concerned, he's dead to us. I know what I said before, but he can't visit my daughter. Not after telling me he was going to take her and raise her with Aubrey. They better have their own fuckin baby.

My phone rings and I hurry up and answer it. It's James. "Hello? Baby, I'm so scared. Please come home. That nigga had the nerve to call me and tell me he was coming to get Tamia!'

James

So, this nigga think he big and bad, got my girl over there scared! "Baby, I'm on my way to handle that nigga. Just make sure everything is locked, including the windows and the back door. Turn the alarm on and monitor the cameras. That nigga is not getting in there. I'll be there as soon as I can. If ANYBODY knocks on the door or you see him on the camera, call the police immediately."

Free

"Oh my Goddddddddd, baby be careful! And please hurry up."

James

"Baby, keep your gun close. Remember what I taught you. I love you and Tamia, and I'll be there as soon as I can." James assured her.

"Boss, we gotta go now! Fresia said that the lil nigga called her and said he was coming to take the baby." I started running out to the car with Money and Joe behind me. Joe had questions, but his ass was just gonna have to wait. Fuck that, I gotta hurry up and kill this nigga.

Monroe

Joe came in the office when James and I were talking. I couldn't answer his questions right now because Free just called. We were on our way to Rob's apartment, and I had so many thoughts running through my mind. Sam told me all about his volatile relationship with Aubrey. She also told me what he did to her and her sister. Damn, I didn't realize Jennifer was her sister, but now that I think about it, they do favor, and both of them have that red ass hair.

"Joe, I am a mechanic. I own my own business, but I don't tell many people about my true net worth. I have other businesses as well, but I needed to ensure that what I have with Aubrey was real before letting her in on all of that." I hope this nigga don't keep asking questions, I'm trying not to put his ass in the dirt too.

Joe

"Yeah, whateva nigga. Let's just find Aubrey."

Chapter 6

Monroe

We arrived to the lil nigga's apartment around eight-thirty am. We didn't see his car outside, but I still wanted to go in and look for him. Joe took the back of the apartment building, James was the lookout in the front from upstairs and I went straight to the apartment. The door was locked, but thanks to the people that I employ, we made copies of both Marie's and Rob's apartment keys when we held them briefly before.

Now let me explain my disdain for the "lil nigga" as I refer to him. Rob and I grew up in the same neighborhood and were even childhood friends at one point in time. Obviously, I was the product of a two-parent home and through their hard work, I was brought up to work hard for what I wanted as well. We weren't rich by any means, but if I had to get a job to help out so my sisters didn't have to, that's what I was going to do. And that's what I did. Rob used the excuse that he was brought up without a father to continue carrying a chip on his shoulder and having this bad attitude.

I always tried to encourage others, including Rob, to do things for themselves regardless of where we came from. Black men in America can't afford to make excuses, let alone be angry about our station in life without trying to change it. We lost touch for some years when I started high school, due to my top grades. Needless to say, I went to college and Rob went to the streets. When I came home on a break and my sister had a bruise underneath her eye. She did a poor job of covering it with makeup. I asked her about it and after some prodding, she told me she was dealing with one of Rob's boys. I hit him up and let him know I needed to holla at him about something.

Some years ago...

Rob

“Wassup college boy?!”

Monroe

“Hey what’s goody?” We dapped each other up. It was good to see him, but I was here for something else. “Hey, do you still rock with a dude name Jeff? My baby sister has a black eye and she said he did it. I need to find him.”

Rob

“Oh word?” He took a drag from his blunt but wasn’t looking at me. “What you tryna do though?” Rob asked me, uninterested in what I was saying.

Monroe

“You haven’t answered my question. Is this one of the dudes you rock with or not? If so, where can I find him?” I asked quietly. I was starting to get angry with him. Why wasn’t he tryna answer my question?

Rob

“Yo, from what I heard, your sister was being a tease. Her actions wasn’t matching her words, you know what I’m saying? Jeff got tired of her leading him on and he tried to take it. What you want me to do man?” Rob shrugged.

“So you supposed to be my mans, but sitting up here in my fuckin’ face tryna make it sound like it’s ok that dude tried to rape my sister? What the fuck you think I want you to do?” By this point, I was in his face, fists balled up and I wanted to kill that lil ass nigga. He was older than me, but I was taller than him. I knew it got under his skin when I called him short back in the day, so anytime I can, I do it by calling him lil nigga.

What I can't for the life of me understand, is why Don continues to want to save this nigga that don't care about shit but himself. His nasty ass used to fuck his cousin and I believe her son is his. And his mom, he drove her right into her grave. He used to beat on his little sister and they always had to run away but for some reason, he was always able to convince his mom and his sister to come back. He's just a fucked up individual overall.

Present Day

I walked into the apartment with my gun cocked. It looked like there was a struggle, and I saw torn panties on the living room floor. I'm thinking to myself, please don't let that be my baby's underwear. I felt my jaw tighten with anger at the thought of him assaulting her. I walked into the bedroom and saw clothes laid out on the bed. I eased into the bathroom, but no one was there. I noticed that there were tissues with blood on them in the wastebasket in the corner. I had a bad feeling in the pit of my stomach, but I continued my search for clues. He wasn't here. Neither was Aubrey.

Dee Dee

Aubrey hasn't contacted me in a couple of days. I do try to give her her space, but she's still my baby. We always text, and although I'd like to hear from her every day, I know she has to live her life. Two days is not much for most people to not have spoken to their grown child, but I just have a bad feeling. I dialed her cell phone again, and this time the phone goes straight to voicemail. I know who to call though. Between Sam and Monroe, someone will be able to tell me something. "Hi Sam, how are you?"

Sam

What in the world am I supposed to tell Ms. Dee Dee? I'm not sure what to do. "Hey Mrs. Dee Dee, I actually have a patient entering my office. Can I call you right back?" I hate that I had to end the call so abruptly, but I'm going to call the police station and the hospital as soon as I hear something back from either Joe, Monroe or Aubrey herself.

Dee Dee

Sam didn't even give me a chance to respond before disconnecting the call. I'll try Monroe to see what I can find out from him. I headed home early because I couldn't wait to hear from Aubrey and Monroe any longer.

Monroe

Damn, Aubrey's mom is calling me. I can't answer until I have something to tell her. I need to find out where Aubrey is and fast. I know Mrs. Dee Dee will get on a plane in a minute. It doesn't take much. But we're back at square one, so I need to at least figure out my next step. I sent her call to voicemail. "Alright, so now that we know he's not home, I need to figure out our next step."

James

"Boss, in the meantime, I need to check on my family. Joe, I need to drop you off, I don't like many people knowing where I lay my head. I need to put eyes on Fresia and the baby before we do anything else."

Joe

"Can you drop me off at my girl's house then? We'll try and go another route to look for Aubrey." As I rolled my eyes. I could give a fuck about knowing where this nigga lived.

Monroe

"I appreciate your help, Joe. The sooner we find her, the better. I know what that lil nigga is capable of and Sam filled me in this morning about her sister's relationship with him."

Joe

“Don’t thank me, ‘mechanic’, she’s my friend.”

Monroe

I turned around to face Joe in the back seat so that he would know how serious I was with my next statement. “Look Joe, and I’m only going to say this once. Don’t disrespect me, my reach is very far in this town and you don’t want to be on my bad side. I’ve explained to you why I didn’t want Aubrey to know the extent of everything I have going on. If you can’t respect it, just say that. But what I will not tolerate from you, nor anyone else, is the disrespect. Are we clear?”

Joe

He’s really feeling himself right now. “Look dude, it’s no disrespect, I just don’t like how you’re trying to handle Aubrey. She’s been through enough with that fuck nigga Rob to have to deal with anything other than what she signed up for with you. Now be clear on this, I don’t work for you. There’s nothing about your little ‘statement’ that puts fear in this heart,” as I pointed to my chest. And with that, I stepped out of James’ car and went into Sam’s apartment.

Sam

I heard someone knock on my door and rushed quietly to see who it was. It was Joe!! I snatched the door open so fast and jumped in his arms.

“Baby!” I cried. “What happened to you? Aubrey’s mom is calling me, where is she?” As I looked behind him.

Joe

"Samantha, I'm so sorry to have you worrying about me. I knew before we went over there, it was such a bad idea. I can't even remember what happened, but I passed out for sure. I ended up at some warehouse and Monroe ended up there as well. He's keeping something from Aubrey about himself, but that will have to wait. The primary thing is to find Aubrey. I just hope Rob doesn't have her or hasn't done something to her."

Sam

"She called from her phone late last night and I could have sworn that I heard a commotion and I also thought I heard Rob in the background yelling at her." I started to cry, now that I realized that he did have her. "What if he hurt her like he hurt me?" From the look on Joe's face, I knew that at that point I said too much.

Chapter 7

Taisha

It's almost time for me to go back to work, and believe it or not, I'm a little nervous about my visit with Don tomorrow. First of all, I'm starting to feel like I'm disrespecting Monroe, but I try to reconcile it with the fact that *he* got rid of *me*! But there was just this nagging feeling that was in the back of my mind telling me not to go. But I wouldn't dare renege on Don. His reach was way too long. It didn't mean shit that he was in prison.

Crystyle

"Tai, the boss told me to let you know that it was almost time for your next set on stage three."

Taisha

"Thank Crys. Curt knows I hate stage three! That petty ass muthafucka though!"

Crystyle

"Don't kill the messenger boo. You know what to do if you don't want to be on stage three. At least the club is packed though." Crystyle shrugged.

Taisha

Crystyle was right. At least it wasn't dead tonight. And it's ten pm, on a Thursday so it was a great night. Stage three was in the cut, so niggas thought because it was pretty much out of the way of the cameras, that anything goes. And it didn't help that some of these bitches would be over here sucking dick, fucking and letting these dudes do whatever to them. So they always thought that all of us were like that. I mean I will fuck and suck, but you gotta be making some major money for all that. And I ain't doing that shit in front of everybody!

I made sure to wear turquoise and silver tonight. Picture a sexy genie that will make all your dreams come true. I always went all out, no matter what stage I was on. I even had on the sheer shimmery face mask that covered my mouth and the little genie hat. I wasn't using one of my good routines though. This was one of those nights that I would let the music speak to me and my body would just go with it. At least I didn't have to work too hard. This was the cheap nigga corner. That's why I walk around the club first to let all the big timers see what they're missing being stationed in front of the big stage.

My ass was out, but it was showcased with a silver rhinestone thong on with sheer turquoise paneled pants with the silver rhinestone band around my waist and ankles. I never got truly naked at stage three. These niggas went crazy over me. Remember, I keep this body on point. Washboard abs, thigh gap, and wide hips in addition to my pretty ass face, smooth caramel skin and voluptuous ass and tits. I knew I was fine!! And I sold a fantasy so good, that everyone thought they had a chance with me when I was on that stage! And I knew that shit. My confidence was through the roof.

I also never got it twisted that real relationships don't ignite at the club often. I did hear that the bitch Free ended up getting pregnant and James proposed to her. Getting pregnant wasn't one of those things on the top of my list. I always envisioned getting pregnant at like thirty-five when I knew I wouldn't be doing this foolishness anymore. But now that Monroe dismissed me, I was starting from scratch. I just knew we were forever. Damn!

But back to that feeling in the pit of my stomach about seeing Don tomorrow. I had already picked my outfit out yesterday when he called me. I was going to wear my lingerie underneath my clothes. I had my perfume picked out, Lolita Lempicka, and I would bring a little oil in to refresh my skin for him. The lingerie I picked out was pink, with black piping. My C cups were going to be pushed up to my chin and I had the garter belt to match with the crotchless thongs. I knew he would want me to dance for him, so I was hoping I would be able to bring my little portable radio and play my music. But, lemme get back to the present and keep on knocking these niggas hands away from tryna get underneath my sparkly ass thong. Ugh, here we go with this shit.

Dee Dee

"Mike, I need you to go with me to Maryland this time. Something is wrong with Aubrey. I'm scared of what I might find. Samantha hasn't returned my calls, nor has Monroe. Aubrey's phone is going straight to voicemail, which means either she doesn't have it, it's off, or the battery is dead." Dead. I never want to use that word in a sentence when I'm talking about my Aubrey. Until I met Mike twelve years ago, Aubrey was the absolute center of my universe. Raising her as a single parent in the military was hard. Her father disappeared when she was still baking in my tummy.

Her father, August, was such a beautiful man. He was from the Virgin Islands and I met him during one of my temporary duty assignments. The Air Force was conducting a secret intelligence operation, and as an Intelligence Officer, it was one of the first times that I was allowed in the field. I met him one morning after finishing my run on the beach. Now at fifty-seven years old, I looked damn good! But at twenty-four, standing at five feet, six inches, with an ample bosom, tiny waist and a generous booty, I was what these kids refer to now as 'on fleek'! Long sandy brown hair, full pouty lips, caramel complexion in that Virgin Island sun, I was stacked! I met this beautiful, dark chocolate man with this gorgeous, thick and curly jet black hair and these seductive hazel brown eyes.

As soon I saw him, I was in love. I was there for three months and we had a whirlwind romance. I got back to the United States and we still kept in touch. We were making plans to see one another, but then I found out two months after I returned home that I was pregnant with Aubrey. I called August and I was so excited because we were already talking about marriage and trying to build together and having kids was something he told me that he wanted with me. I was so young, that I didn't realize that he was just selling me a dream.

Twenty-five years ago

Dee Dee

"Hello August, it's Denise."

August

"Hey my lady. What are you doing? I was just thinking about your body on top of mine the last time I saw you. I can't wait until it's every day." August said in his sexy ass accent.

Dee Dee

"Me too baby, me too. But um, I um, have something to tell you about… that um, probably happened the last time my body was on top of yours." I paused for what seemed like an eternity. "I'm pregnant." He got quiet for afterward, just briefly, and then he started talking again after what seemed like forever. I was so nervous!

August

"Oh baby, you're having my baby? This is wonderful news! I cannot wait to tell my mother! Let's get married as soon as possible. Let me go tell everyone the great news! Can we talk later?" He asked me.

Dee Dee

"Yes love. Call me later. I love you."

August

"Ok, goodbye." August said as he hurried me off the phone.

Dee Dee

I was a little confused, yet I was excited at the same time. I started shopping for dresses, so that we could have a beach wedding. I didn't have much family, as I grew up in a foster home. But as soon as I turned eighteen, I was out of there! It wasn't bad- it just wasn't a loving environment. I told my closest girlfriend and she was excited for me. She also agreed to be my Maid of Honor.

He didn't call me back that night, but I continued to call him with no answer. Once the call did go through, and he answered on the first ring and seemed surprised that I was on the other end. "August, is everything ok? I've been calling you to make plans for the wedding. Why haven't I heard from you?" I asked him.

August

"Denise, I'm sorry. I cannot marry you. I cannot be the father of your baby. My mother would not approve. Sweetheart, I'm so sorry. Please do not call me again." He said very matter-of-factly. I just hung up the phone because I couldn't believe that this sweet, beautiful man that I had come to know, would say that to me. After all the plans and promises. He could just say that to *me*? What did his mother have to do with our relationship? I just didn't know what to think.

Present Day

Mike

"When do you want to leave baby? I'm there." My husband, Mike asked me.

Dee Dee

"They didn't have any flights tonight, so tomorrow morning. I can't go another day baby. I have to see my baby." He held me in his arms for a while until I calmed down. Once I did, I started calling Monroe and Sam again. They were going to tell me something.

Joe

What the fuck did Samantha mean "like he did me"? She had some serious explaining to do. "Samantha, please tell me you were not with that clown ass nigga too baby. You're so much better than that. Please tell me what you mean." I'm trying my best to keep my anger at bay, but she just threw me for a loop with that shit.

Sam

I wanted to open up to Joe in my own time. I knew how he felt about Robert. I told him about the rape, just not about who did it to me. It was just too close to home. I thought maybe he would have done something to get himself into trouble. But now, I've put my foot into my mouth.

"Baby, I told you that I was raped, but I didn't tell you the details. The reason why, and I want you to remain calm, is because Rob raped me in my dorm room and shortly thereafter, I became pregnant. I told Aubrey very recently and she took it very hard, like it was her fault. I knew that you would have a similar reaction and I was trying to figure out how I was going to tell you as well. I'm so sorry it came out like this." Joe sat there and was very quiet for a good little while. He seemed like he was calm and collected, but once he spoke, I knew otherwise.

Joe

"Sam, I'm going to find him and I'm going to kill him. Where are your car keys?" Joe said emotionlessly.

I sat there quiet for second, but when I looked at his face, I knew there was no convincing him otherwise. "Baby, I'm coming with you. I want to see him take his last breath." I told my man, surprising myself.

Chapter 8

Dee Dee

We're finally on the way to the airport to fly to Baltimore Washington International. I need to see my baby; it's now been three days since I last heard from her. My phone vibrated and I answered immediately. "Hello, Aubrey? Baby are you ok?"

Unknown Caller

"Hello, may I speak to Mrs. Roberson please?"

Dee Dee

"This is she. What can I do for you?" I started to get worried. Who was this calling me from a Maryland number? "Who is this please?"

Unknown Caller

"Mrs. Roberson, this is Dr. Sawyer from Prince George's Hospital Center. Do you have a relative by the name of Aubrey Denise Collins?"

Dee Dee

This feeling of dread just made me start sweating profusely. I had to calm myself down mentally, so that Mike could continue to focus on driving us to the airport. "Um, yes, that's my daughter. Is she ok? Please God, tell me she's alright. Please…" Dee Dee shrieked.

Dr. Sawyer

"Mrs. Roberson,-", Dr. Sawyer started.

Dee Dee

"Please call me Denise. Go on." I was dreading this conversation, but I needed to hear exactly what she was going to say. Mike comforted me with his right hand as he steered the car with his left to help me calm down. I found myself holding my breath as the doctor resumed speaking to me.

Dr. Sawyer

"Well Denise, Aubrey has been in a bad car accident and is currently in surgery. Would you be able to come to the hospital to handle her affairs in case of-" Dee Dee cut the doctor off again, for fear of what she was about to say.

Dee Dee

"Dr. Sawyer, there is no other conclusion to this situation other than my daughter making a full recovery and I won't hear anything else concerning this matter. My faith won't allow it. I am currently on my way to Miami International Airport to fly there today. I encourage you to do your very best, as I cannot and will not live without my daughter in this world. She's a strong young lady, and I want your mind and your total effort concentrated on her. I will be there shortly, and I'm counting on you." I disconnected the call with her as tears were spilling down my cheeks.

"Mike, I need you to get us to the airport safely. But I want to let you know that my baby is in surgery because she's been in a car accident. I need to get to her as soon as possible." With that, he got us to the airport in record time. He handled everything, coordinated with the airline to get us on the earliest nonstop flight to BWI. He also arranged the rental car and hotel room closest to the hospital my baby was in. I texted Monroe and Sam to let them both know that I was disappointed in them. But I also let them know where Aubrey was, so that she wouldn't be alone and that I was on my way.

Monroe

"SHIT!" Ms. Denise just texted me. I feel so ashamed about not letting her know what was going on. But I truly didn't have anything to tell her. I could have at least let her know that I was looking for Aubrey. My baby has been laid up in the hospital. I saw that the text also went to Sam so I didn't have to call her and Joe.

"James, as soon as we get to Free's house and make sure she's good, do you mind if I take your car to the hospital? Aubrey was in a bad car accident."

James

"Sure, no problem Boss. I don't need to be anywhere else. I'll put a couple of guys as security on her room. Just let me know the room number as soon as you get there."

Monroe

"Thanks bruh, I really appreciate you." I replied to James. It truly felt like my head was spinning. Like nothing else in this world mattered at this moment. Why didn't I think to call the hospitals? I was too fuckin' busy thinking about that lil nigga to see anything else. I would never have forgiven myself if my baby died all by herself in that hospital. I had to stop thinking like this. She was going to be just fine. She had to! We pulled up to Free's house and as soon as James cuts the car off, he runs inside the house with his weapon drawn. I follow behind him with mine drawn as well.

James

"Fresia, baby, you ok? I'm here baby." I head upstairs to the computer room where she should have been locked in with the baby. When I got to the top of the stairs, the computer room door was hanging open at an angle and I could tell something was wrong. I went into the room and she nor the baby was there. I went throughout the rest of the house and instructed Money to keep watch for Free's car, because it was still parked in the driveway. As I continued to go through the rest of the rooms, I realized she wasn't there. I went back to the computer room to review the tapes.

"Money!" I yelled in a panic. "Come here!"

Monroe

I heard the desperation in James' voice, so I ran up the stairs to find out what was going on. When I got to the room he was in, he was watching something on the screen. There was no sound, but there was Free with the baby in her hands. She looked scared like someone was in the house. I could see her fumbling with the phone as she was trying to soothe their crying daughter at the same time. Someone busted into the room at the moment that she was speaking to someone on the line. It was Rob. He tried taking the baby out of her hands, but Free wouldn't let the baby go. He eventually decided to take both of them while slapping Free in the back of her head and pushing her out of the room, and then out of the front door once they got downstairs. He forced her to get into his car, and then drove off. By this time, tears were streaming down James' face. I felt helpless. I wanted to help him find Free, but all I could think about was getting to the hospital to Aubrey. Then I heard police sirens in the distance. At that point, I saw Free's cell phone still connected to the police department in the corner. I took James' gun out of his hand and hid it along with mine deep into the attic before "five-o" arrived.

Rob

I went back to Free's house after Aubrey sped off. I was about to follow her, but she left so fast that I knew my chase would have been futile. She had too much of head start and I had another plan that needed to be put into action anyway. Once I was able to enter her home, I forcefully took Free and my baby girl to a hotel room off of I-95. I was finally able to meet my daughter. She was so pretty! I thought she would end up looking like my mom. My mother was gorgeous. Light skin with beautiful hair and skin. But my daughter looked just like her mother. She just slept in my arms and Free looked like I was going to hurt her or something. Why would she think that I would hurt my own baby though? That's crazy. I love her, but I just realized that I didn't know her name.

"Free, what is my daughter's name?" She just looked at me, until I looked back at her in a menacing way.

Free

"MY daughter's name is Tamia Lavonne Casey." Free said to me quietly so as not to alarm the baby.

Rob

"Casey? But your name is Walker and my name is Williams. Why would her name be Casey?" I was truly confused at this point.

Free

"Because her father's last name is Casey." She said with venom.

Rob

At that point, I snapped and back handed the shit out of her. I placed the baby down safely before I forgot that she was still in my arms. I knew this was my baby. She knew better than to cheat on me. And when Free was getting herself together after she got up off the ground, she went over to check on the baby.

It was then that I remembered that I hadn't had any decent head in quite some time. And she was looking so good as usual. Those full titties, those suckable lips and that phat ass almost made my mouth water. She was the only one that could swallow up this dick like I liked it and she was about to oblige me today. Since I was able to relieve her of her weapon earlier, I made a request. Actually, it was more of a demand.

"Come over here, take off your clothes and suck my dick." She looked at me like she wanted to cry.

Free

"Rob, no. I have my daughter here." Free said with tears welling up in her eyes.

Rob

"It wasn't a question bitch, put her down and come over here. I want you to undress now and suck my dick like you know I like it." I lifted the gun to let her know I wasn't playing with her. "And if I feel your teeth on my shit, I will fuck you up." She came over and reluctantly did as I asked. When she undressed, my dick got hard as a muthafucka.

Her body was even better after the baby. I'm not even sure how she did it, but her titties were even more plump than I remembered. It must have been due to the breastfeeding. Her waist was small again, even though she had just a little bit of loose skin around it. And her ass, man it was phat as fuck! I just wanted to see if she could still clap that shit like she would do for me when I hit it in the past.

She walked over slowly and cowered down in front of me. I took out my dick, and it was standing at attention at the sight of her pretty ass lips. "Get on your hands and knees. I wanna see that ass in the air."

She did as she was told. I ensured that the gun remained in sight so that she would do what I said. This bitch had the nerve to gag a little bit, like I was disgusting or something. "Bitch, you throw up on my dick and I will fuck your ass up. I don't give a fuck if my daughter sees. Hesitantly, she opened her mouth and I guided my dick into it. Her mouth was nice and hot. She started to lower her mouth onto my dick and all I could do was moan softly.

"Ooohhh yeeessssssssss..."

I had the nine in my left hand, so I used my right hand to push the back of her head deeper into my lap. She started to suck me off just like she knew I liked it. I ignored the tears running down her face, and just concentrated on the pleasure she was giving me. I glanced over in the corner and the baby was still asleep, so I figured I had time to do to Free whatever I wanted. I started to pump her face because she was crying too hard so that I could get what I needed from her. It had been a while, so I decided I would take my time to give her this nut. I held the back of her head while I fucked her throat repeatedly. I felt my nut building up, so I slowed down.

"Damn girl. This shit feels amazing, you still got it baby. Keep that shit going." I demanded. Fresh tears rolled down her cheeks, and I kept it steady until I felt my head begin to swell. With the gun still in my hand, I grabbed her head on both sides with my hands and fucked her throat even harder. I released all of my seed down her throat and I dared her to let it come back up.

"Swallow all of this nut, bitch. Don't let none of it come outta your mouth either. Ahhhhhh ooooooooohhhhh mmmmhhhhhhmmmmm." I kept pumping until I was sure that I was finished. "Now I want you to make that ass clap for a real nigga. Get up off your hands and knees and turn around."

She got up like I said and turned around and twerked that ass real lazy for me. I didn't care how she did it, my dick was hard again in no time. I looked over in the corner where Tamia was in her carrier and she was still sound asleep. I laid down on the bed and instructed Free to come over to me. "I want you to ride this dick like you used to. Make me nut again, but catch that shit in your mouth and don't let one drop get on me or I'm gonna fuck you up."

She did what I told her and I was in Heaven. Marie wish she had pussy that felt as good as Free's or even Aubrey's. Free was still crying and shit so I told her bitch ass to turn around so I wouldn't have to see that shit. I was glad I did, because I had a perfect view of that ass bouncing up and down, making my dick disappear and then reappear. I felt her about to cum, and she stopped so that she wouldn't. I pumped that pussy from the bottom while holding onto her hips and brought that shit up out of her anyway. She creamed all over this dick and cried even harder. Once I made her cum, I flipped her over so that I could dig all up in her guts from the back. I hit that shit and made her ass squirt. My dick was magic!

Once I decided it was my turn, I took my dick out of her box and put it in her ass. I hit it like I was trying to punish her, because I was. When I was ready to nut, I tapped her on her ass like I usually did to alert her that I was ready, and she obeyed me like a good little girl and caught all of my flow in her warm mouth.

"Suck that shit bitch, don't be lazy." And with that, she began to suck my dick like her life depended on it, because it did. I felt dizzy, just like I did when I was inside of Aubrey earlier that day. Once she was done swallowing all of my fluids, I pushed her off of me, and laid down beside her with my arm draped over her. I dared her ass to move. I would have beat the shit out of her, but she just laid there. I'm sure she kept her eyes on the baby until she fell asleep as well.

Chapter 9

Sam

Joe and I rushed to Prince George's Hospital to be with Aubrey. She was still in surgery by the time we got there, so we prayed and prayed out in the waiting room. Monroe had not yet made it, but I was sure he was still out trying to find Rob. Joe seemed inconsolable. I'm sure he blamed himself for not talking her out of going to rescue Rob. Now she was here, and we should have stopped her. I was trying to be strong, but I felt guilty as well. Especially after Mrs. Dee Dee's text message this morning. Why didn't I answer the phone and just tell her what I knew?

"Baby, please drink some water and try to calm yourself. I don't need you being admitted today as well." He took the water and drank some of it. I just hugged him from the back until he stopped crying so hard.

Joe

This shit was all my fault! Now, Aubrey was laid up in here with injuries that could possibly take her life. "I'm so sorry Aubrey, I'm so sorry. Why couldn't you just listen to me, then we would just be at Sam's house still chilling. Please pull through, I don't think I would be able to handle your death. I love you." And with that I finished my prayer and just sat there, just numb.

Sam

I'm really not sure about how to feel right now. It sounded like Aubrey was Joe's girl with that prayer. Once I heard him say that he loved her, I removed my arms from around him and moved away. Does he still have feelings for her? I guess I'll find out soon enough, huh? Sam worried.

Free

I forgot to lock the damn back door. I always forget that door, but James is always there to lock it for me. How could I be so stupid? I got my baby here with this lunatic, and it was all my fault. I called the police and as usual, they took too long to respond. I mean, what if me or my baby were dying? My house alarm started blaring when Rob entered my home. The patio is where I have my coffee each morning. And he distracted me with his call after I stepped back into the house. I just can't believe that I didn't remember to lock it. The kicker is, James even reminded me! I couldn't run right now if I wanted to. My pretty baby... I'm so sorry Tamia, I'm so sorry baby.

She woke up a couple of times last night and luckily, she's on breast milk because there is absolutely nothing here to feed a baby. I know James is worried out of his mind. I have to figure out how to get us out of this room. Why couldn't I pull the trigger? WHY? I thought I was comfortable with my nine-millimeter. I had trained on it, more than once. Why couldn't I just injure him? I knew I didn't want to actually kill him, but if I did kill anybody it would be his ass. But let me get my hands on my gun now, I'm gonna shoot the shit outta this muthafucka for what he just did to me! All these thoughts were racing through my mind.

It wasn't until Tamia started crying again, that I was jolted back into the present. I knew she wasn't hungry, I had just fed her. She was wet. I had no diapers. "Rob, my baby needs pampers." He was still trying to sleep, but he held on to me so I wouldn't try to run.

Rob

Why was this baby crying again? I'm trying to sleep. Why didn't she grab the bag before we left the house? With her stupid ass. She knew she was gonna need it. "Gimme the baby." She looked at me like she was scared I was going to do something to her. "Why do you keep looking at me like that when I want to hold my daughter? Bitch, if I'm gonna hurt anybody, it's gonna be yo' ass. Keep looking at me like that! Now give me the baby." She hesitated but relented and handed her to me as I requested. "Now go in the bathroom, get a towel so you can wrap it around her."

Free

"These hotel towels are going to irritate her skin. The chemicals they wash them in are too much for a baby. We can handle them, but she can't. Her little vagina will be all messed up if I were to do that. Please let's just go to the store and get her some pampers. I can't stand for her to be uncomfortable." Free cried.

Rob

"You think I'm stupid, huh? You wanna go out in public so that you can tell somebody what happened. I'm not stupid, Free." Rob said menacingly.

Free

"I'm not going to say anything to anyone, I just want to take care of my baby." I said as I reached for her. I had to convince him to get us out of here. By this point, she was screaming her little head off. I removed her pamper while trying to soothe her. "It's okay mama, mommy's here. It's ok baby. I was trying to rock her without making him aroused again. I was still naked from hours ago when he made me fuck him.

My very first time having sex after having the baby was supposed to be special. I was looking forward to making it special for James. As usual, Rob took that experience away from me. My pregnancy started out rough because of him, but at least I was able to enjoy the rest of that experience with James. He told me to lock that back door, I should've double checked. Why in the world did I freeze up like that? God please help me.

Rob

I had no other choice but to take her to the store with me. I couldn't leave her there, she would call someone for sure. I couldn't just take the baby with me, I didn't have a car seat. Shit! I didn't think this through. I started pacing the room trying to think of a plan. "I got it!" Rob exclaimed.

"Get dressed, let's go to the store. You try anything funny Free, and I'm going to kill you and take her away with me." The only reason she's still alive, is because I don't know anything about taking care of no little baby. Plus, she supplies the baby with milk. And as long as she's alive, she supplies me with that amazing pussy!

Free

As I started getting dressed, I'm trying to think of a plan to get away from him. "Come on Free!" I said to myself in the bathroom. I gotta think of something and quick! I was getting hopeful. I had to do this for my daughter.

Dee Dee

We finally arrived at BWI airport. I was on auto pilot the entire time with getting to the hospital as the only thing on my mind. I just wanted my baby to be alright. I kept my shades on, because I was a mess. Mike was so helpful, he retrieved our bags from baggage claim, pulled the rental car up to where I was, loaded it up and we headed to the hospital. On the way, I felt my chest tightening, and I knew I was having a panic attack. Mike pulled the car over and began to pray over me and for Aubrey.

Mike

"Breathe, my love. The Lord has Aubrey in His hands, and she's going to come out of this just fine. He has anointed those doctors with the ability to save her life and she is going to fully recover in Jesus' holy name. We are going to get through this minor set back as a family, as God intended and with His love and grace, Aubrey is going to be better than ever. Lord God, please lead us through this to support Aubrey with Your strength, oh God, and we shall continue to bless your Holy name. In Jesus' name, Amen."

Dee Dee

"Amen." I felt those words through my entire being and I believed with all my heart that He was going to pull Aubrey through this. I just chanted the rest of the way to the hospital as I held Mike's hand. "Thank you, God, thank you Jesus. Thank you, God, thank you Jesus..."

Sam

I went to the nurse's station every few minutes it seemed, to check on Aubrey's status but they would only tell family. I tried to tell her that I was her sister, but she was being such a stickler and told me she would only release information to who was on her next of kin form. I was so stressed and on top of that, Joe still wouldn't eat nor speak. He felt so guilty. "Baby, please eat something for me. You're going to end up in a hospital bed as well and what kind of help will you be for Aubrey? Huh? Baby please, just eat a little something for me."

He looked at me and decided to take a couple of crackers and ate them. I handed him some water and he drank some of that too. Then he resumed that blank stare until I told him that her mom and stepdad had walked in. We met them at the desk and waited for the nurse to tell Ms. Dee Dee what she wouldn't tell me. Bree had swelling on the brain, a broken leg, and a fractured wrist, so they induced a coma to allow the swelling to go down. Right now, it was a waiting game to see what happens.

Dee Dee

"Can I see her?" I asked the nurse.

Nurse

"Ma'am, let me see if the doctor is out of surgery. Dr. Sawyer gave me instructions to inform you of your daughter's injuries in case you arrived before she was done. I have a private waiting area to take you to in the meantime, and she also wanted me to let you know that she was doing absolutely everything she could to ensure your daughter would be ok. I placed some water on the table in the waiting area, and I'll be back to give you any information that I receive."

Mike

"We thank you so very much for your assistance. Come on Dee, let's go sit and pray."

Dee Dee

"Yes, thank you so much." I told her, as I laid my head on Mike's chest and let him guide me into the private waiting area.

Mike

"She's going to pull through baby. She's got God on her side and all this love surrounding her from us and her friends. Can I get you anything? You haven't eaten today my love."

Dee Dee

"I'm alright for now baby, thank you so much." We just sat and prayed. I just wanted to give up so many times and give in to the despair I was absolutely feeling. We had been at the hospital about thirty minutes, but it felt more like thirty hours. To be this close to my baby and not be able to see her or touch her…. Talk to her and hear her speak back, this was my own personal hell. I had to give this to God. It was truly the only way I would get through this.

James

The police had arrived shortly after we did to the house. They reviewed our security tapes and discovered that he entered the house through the back door. I always have to lock the back door when Fresia comes back in after having her morning coffee. Had I checked to make sure we had the right nigga in the first place last night, my lady and my daughter would still be here. I really appreciated Monroe being here with me, but I know he was as worried about Aubrey as I was about Free. He called a few of our street guys and told them that the priority was to find Rob. They were instructed not to kill him, but to take him back to the warehouse. I knew we shouldn't have let this nigga go the first time. Fuck what Don is talking about, when I get my hands on him, I'm gonna do him worse than any voodoo bitch ever could.

Chapter 10

Monroe

I have my goons out looking for this nigga. They have the make, model and license plate number for his car along with his picture. He's a dead man walking, and I can bet *my* life on that! My police connect is also monitoring his credit card activity, and they also have a picture of Free so they can keep a lookout for her.

I'm raced to Prince George's Hospital to find out the status of my lady. As soon as I got there, I saw her mom, stepdad, Sam and Joe sitting in the waiting room. Her mom hugged me, as I apologize profusely. "Please forgive me. I've been trying to find her and to find Rob. He did this, I just know it. I was just so overcome with rage. And I'm so sorry." I also hugged Sam. I shook Mike's hand and spoke to Joe as well.

"Mrs. Roberson, I know that Rob had something to do with this and I've been looking for him since yesterday. I'm so sorry that I wasn't able to tell you anything, because I didn't know where she was. But I will deal with him, you don't have to worry about that."

I felt Joe mean muggin' me for some reason, but I wasn't here for all that. If he had something to say, he could do so. At that moment, the doctor came over to give us more information.

Dr. Sawyer

"Ms. Collins is stable for now, but we're monitoring her very closely. I induced the coma so that we can relieve the swelling from her brain. You can't see her yet, as we want to ensure a stress-free environment for now. Mrs. Roberson, here's my card with my personal cell number. Please trust that my team and I are doing our very best to care for your daughter. If you'd like to get some rest and come back when you're able to see her, please do so."

Dee Dee

"With all due respect doctor, I'm not leaving this hospital until I know my baby is alright. I need to see her." The doctor hesitated for a minute, but finally she yielded.

Dr. Sawyer

"Mrs. Roberson, I'm can only allow you to go in for a few minutes to see your daughter. I have to warn you, that she is hooked up to a breathing machine and she is very swollen. With the extent of her injuries, it's going to be a shock to you to see her this way. I need you to understand that additional stress can affect her very negatively, so I need you to keep your emotions at bay. Do you understand what I'm saying?" Dr. Sawyer asked concerningly.

Dee Dee

"Take me to my daughter." I said.

Dr. Sawyer

"Yes ma'am, please follow me." Dr. Sawyer instructed.

Dee Dee

I tried mentally preparing myself to see Aubrey, but there are no words to explain how I felt when I saw her hooked up to those machines and wires and all those bandages on her. Her leg was slightly elevated, and my baby's beautiful face. Her face! She was so puffy, and her eye was black and blue and I could tell it was swollen shut. I touched her left hand gently and prayed over her. I wanted her to hear my voice, so when I was done, I spoke directly to her.

"Aubrey, baby, it's me, mommy. I'm here sweetie and I need for you to get better. We're all here and we can't wait for you to come back to us. Please come back to me baby. Please. Be strong and know that it's not your time to go yet, baby. Come back to me, mommy loves you so, so much." I rubbed her hand and kissed her. My whole heart was in this room, there is no way I would be able to live without her. I was going to remain hopeful and trust that God's got my baby. The doctor came back to the door signaling that it was time to go. I looked at my baby again. "Mommy will be waiting for you baby, I love you so much."

When I left her room, I made it back to Mike before I broke down. I started to feel the tightness in my chest again and Monroe signaled to a nurse that I needed some assistance. They took me to a room and laid me down for observation. The doctor informed me that I was indeed having a panic attack. She gave me a Valium to relax me. Mike sat beside my bed and assured me that it was ok to fall asleep and that he would wake me up if anything changed.

Monroe

I paced the waiting room, angry that there was nothing I could do. I called Benny, one of the guys that was holding Marie for me. I told him to put her on the phone.

Marie

I started speaking before I allowed Monroe to say hello. "You do know that when I leave this place again, that I'm going to kill you, right? I'm going to kill you, your number two and everyone that is currently involved with my kidnapping." I said as I looked around the room at his "employees".

Monroe

"Whatever bitch… Look, Rob is on the run. Is there anything you can do to help me find him? I know you have some type of voodoo shit that you can perform because of what you did to Demetrius." Monroe replied.

Marie

"Oh, and how is Demetrius? Is he resting well?" Marie laughed. I knew how he was doing because of the mixture I gave him. He will be comatose until I release him from it. "And now you need my help? Why would I help you? You want to kill, Robert, no?"

Monroe

"If you help me, I'll give you whatever you want." Monroe pleaded with her. "I'm desperate, Marie. Otherwise you would already be dead." She was making me angry. I had to let her know that I still had the upper hand. And if she was smart, she would help me out.

Marie

"I want Robert. Will you give him back to me?" She requested.

Monroe

"I can't exactly *give* him back to you just like that, there's got to be something else you want? You name it, if you help me, I'll give you whatever else you want. Is there a way you can help me find him?" Monroe asked, desperate at this point.

Marie

"I told you my condition. I will help you locate him, only if you give him back to me. I wasn't done with him yet."

Monroe

I sighed and removed the phone from my ear. This bitch was being impossible. She said she wanted him back, but she didn't specify what condition he would have to be in though. I suddenly had an idea. "Ok, I'll give him back if you help me locate him. But you have to drop trying to kill James and I. And I need for Demetrius to wake up too." I hoped she went for it. This bitch could be my downfall.

Marie

I thought for a while because that seemed too easy. "Okay, it's a deal. As long as you let me take Robert with me when I leave town *alive*, I will never bother you or James again." Marie agreed.

Monroe

"Alright, done. What do I need to do?" I asked.

Marie

"Well for starters, get me the hell out of here." And with that I gave the phone back to the man holding me. "Take me to your friend Demetrius so I can wake him."

Monroe

"Make sure that Demetrius is alright. Do not release her until I return."

Taisha

It was finally the day I was going to see Don. I took a long bubble bath with essential oils to enhance my relaxation because I was nervous! I can't even explain why, but Big Don was the cream of the crop. I didn't want to go too hard and turn him off. I wanted everything to be perfect. I just had to get that call back, because he was going to be my cash cow for the next year or so, hopefully.

After calming my nerves and getting myself cleaned up, I straightened my hair and got dressed. I made the forty-five minute drive to the prison in Jessup and went through the normal procedure of having my things checked and then I was escorted to a room with a twin mattress on a concrete slab. This isn't very romantic at all, but this will have to do. I placed my bedding down with my recently perfume sprayed sheets to set the mood. I knew I wasn't going to be able to bring in any candles, so the sheets would serve as my aromatherapy.

I set up my small radio, I was happy they allowed me to bring that in. I had my music prerecorded so that I could perform my routine that I choreographed just for him. I pushed Monroe out of my mind, as I did prior to any performance and finally Don was escorted in the room and the door was locked behind him.

In his eyes was nothing but lust and desire for my body. It was showtime. I took a deep breath and went over to him and escorted him to the twin bed in the barren cell turned sex den. I started my playlist with the song "Focus", by H.E.R.

"Me - Can you focus on me?
Baby, can you focus... on me?
Me...

Hands in the soap
How the faucet's running and I keep looking at you
Stuck on your phone and you're stuck in your zone
You don't have a clue

But I don't wanna give up
Baby, I just want you to get up
Lately I've been a little fed up
Wish you would just focus on

Me - Can you focus on me?
Baby, can you focus... on me?
Me..."

I swayed to the music real sexy like, while I unfastened each of the buttons down the sides of the legs of my fitted black satin joggers. I tossed them into the corner of the room, as I made my heart shaped ass "talk" to him one cheek at a time. Next, I shed my sheer black top until I was only clad in my red lace lingerie and my high heeled red pumps. I removed my garter belt and dropped into a full split, which I noticed had him all but drooling by this time.

I finished my performance to the song as I sat facing Big Don in the chair, legs spread slightly so he had a very clear view of my pretty pussy through my red lace crotchless panty set. When I was done, I grabbed Don by the hands and pulled him up off of the bed and proceeded to undress him while the next song played.

"I know you wanna love
But I just wanna fuck
And girl you know the deal
I gotta keep it real
I know you wanna see
I know you wanna be
In my B-E-D, grinding slowly

I know you wanna love
But I just wanna fuck
And girl you know the deal
I gotta keep it real
I know you wanna see
I know you wanna be
In my B-E-D, grinding slowly"

His dick was at attention and I guided him to the bed where I then took him into my mouth and started to pleasure him orally as I kept my eyes on his. The visit was ninety minutes, so I could take my time. I made love to Don like he was my man, over and over again. The only thing was, he said he wasn't using a condom. That was a hard one for me, because other than Monroe and my ex before him, I've never fucked anyone else raw. He told me that his wife was the only other person he sexed raw. Any other chicks he strapped up with when they came to visit. After the first couple of times I sexed him, surprisingly, he wanted to chat.

Big Don

"I've always been curious about you, I just respected the relationship you had with Money. I see why you're so special. I want you to come see me twice a week, on Tuesdays and Fridays. No exceptions. Even during your cycle weeks, I expect you to be here. Now let's talk money, how much do you need on a monthly basis."

Taisha

"Well Don, I don't want to strip anymore. I grew accustomed to the life Money had provided me, so I would like ten thousand dollars a month." I replied.

Big Don

"Now Tai… be realistic with me darlin. You're no spring chicken. This pussy has been sampled by any major player within a fifty-mile radius of the club you worked in that you were willing to bust it wide open for to secure that bag. Now, I'm willing to offer you five thousand a month and I'll also pay your mortgage, but that's it." He countered.

Taisha

Well I didn't plan to have to negotiate. I thought that ten thousand dollars was a fair price. But five thousand plus my mortgage paid would still allow me to do what I wanted. And if I needed extra money, I knew how to get it. "Take it or leave it?" I asked.

Big Don

"What do you think? You know me." Big Don retorted with a grin on his face. This was an easy sell. He was glad that he reconsidered. Taisha was the best lay he had had in a while. She was worth so much more, but he wanted to see what she was willing to do.

Taisha

And with that, I agreed. Where else would I get a steady income for fucking and sucking a few times a month. Taisha thought.

Big Don

"Now come back over here and put that pussy on me again." Big Don requested.

Taisha

I did whatever he wanted, however he wanted. I can't necessarily say that I enjoyed it, but with time, maybe I would learn to. I also made a mental note to get back on birth control. His pull-out game I could tell, was very weak.

Chapter 11

Free

We headed to the store and Rob insisted on holding my baby. I guess that was his way of insuring that I wouldn't say anything to anyone or try to run away. We were in Walmart and I was headed to the baby section with Rob on my heels. I was trying to make eye contact with anyone that I could, but no one was paying any particular attention to me. I suddenly got an idea. Rob knew nothing about James because I made it a point not to tell him my business. I wonder if I can convince him to take me home.

"Rob, why don't we just go back to my house. I'm sure if the police ever showed up, that they've gone by now. I mean, we usually stay there anyway. Tamia will be comfortable there in her crib and we can do whatever like we used to." I was nervous as hell, as this was the only card I knew to play.

Rob

It's gotta be a reason why she wants me to take her home. "Why you really wanna go home Free? You tryna play me or something?"

Free

"Rob, you got me and my baby in that dusty ass room. All of our belongings are at my house. I mean, what's the real reason why we're staying in that room anyway? At least at my house, we have food, the baby has her food and there are diapers and her comfort zone. I just want my daughter to be comfortable. No games, I promise." I hoped this would work, considering I had already said something to him about the baby having a different father. I prayed he forgot about that piece.

Rob

"Well the alarm was going off. You think I was gonna stay there and wait for you to hand me over to the pigs though? Fuck outta here." Then I thought about it. "Do they usually leave after the alarm has been tripped though?" Rob thought curiously.

Free

"I'm really not sure, but if we ride by the house we can at least check." I hope he's thinking about it. "And then we don't have to buy anything new because I have what I need at home." I would like to shower and be comfortable in my own home. "Plus, I pumped and need to use the breast milk I have refrigerated before it expires." Please God, let him take me home, Free thought optimistically. And I'm hoping there are no police there.

Rob

I mean, she does have a point. And her home is comfortable. Money and that big nigga James don't know her, so I can definitely stay there and lay low. That idea is actually great, hopefully "five-o" ain't camped around her house. "Let's go." I said to her. And with that, we headed to the car.

Free

Please, please, please don't let the police be there. James, I hope is out looking for me. Timing is everything, if I can just get Rob really comfortable where he's not paranoid. I just have to act normal. Free thought to herself. I prayed the whole ride to my house.

Sam

Joe remained at the hospital. I care for Aubrey too, but what could he do just hanging around in the waiting room. I mean, he couldn't even see her. I went home so that I could get a bath and some fresh clothes. I told him I would be back the next day and if he wanted me to come back to get him, to just give me a call. Am I overreacting concerning how I'm feeling about him wanting to be near Aubrey in her time of need when I want him near me also? Am I just jealous? As I ride home, and as those thoughts were going through my head, I decided to call Monroe to see how he was holding up.

<<<ring, ring>>>

Monroe

"Hey Sam, how are you? Is everything okay?"

Sam

"Hi Monroe, yes, I am fine considering. I was calling to see how you were holding up and if you needed anything." Sam asked thoughtfully.

Monroe

"I'm still on the same mission. Anything change with Aubrey since I left? How is her mom doing? I spoke to Mike a little earlier and he said she was resting then." I asked.

Sam

"Mrs. Dee Dee is doing alright, they're keeping her overnight for observation. There is no change with Aubrey, but it's better than her condition worsening." Sam replied.

Monroe

"You're absolutely right. But hey Sam, get you some rest, I'll talk to you tomorrow. Good night." Monroe said.

Sam

"Good night, Monroe." I replied as we hung up.

James

"After I was able to get rid of the police, I waited around in the dark for a while contemplating my next move. All of a sudden, I heard movement outside. I hid in the computer room where the security cameras were. I watched the monitors to check to see if I could see someone out there. I saw a man, woman and the man holding a baby. Could it be who I thought it was? I texted Monroe.

"Hey boss, I believe the lil nigga brought Free and the baby back. I'm in the computer room watching them on the monitors. I'm going to wait here until he falls asleep or something. The code to the front door is zero six one six. Bring the goons."

Monroe

"We will be there in fifteen minutes. Will await your signal to enter the house."

James

"Bet." James replied to Monroe's text message.

Free

After leaving Walmart, we headed to my house, which was almost a forty-minute ride. I don't believe I've ever prayed so hard in my life. On the ride to my house, I swear I was sweating and hoped he didn't notice. My baby had soiled her blanket that I wrapped around her a few hours ago, but she stayed sleep while I held her in my arms. Once we got to the house, there seemed to be no one there, and I was able to breathe again. Rob parked his car down the street, he took the baby from me and we walked a short distance to the house.

Rob

"What's the code, Free?" Rob demanded.

Free

"The code is zero six one six. The alarm shouldn't be on and the light switch is to the left."

Rob

"Alright." I opened the door and made sure not to make any sudden movements so as not to wake the baby. But I was watching Free though. I didn't trust her ass. We went inside and there was absolutely nothing going on in the house. I hoped it stayed like that for Free's sake. I wasn't playing around with her at all. I will kill her and not think anything of it. "I'm hungry, fix me something to eat. Where can I lay her?" Rob said.

Free

"I'll take her. I need to wipe her down and put a pamper and a sleeper on her. I'll be right back." I started to walk up the steps with Tamia and Rob was right behind me and pulled my hair hard.

Rob

"Like I told you before, don't fuck around with me Free. I *will* kill you. If you call anyone or try to get slick with me, I will blow your muthafuckin head off." Rob suggested as he pointed the barrel of the nine-millimeter at her temple.

Free

This shit is unreal. Yesterday, before I got his phone call, all was perfect in life. I had James, and we had our baby girl. How could I be so careless by leaving that back door unlocked again. Free thought. "I'm not playing games, I just want to take care of my baby." I said as tears ran down my face. I really couldn't believe that this was my fucking life. James please save me. He followed me up to the baby's room where I proceeded to change her. She woke up and she looked at me with her big bright eyes and I just wanted her to feel safe. I was trying my best to calm my nerves so she wouldn't sense that anything was wrong with me. "Can I feed her before I cook please?"

Rob

"Damn, didn't she just eat?" I was getting annoyed.

Free

"She didn't eat much. I know she's gonna be hungry soon and it'll be better for everyone if I feed her now so that I can try to get her back to sleep." Free replied cautiously.

Rob

"Whatever bitch, hurry up." Rob ordered.

Free

How the fuck was I supposed to hurry a baby? I swear his ass was stupid. Why did I ever get involved with this fuck nigga? I HATE his dumb ass, with a passion. I wiped her down and put a pamper on her. I put some nighttime lotion on her, while pulling her purple sleeper on her with the elephant on it.

I sat in the rocker and got the cover that I used in public to cover my breasts while I breastfeed so that he didn't start thinking about sexing me. I knew how this pervert's mind worked, anything could set him off. Tamia ate really good, but she didn't fall back to sleep right away. I knew she wouldn't because she had pretty much slept all day, which I was so thankful for. I was hoping I could keep her up for as long as I could so that he would fall asleep.

I wrapped the baby carrier to my body and strapped her in so she would be close to me. I went back down into the kitchen to see what I had to cook to feed this nigga. I realized I hadn't eaten in almost twenty-four hours, and I needed to eat but I wasn't hungry. I knew it wasn't healthy for my breastmilk, but I had some in the fridge for the baby when she got hungry again.

Monroe

I arrived at Free and James' house in record time with three of my street niggas that were always ready to go. I explained that we would wait until James gave us the signal before we moved in.

"Alright once I get the signal from James, Stevie and Goldie, ya'll will come with me. Benny, I need you to stay here in the vehicle in the shadows because the lil nigga might be able to manipulate his way out of there."

I saw his car parked down the street and had Goldie flatten the tires on the passenger side. He thought he was slick by doing that, but I'm hip. I'm way smarter than he looks. As of right now, it's just a waiting game.

Chapter 12

Dee Dee

I had a dream that I was with Aubrey walking and talking with her on the beach in Mexico. We had a great time on that trip, and I would give anything for us to be there again instead of in this hospital. When I awoke from my dream, I wasn't sure what time it was, but I knew it was late at night. Mike was in the corner of my room sleep in a chair with his feet propped up on a table. I knew he was uncomfortable, but I also knew that he wasn't going to leave me here by myself. I had to use the bathroom and I got up as quietly as I could, so as not to wake him.

I felt a lot better by now and was able to use the bathroom without awaking Mike. I peeked out of my room, and it was pretty quiet in the hospital and no one was moving around. I walked down the hall, trying to remain inconspicuous. Nobody said anything to me, as I made my way to Aubrey's room. She was in a more secured area of the hospital, but as I said, no one challenged me in any way. I went to the room that she was in earlier that day when I saw her and there she was.

She looked so peaceful accompanied by the beeping and whirring of the machines surrounding her. I got a chair and quietly brought it over to the side of her hospital bed so that I could sit with her. I took the hand attached to the arm that had no bruising or bandages as I did earlier. I quietly prayed. I prayed harder than ever.

I tried channeling all of the strength from all of the parents before me that have been in this very position. My baby had to live and fully recover. She MUST! Death was not welcomed in this room. I would not allow any of the negativity or stress that she has been through in recent years to cloud her mind! She must think *and* dream positively, she must bring herself out of this coma.

While I understand the reasoning for it, I just wish there was another way. "Lord, I just need a sign!" Ok, back to praying. "Lord you know my heart and You know my baby is a good person and she belongs to You. Please save her! Through saving her, you'll be saving me." And then it happened... Aubrey squeezed my hand.

Rob

"What's taking you so long to cook, bitch? What are you making? A nigga hungry as fuck. If it was gonna take this long, we could have picked something up." Free has been cooking for a minute. I hope she's not trying to stall me out. Good as that pussy was earlier, I'm getting some more. I can't understand it, but for as long as Marie was holding me in her apartment, I could never get the feeling of Free's pussy out of my brain. I guess I was addicted to that shit. But I'm back!! And I ain't never letting that ass go.

I mean, I love Aubrey, but her bitch ass ran away from me, and I could learn to love my baby mother right? Especially since that box is so fire. How the fuck was she still so fucking fine even right after having the baby though? I truly thought she wasn't going to be good mother because she's a hoe. But I can tell she loves my daughter more than anything. How the fuck was I supposed to know about chemicals a hotel towel was washed in?

Free

Tamia was just laughing and smiling at mommy as I was cooking for this nigga. I just kept talking to her and she just cooed. It was absolutely precious. I'm thankful that she is oblivious to this damn devil that was here invading our space, making demands and shit like he's supposed to be here. I know this nigga thought he was fuckin on me tonight, but he was sorely mistaken. I put some sleep aid in his mashed potatoes. He was going thee fuck to sleep! I also put some in his kool-aid, I'm not playing with this fuck nigga tonight.

"I know how you like your steak. Gimme a minute and I'll bring you your plate. Do you want broccoli or peas?"

Rob

"Free, now you know I want broccoli. I don't even know why you asked me that." That ass looking real good in those sweat pants, but why is the baby still awake? I ain't gonna be able to hit it like I want to if the baby woke looking dead in my face. "I thought you said she should be sleep by now?" Rob asked.

Free

"I think it's because you're here. She's curious." I lied. "She'll fall asleep eventually. Damn these potatoes good!" I made it a point of tasting them before I placed the sleep aid in his portion so he wouldn't think I did anything to his food.

Rob

This girl know she can cook. I guess I could be a bit nicer to her. I know she's not feeling me right now, but we could get it back. Yeah, we'll be together and raise our daughter. No reason we can't get back to normal. But how did Aubrey fit into those plans? I guess I would have to figure that out later, when my ass wasn't hungry or horny for Free's fine ass.

When she brought over my plate, I grabbed her hand and kissed it. She put the plate down and she didn't even acknowledge the kiss. I'll convince her to get back to liking me, hopefully. It shouldn't take that long. I mean, she did just have my baby. Don't all new moms want to be with the baby daddy?

Free

What the hell was that? Well at least he wasn't shoving his dick down my throat. I guess. Ugggghhhhh! This nigga looking at me like he's trying to be a family. Whatever, pass the fuck out already. Anyway, I grabbed my salad and sat opposite him. I didn't want to risk him EVER trying to touch me again.

Rob

"Why you eating *that* when you cooked all this food though?" Fuck she over there with that big ass salad for? Rob thought.

Free

"Nuh uh… Those leftovers are for you. I still have fifteen pounds I need to lose. No carbs. No meat. And you see that treadmill over there? I'm on it every time she's asleep. And when she's not, I'm either feeding her or playing with her or we're walking up and down the steps. I get it in however I can. And now that I'm back in school, I have to wear real clothes. I'm not feeling the size I have to wear right now."

I was trying to be as ordinary with him as possible. Trying to talk as normally and as much as possible, so he would scarf down that food and that kool-aid as fast as possible. "Is the food good? You need me to get you anything else?" Trying to sound concerned, when I could give two shits.

Rob

"Oh yeah, this food is fire. I've always meant to ask you what you marinate your steaks with."

Free

"That's for me to know...". As I laughed genuinely. I never told anyone what I used when I cooked. Not even James. He smiled when I said that and downed his juice. "I need some more salad dressing." I walked over to the refrigerator and got the salad dressing and the kool-aid that was already mixed with the sleep aid. I don't drink kool-aid, and he already knows that. I think it makes your breath stink. I filled his cup up again and watched him drink a little bit more with his meal.

Rob

"Well as long as you keep cooking these steaks as good as you do, I don't even need to know what you marinate them with. Appreciate the refill." Rob said genuinely.

Free

"No problem." Not a problem at all. Just continue to eat all of those damn potatoes and drink that second glass of kool-aid, muthafucka.

Monroe

We were still sitting out in the car with no word from James. I decided to text him to make sure he was alright.

"Yo, everything good? Plan still on?"

James

"Yeah Boss, he's eating right now. Free doesn't know I'm here because he won't let her out of his sight."

Monroe

"Well we're still out here and ready whenever you give us the word. Just don't kill him, I want that shit to be drawn out." I said.

James

"Gotchu, I want the same. Hit you in a bit, hopefully." Just waiting this nigga out for now.

Monroe

"Bet." I replied. I'm anxious because I'm ready to get this show on the road. I didn't fuck him up last time, but this time will be fun for me. I know for a fact he did something to Aubrey before she got away from him. He's gonna pay for that shit dearly. I called Mike and he said everything was the same. He found Mrs. Denise in Aubrey's room praying over her, so he didn't interrupt. That was about thirty minutes ago. I'll call them back in another thirty, if I was still sitting out here.

I hate that I'm not there at the hospital with Aubrey, but I know her mom understands that I'm out here to ensure that lil nigga never even speaks to her again in life. I miss Aubrey so much. This situation has proven to me that I'm totally in love with her. I've never felt this way before, and I love it. She completes my life and I know she will be my wife. Please God bring her back to me. Amen.

Taisha

After quitting my job at the club, I feel like I'm back on top. I was here to tell Curt to go fuck himself. I know he thought the reason I was in his office was to let him rip through my walls with that big ass ugly dick of his. He was too ready when I came in there. Because you know I was looking good. I had on my favorite black leggings, with a crop top, black and gold combat boots and an oversized camouflage jacket with gold and red embellishments. My hair was sleek in straight back long ponytail. My face was beat, per usual with sculpted brows, luxurious mink lashes, winged eyeliner (so sharp it could cut a bitch, ok!) and my MAC Ruby Woo on my lips. I also wore my red Christian Dior fanny pack with the gold chain links that completed my outfit for today. I looked like money, so I be damned if I was to entertain anything that didn't involve it.

Curt

"Hey Sapphire, you came to twerk that ass on this dick for a real nigga?" I instantly smiled at the prospect getting up in some of the best pussy I've ever had. Of course, she didn't need to know I thought that. I told her that, because she was getting older, that she needed to prove to me that she deserved to be here. And that was in the form of a lil sample after a private show every now and then. Truth be told, it was hard for me not blow my load just off of watching her dance.

Taisha

I almost threw up in my mouth at the memory of our last encounter. "Curt, I came to tell you that I will not be dancing in this piece of shit club anymore." His facial expression looked like his dumb ass was confused or something. I hope he doesn't try and jump bad or nothing, because I got my taser with me today and I will light that ass all the way up! If I can, I'll place that shit right up in them nuts!

Curt

"Fuck you mean you not dancing here no more? Your shift starts in an hour. Who I'mma get to fill that spot on such short notice?" Curt asked, genuinely confused.

Taisha

"Not my problem. I'm out." And with that, I turned around and chucked up the deuces just before the debut of my elegant middle finger. Then his ass had the nerve to grab me by the arm! It wasn't rough or anything, but the audacity of this fool!

Curt

"Sapphire, just let me sample that pussy one more time and I'll let you leave. You know you like it." I said while grabbing on my dick. "I'll pay you this time and everything." I took my stash out of my pocket that totaled about fifteen hundred dollars. I was willing to give her everything in my hand, too. She was *that* good!

Taisha

This was just what I was waiting on. "What would you like me to do?" As I licked my lips seductively. He started pulling his pants down revealing that he was semi-hard. With that big ass, ugly ass dick. "Money first though Curt. I'm not playing with you, today."

Curt

"You know what I like baby. Come on over here and let Big Curt feel that wet pussy."

Taisha

He tried peeling off a few twenties, and I wasn't having that. "All of it if you want anything from me today, nigga." I was dead serious too.

Curt

"Alright Sapphire, damn. Here." I didn't care about that little bit of money. My shit was hard as a brick now. I sat down on my couch after pulling my shit out to show her how ready I was for her. Nobody worked that shit for me like she did. These other bitches in here were lazy. And most of the time complained that I was too big. I still made them give it up though.

Taisha

After I stashed that money in my Christian Dior, I sauntered over to him and he leaned his head back on the back of that nasty ass couch that was in his office. It was like a grayish colored, microfiber piece of shit that appeared like it hadn't been cleaned in twenty years. It was all sticky and I made sure never to touch it. He had his eyes closed in anticipation of the pleasure I usually put on him, but he was in for the shock of his life, literally. I pulled out that taser, aimed it at his nether region and let it flow. He couldn't even make any noise at first. His face was fashioned into the most grotesque image I'd ever seen. There was no sound at first, and then after what seemed like forever, he let out this high-pitched squeal.

"Yeah nigga, you will never get none of this good shit again! Ole nasty ass, perverted ass nigga. Kiss my muthafuckin ass and don't you *ever* speak my name again!" With that, I grabbed all of my belongings I packed from my locker and ran out of the building. As soon as I got in my car, my phone rang, scaring the shit outta me!

<<<ring, ring>>>

"Hello?" I pulled off and answered it in a huff.

Automated Prison Operator

"You have a collect call from...". It was Don. I wonder why he was calling me. I just saw him. I accepted the call.

Big Don

"Hey baby, what's going on?"

Taisha

"Nothing much, hun. Just collected my belongings from the club. What's going on with you?" I replied as I tried to regulate my breathing. I was trying my best not to keep checking my rear view mirror to make sure that nigga Curt didn't come fuck me up. Luckily, I only placed my post office box address on any of my paperwork, so he wouldn't know where I lived.

Big Don

"You sure? You sound a bit rattled."

Taisha

"Nah, I'm good. Just picked up my stuff from the club.

Big Don

"Oh alright. I was just thinking about you… Can't get you out of my mind ever since you came to visit a nigga. I need you to come back in the morning. Set that shit up again for us."

Taisha

Okay, now our terms were Tuesday and Friday. I didn't want to fuck this up, so I had to figure out how to approach this gently. I didn't want to fuck my money up. "Did you want to change the terms of our contract? We agreed to the five thousand dollars and my mortgage payment. You want to change it?" Taisha countered.

Big Don

"Come on Tai, I need that a little more often than twice a week. How about we up it to three times a week, and I'll increase your money to seventy-five hundred, plus your mortgage. Didn't you get your money?" Big Don said, almost begging.

Taisha

Now money talks. And to make the forty-minute drive from my house up to Jessup for a ninety-minute visit three times a week? I can absolutely do that. But I gotta play it cool so he doesn't think that he can just change the terms whenever he felt like it.

"Well, I had some things set up for tomorrow, can we make it Thursday?" I paused. "I mean, I may be able to change a few things around if you can get me that additional twenty-five hundred in my account today." I tried sounding seductive while saying that.

Big Don

"Done. See you tomorrow and wear that perfume again." Big Don requested.

Taisha

"I can make that happen for us baby. I'll see you tomorrow." *Jackpot!* Now I'm sure he's gonna wanna change the terms again sometime in the future. This pussy I'm sitting on is fire, but I already knew that. Now let me head to this clinic to get these birth control pills like I was supposed to do this morning."

Chapter 13

Dee Dee

After Aubrey squeezed my hand, I kept talking to her to keep her in whatever space she was currently in.

"Aubrey, it's mommy. If you can hear and understand me, squeeze my hand again baby." Nothing happened. I repeated myself, and nothing happened still. I refuse to give up hope, so I started praying over her again. I sensed that someone entered the room, but I didn't open my eyes and I did not stop praying. Nothing in this world is more important to me at this moment, than to pray for my baby.

After a few seconds. I opened my eyes and saw Mike doing the same. He had his hand on Aubrey's uninjured leg while he prayed over her. I wouldn't change anything about my relationship with my husband, other than when it started. I met Mike when Aubrey was fifteen, almost thirteen years ago. He was a contractor that worked for the same company I worked for at Charleston Air Force Base in South Carolina. I had already retired a few years before and started my second career to work on a second retirement check. I was about that money so I when I did retire from this job, I could travel the world while collecting all my government money.

Almost thirteen years ago

We saw each other in passing, but never actually struck up a conversation until I saw him at the building cafeteria during lunch. It was packed in there. I went over to his table once I paid for my food because he was sitting by himself and I didn't want to eat my food at my desk. "Hey, it's Michael, right?" I said.

Mike

"Yes, but you can call me Mike. Denise, is it? You work in acquisitions, right?" She was breathtaking. I had been seeing her around, but I didn't approach her because honestly, I thought she had a man. But I definitely knew who she was.

Dee Dee

Wow! I had no clue he would know who I was and all of that. And for the first time, I realized how fine this man actually was. "Yes, to both, but you can call me Dee Dee. Is anyone sitting here with you? Would you mind if I joined you?"

Mike

"No, to both. Please, have a seat." As he got up and pulled my chair out for me. I was truly impressed by his gallantry! It wasn't a spectacular act or anything, but not many men these days had manners. Or they didn't bother to show that they were raised right. One or both, I couldn't be too sure anymore.

Dee Dee

"Why thank you, kind gentleman." During our lunch meal, I discovered that Mike was from Newark, New Jersey and was the youngest child of three. He had two sisters and wasn't your typical 'baby of the family'. I could tell he was very responsible, financially and otherwise. He had two sons, Marsai and Maddox, both in their late teens from his previous marriage. Mike was forty-seven, just three years older than me, and his birthday was two weeks before mine. His skin was mahogany, with a red undertone and his hair was very thick and wavy but he kept it faded low. He was slender, about six foot even and in excellent shape. He had broad shoulders, with the most beautiful arms and legs I had ever seen on a man. I first noticed him because of how he dressed. But his walk… Denzel had *nothing* on Mike. This man had it going on!

We started dating shortly thereafter for about fourteen months and then we got married in a small ceremony. Since then, we'd moved into an ocean front condo on the beach in Miami. We travel whenever we get the itch, since we both had retired from the government. He's always loved Aubrey like she was his own, and their bond was special. I loved my family. I appreciated him stepping in when he did. I've never introduced my daughter to any other man, because I'd never gotten serious with any other man. So, to see this man, who is not my daughter's biological father, praying over her like his life depends on it, is oh so special to me. He is truly remarkable, and God couldn't have blessed me with a better husband and father to my Aubrey.

Present Day

A few hours after we prayed for her, we left and went to the hotel to shower, get something to eat and came right back. Aubrey's condition was still serious but showed slight improvement, as her swelling subsided on a very minuscule scale. I will take anything at this point as a victory! Finally, I was allowed to sit in her room and read to her around the clock. I guess Dr. Sawyer figured out that I wasn't going to have it any other way. When she came to check Aubrey's vitals at the beginning of her shift, that's when we were praying. She left and came back but did not bother me. I was grateful to her for that. I'll be sure to send her something very nice for the way that she took care of Aubrey... and me, during my episode yesterday.

Two Nights Ago

Rob

After I finished picking over my food to Marie's dismay, I realized just how tired I was. It had been a long time since I was able to get a good night's rest. When Aubrey showed up to the apartment, she made me get in the closet and then tied me up and gagged me so whoever was at the door couldn't hear me. I had already started weaning myself off of whatever she was putting in my food to control me, so when Aubrey let me out, I was already back to my old self.

Present Day

Free had already finished her salad and started feeding the baby again. I don't know why she put these big ass clothes on once she got out of the shower. And why she was covering herself and the baby up like that while she was feeding her was beyond me. When she fed her in the hotel room, she was totally naked, and I was able to watch her breastfeed the baby. That shit was so sexy to me because I imagined myself sucking those big ass titties. "You ready to go to bed yet? Is the baby sleep?" Rob asked Free.

Free

"She's still eating, but after that, I'll be ready once I clean up the kitchen." I was really stalling him out. But I was also wondering why his ass wasn't knocked out yet. Maybe I should give him more juice with the sleeping pills in it. He's not touching me again tonight, I bet my life on it.

James

I'm still waiting for this nigga to come up these steps. I know he has Free's gun in his possession, so I can't sneak up on him while he's facing the stairs. He'll spot me immediately. Free usually has the baby down by now. It's a reason she's stalling. He must think she's gonna fuck him or something. I just saw him get up and he stumbled slightly. I was watching Free, and I couldn't read the look on her face. I noticed that she saw him when he stumbled, then he tried to shake it off. He started walking and then he had to grip the kitchen counter to keep from falling.

Rob

"WHAT THE FUCK did you give me, you bitch? What did you put in my food?! Bring your ass over here *now*!" Rob yelled.

Free was backing away from him by going around the kitchen island while trying to soothe the baby. Tamia started wailing when he started yelling.

"I'm gonna kill you bitch. Just wait... wait 'til I catch your sneaky ass. I'm... gonna... kill... you..." Rob slurred.

Free

Rob started dropping to the floor and while on his hands and knees, he was shaking his head and trying his best to regain focus. I crushed up enough sleeping pills to stop a horse in its tracks, so I knew he was not going to be able to get at me. I just wondered what was taking so long for him to go down. Finally, he was starting to slow down tremendously. He was fighting it hard though, but it was just a matter of time. And when he did, my baby and I were out of there. Free thought excitedly.

James

I started creeping down the stairs. I got Free's attention and I could see that she was relieved. I motioned for her to come to me, but she looked so afraid because she still had to pass him. He had stretched across the floor still trying to reach for her, but I could see that whatever had him down was working just like Free intended for it to.

"Come on baby." I whispered, and at the same time, I had come all the way down the stairs, Money and two of his guys entered the house with him. She ran past the lil nigga quickly with Tamia in tow and I hugged her so tight. I was so glad my girls were safe.

"Did he hurt you baby? Is Tamia ok?" I asked her as I kissed her all over her face and looked at my baby girl with tear stains on her face. Free had tears streaming down her face in relief as she held onto me for dear life. I could tell she was so relieved that we were here.

Free

"Oh my God! James!" I exclaimed. He was here! I'm so glad he came when he did, because I was about to take my baby and go. Monroe and two other guys came through the door about the same time that I saw James and they collected Rob and took him out of my house. He looked at me right before his eyes closed, from all of the exhaustion from the pills I tainted his food and kool-aid with. His eyes told me that he was serious when he said he would kill me. I hope they take care of his ass this time for good, or I may have to move away to keep Tamia safe.

"The baby is fine. But he…" I paused, "he raped me twice." Free whispered into James' ear. With tears streaming down my face and sobs wracking my body, I was relieved beyond measure that I was back with my man, but I was so ashamed of what I let him do. While I hated Rob, I enjoyed what he did to my body. What did that mean? Did I still have feelings for this clown? I felt so stupid and disloyal for betraying my man in this way.

James

"I'm so sorry my love for not being here when you needed, no one will ever hurt you again. Especially not this nigga." I said. I hugged them both as Free's body trembled. She was hugging me so tight, I was never gonna let her go. "Shhhh, I got you now sweetie. Your man is here. I love you." The realization that I was going to have to step away from her again albeit briefly, was disturbing me because I had just gotten her back. But we had to take care of this nigga immediately! He was not about to get away from me this time.

"Pack a bag for you and the baby. I don't want you to stay here tonight. I made a reservation at one of the resorts in town for tonight. Tomorrow we're leaving town for a few days just to get away. Call your school and tell them you had a family emergency and that you'll be back next week."

I walked outside and told Money that I needed one of his best men to guard my lady and my daughter until we took care of this nigga. "Boss, it has to be someone you trust with your life. I can't have anything else happen to her. Also, I'm taking her away for about a week starting tomorrow. I hope you don't mind."

Monroe

"Anything I can do, man. I got your back. I'll set it up. Get your family situated and meet me at the spot. I'll wait for you before I get started." I replied, reassuring him that I had his back.

James

"I really appreciate that man, truly." After we dapped, we then embraced with the other arm. He was not only my boss, but my true friend. I went back into the house while Free was packing and picked up my baby girl. She fell asleep in my arms after what I'm sure was a very trying day. I just held her close to me and rubbed her little back. I'm so thankful to God that they are alright.

Monroe

I wasn't taking any chances with the lil nigga this time. I took him to the warehouse and had Stevie and Goldie carry him from the trunk. He was passed out, but I knew how to get that niggas attention. I was just waiting for James to get Free and the baby settled. I pulled Benny aside, I needed to talk to him privately because what I was about to request of him wasn't for everyone.

"Benny, I need you to do me a solid. The reason I'm asking you is because, besides James, I trust you way more than these other niggas." Monroe said while Benny nodded his head.

Benny

"Money, whatever you need me to do, you know I got you. You always been there for me since my father died. I'll go in here and murk that nigga right now if you want me to. I ain't never liked his shady ass anyway." Benny responded.

Monroe

"I appreciate it, but that's not what I need. What I need for you to do is guard James' family until we're done here. I don't trust nobody else to do it. I got a rack for you tomorrow for helping me out with this." Monroe pleaded.

Benny

"Money, don't worry about that. Ya'll been taking care of me for so long. You're family, and that extends to James' family as well. Don't even worry about it. I'm there." Benny replied.

Monroe

"Man, I really can't thank you enough." I said thankfully. With that, I dapped him up and told him to touch base with James to get the details. I walked back inside the warehouse and the lil nigga was still passed out. "Undress that nigga and chain him up." I went and got a bucket of ice water and sat it down in front of him. He was chained to a heavy duty wooden pallet rack in the upright standing position, with his feet and hands bound up against the wall.

"Aye Stevie, go get the blow torch and Goldie bring me my tool box from my office." Let the muthafuckin games begin.

Chapter 14

Taisha

After talking to Don and confirming that extra money hit my account, I headed to The Ritz-Carlton spa in Georgetown with plans to hit up the CityCenterDC high end shops in northwest for a little relaxation and retail therapy before my next visit with him tomorrow.

Spa Attendant

"Good afternoon and welcome in. How may I assist you? Do you have an appointment with us today?"

Taisha

"Hello, no I don't have a reservation, but I would like to take advantage of a few of your services as well as gain access to your spa for the day. Will that be possible?" I replied in my most friendly voice.

Spa Attendant

"Of course! Are you a guest at the hotel?"

Taisha

Damn she nosy. "No, I am not." I said with a phony smile.

Spa Attendant

"Well that's no problem, ma'am. Here's a menu. We have a pretty full staff today, so after you peruse the menu, I can let you know how we can accommodate you. Please follow me into the tranquility room. May I get you anything to drink?"

Taisha

I forgot just how nice this place was. I hadn't been here since Money spoiled me for my birthday a couple of years ago. I easily blew a rack in here just on spa services that day. "Yes, I'll take a glass of Champagne, please. Thank you." Money didn't even blink at me fuckin off that kind of cash at a spa or shopping. Those were the good ole days. Now I couldn't get near him.

All I had been doing before hooking up with Don, was saving my coins since I felt like Curt would fire me anytime I refused to give him some ass. The reason why I didn't fuck with any of the other clubs was because the security was tight at Sugar's. You always heard about rapes and sometimes even murders at or around the other clubs in this area. And most of them other girls were so strung out, that most of the time they didn't know if they were coming or going. I stopped fucking with drugs in my college days prior to meeting Money.

I started to actually have quite the little nest egg. And I've always paid attention to stock market trends since learning quite a bit about investing from this white girl, Hannah that I went to college with. Hannah was a dyke and she tried to holla at me one night at a party where I met her. I refused her time and time again, and eventually she wore me down enough to hang out with her crazy ass. She claimed she understood I wasn't gay and just wanted to be my friend, but she would always try her hand on the sly. We lost touch in college, after some fuck shit went down, but when I met my ex-boyfriend and Don, I was able to get back to the real me.

I feel like I owe Don a lot, so being there for him was easy. But after today's visit, it seems like he wants more than I'm willing to give. I'm good at offering the fantasy, but if it ain't Monroe, I don't want nor am I claiming nary a man.

Sam

After getting a bit of rest, I headed back to the hospital to check on everyone. I stopped by Charlie's Philly Steaks to grab something to eat for Joe. He hadn't called me all night. He also wasn't answering his phone. So, once I got back to the hospital and saw that he wasn't there, I was just hoping he wasn't anywhere else doing anything stupid. Like trying to find Rob. I still wasn't able to visit with Aubrey, but I did run into Mrs. Dee Dee and she hugged me and let me know that she was improving.

"Are you sure there is nothing that I can do for you? Have you eaten? Do you need me to sit with you?"

Dee Dee

"No baby, I'm alright and you being present is enough. I know Aubrey feels your love and support. You go ahead and get you some rest. I'll keep you posted, sweetie."

With that, we embraced once more, and I also hugged Mr. Mike as well. I asked him if Mrs. Dee Dee was really doing alright. I knew she was strong, I just felt I should have been doing more. He told me that he would let me know if she needed anything and thanked me for the love and support as well.

After leaving the hospital, I stopped by Joe's house to see if he was there. The house was dark, and he didn't answer the door nor his phone when I called once more. I was very disappointed, and was trying not to worry, but it was so hard. I just went back to my house and cried myself to sleep. I'm not used to this version of myself. I've never been in love before. But what was killing me even more, was that I wasn't sure if he was loving me back the same way or if he was in love with Aubrey.

Joe

After Aubrey's mom and stepdad left the hospital today, I snuck around trying to find out where Aubrey's room was. A dude, that I assumed to be a nurse stopped me to see where I was going, and I lied and told him that my grandmother was on the floor I knew Aubrey was on. I figured, somebody's grandparent is always at a hospital for one reason or another and he seemed to believe me and asked if I needed help. I politely declined. I went into the bathroom on the way and I'm glad I did. I had some crust around my puffy ass eyes from when I fell into that uncomfortable sleep and I looked a mess. I just splashed some water onto my face a made a mental note to make an appointment to get my locs redone.

Samantha called again. She's been calling me all night and all day. I haven't been answering her calls because I just don't wanna talk to nobody. It's totally my fault that Aubrey even got into this situation. Had I not shown her where Marie lived, I would have never fucked around and ended up being separated from her. Things were still foggy with that shit. And Reggie, I mean James, tried to explain some fake ass story to me.

I tried not to be hateful towards Monroe since she was happy with him, but now I know for sure now that he's shady. He's hiding something a little more than his net worth. And I'm gonna find out what it is. But I just had to put my eyes on Aubrey before I left. I walked the halls and ended up by a desk that had A. Collins on the board with the room number. It was two doors down, so I walked like I was supposed to be there and went into the room and shut the door behind me quietly.

I opened the privacy curtain and saw her hooked up to all this shit. Her face was black and blue. Her arm was in a cast and so was one of her legs. What the fuck, man? I could still tell how beautiful she was. Tears just started pouring out of my eyes as I stroked her hair softly. I watched her chest rise and fall as she breathed in and out. I kissed her hand gently and apologized profusely. I hoped she could hear me because I missed her so much.

I felt so guilty for shutting her out when I did. It wasn't her fault that I fell in love with her. It's also not her fault that I still am. How the fuck can I reconcile my feelings for her *and* Sam? I just didn't have the energy for all of that right now. I know what I do have the energy for. I'm gonna find the nigga that's responsible for her even being here and I'm gonna kill his ass. I kissed her lips gently and was startled when the doctor entered her room.

Dr. Sawyer

"What are you doing in my patient's room? And why are you kissing her on her lips?"

James

After getting Free and Tamia settled into the Mandarin Oriental hotel, I spoke with Benny briefly to ensure he understood what he was here for. "Hey man, I appreciate you doing this for us. If Monroe trusts you, I know you're the real deal."

Benny

"No doubt man, just like I told him, your family is my family by extension. Plus, you've always been around since I've been part of this organization and you've shown me nothing but respect. I appreciate you for that, because as a young nigga trying to come up, it doesn't go unnoticed."

James

"Man, you've always been one hunnid with me. I got something for you when I get back from outta town. Those two are my most prized possessions. My life is in that room, and I'll be back as soon as I can. Thanks again, man." James said as they dapped.

Benny

"No doubt, fam. Go ahead and take care of your biz. I got you." I replied.

James

After that, I checked in on Free and Tamia. Once I made sure they were good, I headed back to the warehouse. I had nothing but murder on my mind, and he was gonna die slow. Trust that. This nigga's time has been up. And he was about to find that shit out for sure.

Free

I really didn't have any objections to leaving my house tonight. I'm seriously considering selling it or renting it to a nice family because my memories in there are clouded with negative images and nightmares of Rob right now. That will probably be best, but for now, I'll take a bubble bath in this luxurious bathtub while the baby is sleeping. I kept her tucked in the car seat and just sat her down on the floor at the side of the tub while I relaxed. I looked out at the waterfront through the large eight-foot bay windows in the bathroom. Everything about this suite was absolutely breathtaking, along with the one hundred and eighty-degree penthouse views.

I wasn't supposed to be drinking wine, but I felt like I really needed it to bring my stress level down. I missed my Prosecco so much. I said I'd only have a glass, but I ended up having two so far. I would just have to 'pump and dump' over the next couple of days just to be sure my milk isn't tainted with alcohol. Luckily for me, I decided to stockpile when my breasts became really engorged or felt like they were getting hard. I hated that feeling, so much so that I kept my breast pump with me everywhere I went. It became my best friend, indeed. I hit play and the music softly coursed through my

Bluetooth speaker, and one of the songs I loved dancing to for James played first.

"I like it when you lose it
I like it when you go there
I like the way you use it
I like that you don't play fair

Recipe for a disaster
When I'm just try'na take my time
Stroke is gettin' deep and faster
You're screamin' like I'm outta line

Who came to make sweet love? Not me...
Who came to kiss and hug? Not me...
Who came to beat it up? Rocky...
And don't use those hands to put up that gate and stop me

When we... fuck
When we... fuck
When we... fuck
When we... fuck"

I started caressing my soapy breasts and imagining it was James' hands on me instead. I pretended it was him exploring my body lovingly, looking into my eyes and telling me there was no other woman for him. In my mind, I saw him kissing my breasts as I touched them and then licked along the curve of my nipple, down to my stomach, and then making love to my center with his tongue. I brought myself to climax just thinking of him pleasuring my body, as Rob's face entered my mind and then the thought of him bringing me to the last climax I had, resurfaced. How could I even be thinking about him at a time like this? I was so ashamed of myself and felt so unworthy of James' love.

I dreamt of having the perfect life when I become married to James. We would have more kids and raise our family as if none of this ever existed. But how could I forget how Rob used my body and my mouth for his pleasure? I felt dirty and just... just fucking contaminated. And then I tried to wrap my mind around how I allowed him to use my body like that before any of this crazy shit happened.

I thought it was cute when he threatened to hurt me if I told Aubrey about us. He wasn't doing anything to me yesterday that was different from what he did to me before. Why should James even want to marry a whore like me? Tamia damn sure doesn't deserve a whore for a mother. She would be better off with James raising her and finding a decent woman to be her new mother. I just stared at the razor blade that rested on the surface of the garden tub with tears in my eyes as I took another swig from my champagne flute.

Joe

I rented a car once I left Prince George's Hospital. I wasn't in the least bit concerned about my car being totaled. Aubrey was my concern at the moment, although the insurance company tried contacting me today. I was driving around like a mad man, wishing that I had paid more attention to my surroundings when I was there. I remembered it was a white building just outside of a nice neighborhood that had nice houses with white picket fences, well to do families and their dogs. I had one goal in mind, and the images of the plans that I had floating around up there didn't match the scenery that I was lost in. I just felt it in the pit of my stomach, that I was in the vicinity of that building. I headed down Madison Street and took a right onto Golden Avenue. I continued for about seven minutes until I reached the Frontage Road that would take me to Interstate 495 which was to my right. I took a left instead and I slowly coasted down Stith Lane. And there it was... King Enterprises. The white building with the green door. Monroe King's warehouse... right there in front of me on Murray Circle.

Chapter 15

James

I arrived at the warehouse and entered the room just in time as Monroe had prepared his tools on this table in the lil nigga's direct view. He was still knocked out, but he was chained up, butt naked to the wall with a very large plastic tarp behind and underneath him.

Monroe

"Wassup Jay? You ready?"

James

"Let's get it, Boss." I said.

Monroe

"Goldie, wake his ass up. Throw that bucket of ice water hard as you can on that bitch!" Goldie was about five foot six or seven probably around two hundred and fifteen pounds of nothing but muscle because his short ass was always at the gym. Even his neck was massive, so I knew lifting that big ass bucket of ice water was gonna be nothing to him. Goldie threw that ice water at that lil nigga like it was *his* girl in the hospital. I appreciated that shit too, because I knew that shit hurt.

Rob

"AHHHHHHHHHHHHHHHH!!!!!!!!!!!" What the fuck is going on? There was this bright ass light beaming on me and I felt constrained by something. The coldness from that ice water assaulted all of my senses and nerve endings and was now in my eyes. I could see that there were people standing around, but nobody said shit to me. I was so fucking cold, and my dick felt like somebody drove a fucking semi-truck over it. This couldn't be happening! "FUUUUCCCKKKKKKK!!! What the fuck! Who is there? Let me go and let's throw them hands! Pussy ass niggas. Got me chained up and shit. Bitch ass niggas ain't man enough to face me!"

Monroe

"Shut the fuck up you lil ass nigga. You wanna fight somebody fair and square while you out here raping women? Fuck outta here with your bitch made ass." Rob's eyes widened at the realization that I had him chained up with his ass out. "Yeah nigga, what you got to say now? Aubrey fucking laid up in a hospital bed because of your bitch ass. Goldie..." At my instruction, Goldie punched the side of his torso. From the way he cocked his fist back, it seemed like he was trying to punch a hole through Rob's dumb ass.

Rob

I tried drawing in the largest amount of air that I could as Goldie all but obliterated my lungs on my right side. I began to cry as I started writhing and gasping for breath. That hit felt like my entire body was about to explode! Damn, they caught me slipping. That bitch Free had me thinking that she was considering being with me. How did she even know these niggas? How did this happen?

Monroe

"Goldie..." I prompted as I did before and he hit him in the same spot again. That lil nigga couldn't even open his mouth to scream. It was a sound I never heard before, and it would have been a horrible sound coming from anybody else. This nigga was the devil's spawn. He needed to be eradicated from this universe. And I was the *Dark Angel* to deliver him right back to Hell.

James

I removed the white napkin that covered my first weapon of choice. I grabbed the scalpel that was on the table among the assortment of knives from all the sizes I had arranged there. I dramatically made a scene about picking up the scalpel and examining it. I held it right in front of my face like I was checking its sharpness. I was just playing around with the nigga though. I knew he was getting more and more scared as time went on. I wanted this nigga to beg for his life! I want him to feel as violated as I'm sure he made the women in his life feel. Fuck his cries, fuck his whimpers and his pain. He deserved all of this shit.

Monroe

The way James just introduced that scalpel like he was about to perform surgery had that lil nigga shook. Shit, I even shivered a bit. I've seen him in action before with some of the jobs I've ordered, and he never looked like he was enjoying himself as much as he is today. And he hasn't even started yet.

James walked over to Rob, who was now drooling at the mouth, and pinched his right nipple and sheared that shit clean off. That lil nigga's body was bucking so hard, that I thought he was going to hit his head against the wall and knock himself out.

"Stevie, Goldie, pull that apparatus from against the wall so he doesn't kill his damn self." He continued thrashing about for a good while. I know that shit hurt! But I was enjoying myself and I hadn't even gotten started on what I had in store for him. Once that lil nigga started settling down, the foaming at the mouth he was doing had a little blood mixed in with it. I believe he bit his tongue so hard that it was bleeding.

James calmly walked back over to him, pinched his left nipple and repeated the same procedure. He screeched so loud, he sounded like we were cutting off his dick. Not yet, lil nigga, not yet.

Joe

As I parked the car and looked around the parking lot, it seemed as if no one was here, but I know these niggas are here. And

I have a feeling that something is going down or at least about to go down. I approached the front door and tried the handle. It was locked. I walked around to the east side of the building and got close enough to try and peer through the heavily tinted windows. I could see one person walking toward me through a small slit in between the door and the frame. I backed up when the door opened, and I was suddenly eye level with the barrel of a sawed off shot gun. It wasn't anyone I recognized, but I knew that he was a paid hand. I put my hands up and simply hoped for the best.

Henchman

"Who the fuck are you and what are you doing here?"

Joe

This guy looked "John Coffey" from *The Green Mile*. Tall, dark and humongous. He had to be about six-five, six-six. He had muscles every damn where. "I was looking for Mr. King." He just continued to stare in my face and with the gun pointed at the middle of my forehead. He stepped aside, with the shot gun still fixed on my face, and pushed me up against the wall roughly. He closed and locked the door with his left hand, with the shot gun still pointed at me with his right. Once he finished, he grabbed a hand full of my shirt, and told me to walk into the next room. I guess I wasn't moving fast enough for him and he pushed me again.

"You don't have to be so rough, sir, I'm just here to talk to Mr. King about my car." He checked to see if I had any weapons on me. Once he was satisfied that I didn't, he motioned for me to sit in a metal chair that appeared to be attached to the concrete on the ground. He then cuffed me to the arms of the chair and left the small concrete room and locked it. He must've smelled my bullshit from a mile away. So, I guess I'll just wait until someone remembers that I'm here. I guess.

Free

I made a few shallow cuts on my forearm. I knew if I were really serious, that I'd have to cut deeper. Then I noticed my baby girl's eyes were wide open, staring at me whimpering with tears running down her precious little face. All while I had a blade in my hand. I put the razor down and immediately realized that I was contemplating taking my life. And my baby daughter was almost about to witness it. How long would she be in here by herself, next to my lifeless body before someone rescued her? As soon as I came to my senses and talked myself out of taking my own life, she was already back sound asleep. Nothing but God.

I got out of the tub, wrapped my arm in a hotel towel and applied pressure. I sobbed at the prospect of how close I had come to what I was about to do. I need James. I let the water out of the tub, cleaned up my mess, got dressed in my pajamas and once I was convinced my arm was okay, I picked up Tamia and cuddled with her in the bed. I fell asleep as I wept.

Monroe

Carlos, who is part of my security detail, called the phone in the corner of the room to let me know that I had a visitor. I asked who it was, and he told me some guy pretending that he was here to talk about his car. Carlos knew he was lying, because customers were never invited or allowed out here. He informed me that he was in holding room one until I was ready to deal with him. By the time our uninvited visitor arrived, Goldie had knocked out a few of the lil nigga's teeth and he appeared to be on the verge of passing out.

"Goldie, the bucket." With that, Goldie threw more ice water on him. It took him a little while to catch his breath once that cold sensation was introduced to his newly mutilated deformities. Stevie grabbed the sledgehammer from the table as it was his turn to do whatever tickled his fancy. He swung that sledgehammer from behind his back and down onto the lil nigga's left foot. Once that happened, his eyes got wide, with his mouth in an "O" shape and then he passed out.

We decided to take a break for a minute and then I went to the holding room to see who was trespassing on my property. As soon as Carlos unlocked the door, I recognized from the back of his head, that it was Joe.

"Joe, why are you here at my warehouse? I know I did not invite you here. I will reimburse you for your car since my lady was driving it. Was that what you wanted to discuss?" Aubrey's car wreck beyond totaled Joe's car. Not only was I going to replace it, I was going to upgrade it. If he allowed me to do so. I know Aubrey would want me to do that, but I also know a man's pride.

Joe

"No, you did not invite me, but I would like to find Rob just as much as you and James. Or is his name Reggie?" Joe snapped.

Monroe

Reggie was the name that James used as an alias, so as not to have anything leading a trail back to him. Joe didn't realize that I was just protecting him. Most people cannot stomach all that occurs with this life. I don't nor have I ever hesitated to take a life, since I became Big Don's protégée. What Joe doesn't understand is, once you cross that threshold, there's no going back. I just decided to listen to what he had to say. I walked to the back of the room, so he would no longer need to crane his neck around. "Don't worry about his name. Your business is with me, correct?" Monroe replied.

Joe

Monroe is trying to handle me. I'm sure it would be intimidating if I wasn't the person that I was. But I ain't ever gonna let no nigga put fear in my heart, and I wasn't about to start now. Fuck this nigga. "Yo, get me out of these handcuffs and this room. I don't work for you. I don't have to stay here. My business is with you, nigga. But we ain't talkin about shit while I'm handcuffed to this hard ass chair." I fumed. He was getting me madder than a muthafucka.

Monroe

I walked slowly around the room. It was at a very leisurely pace and I was just waiting for this nigga to shut the fuck up. "You're in no position to make any demands. And I warned you about what I don't tolerate. I would hate to remind you." He looked at me incredulously, like he wanted to refer to ME as 'lil nigga'. "What was your purpose for coming here? If you wanted to find Rob, then why are you here?" Monroe questioned authoritatively.

Joe

This nigga really thinks he's big shit. Remove these cuffs, I dare you. I wanted to show his ass exactly who I was. But he was right. I'm in no position to make any demands *and* I can't defend myself if something were to pop off right now.

"Look man, Aubrey is one of the most special people to me in the world. I want that nigga to pay. I want to torture him slowly and deliver the final blow. The way he got Aubrey laid up in that hospital, I just can't get that shit outta my mind. She don't deserve none of the shit she's going through, and part of it is my fault. Had I not shown her where Marie lived, she would have never gotten tangled back up with that clown ass nigga man!" I was on the verge of yelling at him. He didn't understand how bad I felt about everything.

Monroe

The nature of Joe's interest in Aubrey is not simply on a platonic level, nor is it innocent. This nigga was too emotional, but it makes sense. I just hate that Samantha is in the crossfire between him and his lust for Aubrey. "Have you ever told Aubrey that you're in love with her?" Monroe asked curiously.

Joe

Huh? What is this nigga talkin' about? I remained quiet for a few minutes before I said... "I'm not sure what type of operation you are running here, nor do I care to go into all of that. I would like to know, where Rob is, so I can kill him myself. If you don't want to help me, just let me go. I'll do it my damn self!" Joe proclaimed.

Monroe

"Come with me, I want you to see something." Monroe suggested.

Chapter 16

James

This bitch ass nigga passed out from all of the pain that was being administered to him. But I got something that will wake him up though, plus keep him from dying right away. I wanted him to *wish* he was dead. To beg for that shit, but we were gonna deny that relief for as long as possible. While we were on "break", I called Free to see how she was doing and if she was able to relax.

<<<ring, ring>>>

I got her voicemail, and it was still early, so I decided to call her again.

<<<ring, ring>>>

She didn't answer the second time either. I hit up Benny, to see if she had said anything to him or needed something. He told me that there was no movement from the room, and I asked him to knock on the door for me. She didn't answer. I was trying not to worry about her, but this situation was like none other with her and the baby being kidnapped and held against their will by this fuck nigga. I was about to head out there when I saw she was now calling me.

<<<ring, ring>>>

"Hello, Fresia? You okay baby? Is Tamia alright?"

Free

"I'm ok James, just tired. Do you know when you'll be back? I just need you to hold me. Make me feel like everything is alright. I'm in a really bad place, and I'm scared."

As the rain continued to spill from the skies, it imitated my mood. The tears continued to stream down my face as I rocked the baby as she slept. I left the bay window and curled up in the big, empty king-sized bed that just reminded me that James isn't here with me. But I guess I'll try to go back to sleep now.

James

I felt so selfish. Here I am, way out here trying to exact revenge and not taking care of my lady. This nigga should have never been my priority. Instead of trying to make myself feel better about what he's done to her, I should be there for her. She's the one that went through it with this lil nigga. I should be making sure she knows I love her, and that what he did to her was not in any way her fault. We have this beautiful little girl that through our love, will be as much a gift to this world as she is to us. I gotta get up outta here. "Aye Stevie, you seen where Money went?"

Stevie

"He went to the holding room. Somebody showed up unexpectedly."

James

"Aight, thanks." As I left the room we were punishing this nigga in, I closed the soundproof door behind me. You see, Money took his time when fortifying this place. Each "conference room" had a purpose. The one we were in obviously was for what we were currently using it for. He had two others like it in the building. All of the rooms except the storage area, the lobby and the actual spot we stored our auto parts in, for auditing purposes were soundproof. The product room had a fingerprint and eye scan associated with it to be able to enter that area. Only he and I could go in and out of there unescorted.

As I walked down the hall, I noticed Money and that nigga Joe walking towards me. "What's going on boss?" I asked, because he looked as if he was about to take him down to where we were about to kill the lil nigga.

Monroe

"James, you remember Joe. He thought he would stop by and I decided to show him the business we're conducting today."

James

He looked a little different in the face, and I could tell he was very aggravated with Joe. Usually when he got that way, murder was on the horizon. And I don't think Joe knew what he was actually in for. He wouldn't have left that room alive; he just would have been our next casualty. "Boss, can I holla at you real quick? It's an emergency situation."

Monroe

"No doubt. Joe, would you mind just having a seat inside of this room real quick? I need to discuss a private matter."

James

Joe went into the room and Money closed the door behind him. "Boss, we can't kill him." I told him.

Monroe

"Kill who?" Monroe asked with a semi crazed look on his face.

James

"Joe." I said. "Once Aubrey comes out of this situation, imagine how she would feel with Joe dead. And his girl, she doesn't deserve that either. I know he can be a bit slick out of his mouth, but we can have Benny and Goldie fuck him up after we take care of the lil nigga. He'll be hurt for a few, but at least he will still be alive."

I could tell what I said got him back thinking straight. We've been working side by side for so long, that I know him just that well.

Monroe

"You just saved his life." Monroe replied ominously. I went to open the door and noticed that Joe was standing very close to it, as if he was trying to hear what we were talking about. I acted as if I didn't know what he was doing, and we turned from the direction we were originally walking in. He just doesn't know that I was about to murk him for being a busybody.

"Unfortunately, I cannot help you with finding Rob. I have your number and if I find him first, I will definitely let you know. I know how much Aubrey means to you. Now if you'll excuse me... Carlos." I said as I summoned him. And I walked away from Joe with no further discussion. Carlos escorted Joe off the premises just like that.

James

Money dismissed Joe without an explanation, and I could tell that he was pissed. Neither of us cared about his feelings though, I just wouldn't want his girl hurting over losing one of her closest friends. Even if that nigga was extra. Money turned to me and asked if I was ready to resume, and I explained that I had to finish my part and get outta there because there was something wrong with Free. He decided to let me get out all of my frustration first, just as long as I didn't kill him. Well deliberately anyway. We weren't aware of how much he could take, and that's why we were taking our time.

Upon entering the room, Money motioned for Stevie to hook up the machine we had Marie attached to last year so we could send a few voltages through him to wake him up. The irony of using the same contraption on his ass, especially since he allowed us to, knowing she didn't deserve that.

Monroe

"And turn that bitch all the way up!" I yelled. Once Stevie started the machine, that voltage passed through Rob's body and jolted him awake quickly. You could see smoke coming off of his body in various places once Stevie turned it off.

Rob

"PLEASE man, please stop! Just kill me! All this shit is too much!" He cried.

Monroe

He started pissing himself uncontrollably and when he was speaking, I confirmed that he had in fact severed part of his tongue so his words came out a bit distorted. James decided to take the pool stick at the biggest end and jam it into to his anus. Now *that*, I couldn't watch. He roughly inserted it a couple of times and removed it before I had to look away. Having something crammed in your ass hole is what a man has nightmares about. Well straight men anyway. Rob passed out again after screaming in agony. This was the most tortured that I'd ever seen anyone. Whether I was participating in it or a witness to it. Goldie injected adrenaline into his arm to wake him back up, then threw another bucket of water on him. But this time, it was scalding hot.

James

"I bet your bitch ass wished you never did that foul shit to Free or Aubrey now, huh?" I got close enough to him to smell his scorched flesh. He started blistering up immediately. But now that we injected him with that first dose of adrenaline, not only was his heart working overtime to sustain his bodily functions, he felt absolutely everything we were doing to him even more.

I whispered, "You know, me and Free are getting married and we're going to raise *our* daughter together. You won't have a legacy after leaving this earth, and no one will miss your punk ass either." I had a paddle in my hand at this point, so I started whacking him as hard as I could, everywhere I could, and then I saw him starting to welt up.

I hit his ass so hard, I was sweating from the energy I exerted. I wouldn't be surprised if I broke or injured some of his bones in the process. I hope all of what we did here today felt like hell on earth. He deserved that and more. Once I was satisfied, I thanked Monroe, Stevie and Goldie for their support and headed home to shower before I joined my girl and our daughter at the hotel for a much-needed vacation.

Monroe

I was surprised that after everything we had already done to him, that he was still alive. Months ago, Aubrey took me into the clinic after hours because she forgot something. While she was busy, I swiped some of their local anesthetic. It was just one small vial, but I knew it would come in handy. So, once he calmed down from the brutal beating James put on him, I spoke to him in a very even tone.

"I know that you want to die, but I have just a few more surprises in store for you. So just try to relax, I think you will like it." I said ominously. Rob's eyes grew as big as saucers while I was speaking to him.

Rob

"Please Money, please just kill me! I just can't take it no more, man. Shoot me in the head already and just get it over with." Rob cried.

Monroe

"Wrong answer." After all of this, he still didn't acknowledge or show any type of remorse for his indiscretions. A simple sorry would be great, but his bitch ass only thought about himself *still*, even at the prospect of the end of his sorry ass life.

I injected the anesthetic directly into his dick with the needle I had been holding behind my back during our conversation. His eyes shut real tight at the sensation of the prick. I wasn't able to inject all of the solution, because he was bucking his body so hard. Eventually, there was a very loud cry that escaped his lips. He was truly miserable and screaming *'I wanna die! I wanna die!'*

"Not yet..." I teased. "There's still just a couple more surprises in store just for you! We still have so much fun to have together! Don't worry, it's almost over." Once I said that, I saw that a little spark of hope entered his mind. That was exactly what I wanted. Build him up, just to tear his lil ass right the fuck back down. To keep breaking him over and over, at every turn.

I headed back to the table with all of our chosen goodies on it and I decided that the lil nigga responded so well to the scalpel, that I would use it as well. He didn't see what I had for him at first, but when I repeated that dramatic show and tell like performance with the instrument, he cried out and this time, he shit himself. I put a glove on my left hand and grabbed his dick very abrasively. I think he finally got the picture of what I was going to do next.

With a quick swipe of my right hand, I tried slicing that muthafucka clean off. But to my delight, I had to do it again. He started thrashing about wildly, foaming at the mouth and it looked like he was about to shake the rest of his dick off for me through that movement. His body started experiencing a seizure, so I injected him for a second time with more adrenaline to ensure his heart didn't stop. Once he calmed down, I slashed the rest of his dick off and then used the blowtorch to cauterize his skin. I didn't need him bleeding out through where his dick *used* to be.

I knew at this point he was very near to his end. But there was just one more surprise I had in store for him. I went over to the door and opened it.

"Hello Marie. He's all yours."

Chapter 17

Marie

"Um, Monroe…?" He nodded yes, with a half-smile. "What the hell am I supposed to do with him like, like… *this*? He's barely alive. And that beautiful penis!! What have you done?" I shrieked as I noticed it's remains on the floor in front of my man. It was almost hacked into pieces!

Monroe

"You asked for me to give him to you in exchange for leaving me and my crew alone. You didn't specify in what condition. He's been around here raping and abusing women and who knows what else. I think his punishment was just."

Marie

"Well, I guess you're right about the condition. I guess I should have been a bit more specific with the details of this deal." Marie said, looking at Rob in disbelief.

Monroe

"So, we still have a deal, right? You won't try to kill me or my associates?" He questioned.

Marie

"Well, you have honored your end of it, so all is well." I looked over at what was left of Robert and shook my head. "See, if you would have just stayed with me, none of this would have happened. I think I can salvage him. I need one more favor from you though." I said as I turned to look at Monroe. I removed a mixture that I think I had perfected from my grandmother's journal. It contains a binding spell that will link Robert and I forever. It wouldn't make him love me, but he wouldn't just be able to wean himself off of me like he did before by not eating or drinking whatever I prepare. "I need you to help me get this into his system." Marie propositioned.

Monroe

"Well, what is it? And what does it do?" Monroe asked her curiously.

Marie

"Nothing that will make any harm come to you all. But I cannot do it by myself. So, if you would please?" Marie replied. And I gestured to him and his associates to hold him by the arms for me. Robert was in so much pain, but also on the brink of death, so I had to hurry. Once they held his arms and his head in place, I forced a tube down his throat to make him ingest the mixture. His left eye got wide, and I saw the right one trying to do the same, but it was almost swollen shut.

I connected the other end of the tube to a funnel in my hand and began pouring the mixture into his system. Then, I poured an elixir that would help heal his wounds on the inside and out. He would have to recover for at least a month, and his dick was gone, but I still had use for him. His foot was shattered and that would never heal correctly. But if he worked hard enough, maybe he could walk again someday. And without any assistance. "One last favor please," I said to Monroe.

Monroe

"I only agreed to do one more thing for you. This would be two. Don't take advantage of the situation, Marie." I realized that I may need her help in the future concerning the fate of Aubrey. If these mixtures worked for him, then maybe she could create something that would work for her. "What else do you need?"

Marie

"Would you mind unchaining him for me please?" Marie asked innocently enough.

Aubrey *(In Dreamland)*

'Yes, Monroe! I will marry you!! I love you so much baby'! He proposed to me in the same Walmart we met at (the second time). It would have been corny had it been any other man. But he surprised me by showing up while I was shopping. Some of the store associates were in on it. Must have been the most Walmart workers in one store that I had ever seen because you know they ain't never at the register! I had to laugh at myself on that one! Why am I laughing so hard still? Why are these store lights so bright?

"Monroe, where are you? Baby?"

Dee Dee

Is that a smile I see on her face? I got up out of the chair I was in and got a little closer to Aubrey. I was so focused on her that I had to remind myself to breathe!

Mike

"What is it baby?" As I got up and joined my wife at Bree's bedside.

Dee Dee

"Shhhh..." I was still waiting for her to do what I thought I saw her do, again. "Come on baby. Smile for mommy. I know I saw her smile bae. I just know it. She's trying to come back to me. Come back baby, please come back."

Then she smiled again. This time was almost a laugh. "What are you dreaming about baby? Come on and wake up. Wake up for mommy." I was rubbing her hand and moving her hair out of her face. "Wake up Aubrey, wake up and tell mommy what you're laughing about. Come on baby, wake up."

At this point, Mike was praying over her again as he's been doing since the accident happened. He prayed so hard for my baby, *our* baby. She was as much his as she was mine. And I loved him even more in that moment. She smiled again and again. I pressed the button for the doctor to come in here. I swear she was laughing!

Dr. Sawyer

"How's everything going, Mr. and Mrs. Roberson?"

Dee Dee

"Doc, look! Look at her, she's smiling and laughing. This has to be a great sign, right? Please tell me she's coming back to me!"

Dr. Sawyer got out her small flashlight to look into her eyes. Her eyes weren't exactly following the light, but there was some movement. As soon as she started shining the light, Aubrey wasn't smiling anymore. She just journeyed back into her "sleep".

Joe

After I left the warehouse, I drove to my brother's house. If there was anyone that I trusted with everything, it was Alton. He was outside playing with my niece and nephew when I pulled up to the house. This was the life that I wanted with my future wife. He and my sister in law, Shayna, were so perfect for each other. She's been around since I was a little boy, almost eighteen years ago.

Our parents passed away in a car accident years ago when I was still in grade school. My brother, who's eleven years older than me, worked three jobs to support me, Shay and their growing family. The life insurance payouts we received from my family took care of our parent's home and since Alton was nineteen already, I was able to remain in his custody. He ensured I finished high school and was there for me throughout college. I was awarded a four-year basketball scholarship, until I tore my anterior cruciate ligament, better known as an ACL, two years into my contract. That championship game, although I scored thirty-nine points, including the game winning shot, had seven rebounds and six assists, was the end of my scholarship. Once I completed rigorous therapy over a six-month period after two surgeries, I discovered I was not allowed to play for the school again.

Fortunately for me, Alton wouldn't allow me give up. I didn't want him to take on more work to pay for my schooling, that's why I busted my ass for that scholarship in the first place. I limped my ass to my classes and completed my Bachelor of Science degree with a double major in Health Care Management and Dental Hygiene. Took a little longer than the two years I would have had left on my scholarship, but I stayed the course, with a vow to make my family proud.

I was getting my feet wet working at Mountainview Smiles Forever, but I was well on my way to having my own patient load. And with Aubrey by my side… I meant, *Samantha* by my side. Damn, what the fuck is my problem? Here I was daydreaming about this woman that did not belong to me, again. After Aubrey's accident, I've caused major damage to my relationship by not being present for Samantha. I wanted to talk to my brother about it. I needed his advice on what I should do next. That's why I stopped over today.

When I finally got out of the car, my niece and nephew, Dakota and Ahmad, ran up to me as they always did. "Uncle Joey, Uncle Joey!" That never got old. These kids at four and eleven, were absolutely the most perfect kids in the world! Dakota was Uncle's Baby and Ahmad was my boy! "What ya'll up to? Y'all making your daddy run around after y'all?" All my cares went away when I was with my family. I couldn't wait to become a husband and a father.

Alton

"What's up little brother? Shay is in the house cooking right now. You staying for dinner, right? She baked some pies last night!" We shook hands and then embraced.

Joe

"Man, you don't even have to ask! I'm already hungry!" Shay could bake her ass off! I rarely called in advance before I came by, because I knew if I gave her enough of a heads up, she was gonna make something especially for me. She did not need to go through the trouble for me, although I appreciated it. "Lemme go and say hi to my sister."

Alton

"You better not be in there flirting with my wife or hugging her too long, either!" He joked. He got serious for a moment and I knew that look. We would talk a bit later about whatever was on his mind. I knew there was something serious on lil bro's mind.

Joe

I was deep in thought for a moment as I silently acknowledged that I would bring up what was on my mind to him later on. "Well you know how little brothers do!" We laughed a bit before I headed into their home to see Shay. I took my time admiring the home I grew up in. I believe it was Alton that had the green thumb and kept up my mother's rose garden. Over the years, there have been a few additions to the home and also some renovations to allow Shay to make it her own.

The backsplash in the kitchen was upgraded to this textured granite which contained hues of blues and greys, that also matched the countertops and island. Other updates to the kitchen included a Wi-Fi enabled, stainless steel smart refrigerator with a see-through French door, ice maker, water dispenser and bottom freezer. Also, there were now double ovens installed where the old cabinetry used to be. The flooring throughout the home was upgraded to Italian Vincoli Gris Porcelain Tile, with eight-inch baseboard molding in all rooms as well as the office and hallways. I knew, because Shay allowed me to come with.

She encouraged my decorative passion. She assisted me with the décor in my home as well. That's just part of how I bond with my sister in law. I definitely appreciate our relationship outside of my only brother. Shay is one of my best friends. "Who's the most beautiful sis in the world?" I asked as I snuck up on her. Shay was a very shapely woman with thick thighs and hips, radiant dark chocolate skin and almond shaped eyes. She stood at a mere five foot four inches but don't get it twisted, she is a force to be reckoned with. She was just an absolutely gorgeous woman with the prettiest smile I'd ever seen.

And she sported sister locs, so you know we had a special connection. She even took me to get mine started about seven years ago. I remember when I was younger, I would always tell her I was gonna marry a woman that looked just like her if I didn't marry her first. I don't look at her in a sexual way, that's my brother's wife. But she was effortlessly sexy, even with her growing baby bump. They referred to this one as the 'pull out baby'.

Shay

"Oh, and you better know it's me!! Hey Boobah!" As she did a few poses with her hand on her belly. "How's my baby brother doing?" She looked around for a second before asking, "Where's Samantha? Be sure to tell her that I got that chocolate pie waiting for her whenever she wants it."

Shay was an amazing baker. Her baked goods were coveted from here in Maryland and up and down the Eastern seaboard, from New York on down to the Carolinas and the business is booming. She ran a home-based operation called *Shay's Sweets & Treats*, so that she could still be at home with the kids and still contribute to the family. She's currently exploring expanding her shipment area.

Joe

When she mentioned Sam, my mind felt confused all over again and I had this guilty feeling that engulfed me. I shook it off quickly. "She's alright, just loving me. I can't complain. Alright now sis, you know every time you have a baby, your butt gets bigger. How many more nieces and nephews you gonna give me?" I laughed so hard at my own self. She was laughing right along with me.

Shay

"Oh no, no, no… you only get *one* more nephew, and that's it!" I could tell she was too serious about that even with the biggest grin on her face.

Joe

She smirked a bit, then I realized she was telling me the baby was a boy. "WHAAAAT! Congratulations sis! I'm so happy about that, because I was worried about how Uncle's Baby was gonna act when I started giving her little sister my attention too! That's great news sis, I'm happy for ya'll man." I hugged Shay because I truly was nervous about having to split my attention between Dakota and a new baby girl. She had me wrapped around all her little fingers. My brother and the kids came in the house right then. I was cheesing so hard from ear to ear.

Alton

"Aye man, I already told you, you can't marry my wife." We laughed so hard together!

Joe

"Aye man, I stopped trying to marry your wife when you stole her from me on your wedding day! You know I was trying to make her mine." I was cracking up by this point. "But hey bro, I am so happy about my newest nephew! Congratulations man!" We dapped each other.

Alton

"Yep, I remember! You were about to go to the eighth grade, I think. Actually, you thought you had a chance with my dime piece." And he looked at her so admiringly when he said it.

You could tell that they were still very much in love with each other. She was blushing like the teenager she was when my brother met her. I respected their love. I couldn't wait to have that special bond with someone. Samantha was as close as anyone had gotten, and I loved her lil freaky ass. But there was still something missing. A void of some sort. I had to figure this shit out. There was only one person that made me feel whole. But she belonged to someone else.

Monroe

I was finally back at Aubrey's house. Felt like I hadn't slept in days. But now that we had taken care of the lil nigga, it was catching up to me. No time to sleep though, I had to get back to my lady. I missed the fuck out of Aubrey. Her scent was all around me. I missed the way she touched me, the way her body fit me like a glove. The way her full lips felt on mine. It was always electric when she kissed me. I missed those beautiful hazel eyes that just had me mesmerized every time I looked into them. I couldn't sleep knowing my baby was laid up in the hospital like that.

I left the house after my shower. I put on a little of the cologne I knew she liked and dressed in some sweats and a t-shirt. I brushed my hair and made a mental note to make an appointment with my barber. I wasn't feeling the curly bush.

Once I arrived, I stopped at the flower shop for some tulips and another bouquet of the colorful roses that I knew she liked so much. When I stepped into the room, I could tell her mom had been crying. I put the flowers down and went over to her. It didn't look like anything good was going on.

"Hey Mike." As he and I embraced one another. "Mrs. Roberson, please tell me she's getting better."

Dee Dee

"You would know, Monroe, had you been here with her."

Monroe

I knew she was disappointed in me, but I had to do what I had to do. "I had to take care of something before coming back up here. I'm sorry, but I swear everything I was doing, was to ensure her safety when she wakes up. And I know she's gonna wake up," I paused as I looked over at Aubrey. "She has to." Her mom stood up and hugged me. She knew I was being truthful. She knew I loved her daughter.

I held my lady's hand and kissed it. I got on my knees beside her and pulled out a box. I placed the ring on her ring finger and her mom was just weeping. "Wake up beautiful, I want you to marry me. We have so much life to live, don't check out on me now. Come back to us, wake up for me. I can't live this life without you baby." The doctor walked into Aubrey's room at the moment. The look on her face, I couldn't read.

Dr. Sawyer

"Hello everyone, sorry to interrupt. I need to go over the prognosis so that you all are prepared."

Chapter 18

Taisha

I repeated my pre-Don visit ritual that I had done the day before. The difference from yesterday is that I wasn't as nervous. I knew exactly what to expect… or so I thought. As soon as I got there, he tongue-kissed me like we were in love or some shit. That immediately turned me off. But I went with it. Shit, what else was I supposed to do? I always keep the dollar sign at the fore front of my mind. It's only the second visit and he's into me real tough already. I didn't even get to set anything up; not the dance routine I had prepared or nothing else. Unlike before, he was already in the cell awaiting my arrival.

While lying with him after we were done with sex session number one, he was talking about the future. He said he knew that realistically there wasn't much to look forward to in his life as far as a future on the outside, but for some reason he's asking me to contact lawyers about appeals, showing up to court dates, etcetera, etcetera. I'm not ready for any of that, but I do wanna keep this money coming in. What am I gonna do? I had to think of something and fast.

"Donnie, I don't want you to take this the wrong way or anything boo, but me advocating for your release wasn't part of our terms. Don't you think that those things would be better suited for your wife to do?"

He contemplated for a quick second before replying. I really didn't want to come off as cold or anything like that, but I agreed to sex him three times a week and my mortgage payment for seventy-five hundred dollars. This was not a relationship in the least, nor part of our agreement.

Big Don

I thought about what Tai just said. Maybe it wasn't realistic to ask someone that I was paying to suck and fuck me to handle my business. I need to reign it in, this was just supposed to be sex. "Don't worry about it, Tai. Come and put that pussy on me again." I knew how to handle her from this point on.

Sam

<<<ring, ring>>>

Ugh, I wasn't sure if I wanted to speak to Joe right now. He's been calling my phone like crazy, though. "Hello?" I said with as much attitude as I could muster. These emotions are very new to me.

Joe

"Hi Samantha. How are you?"

Sam

"How would you be if I disappeared for almost three days?" I yelled at him. "This is absolutely unacceptable, because I know that you've seen my calls. I told you before Joe, I'm not into games or the bullshit." Sam argued. I felt myself getting worked up, and I know I should not have cursed at him. "I'm sorry. I just don't know what to think at this point. Are you calling to explain yourself?"

Joe

"I feel so badly about how I've handled things. I let my guilt get the best of me and for that I'm sorry. I should have at least picked up the phone to let you know what was going on. I just didn't know how to express what I was feeling." Joe lamented.

Sam

Well… he did sound apologetic, I guess. I sighed before answering him. "I accept your apology. But you can't assume responsibility, nor the blame for all that's happened with Aubrey. She did ultimately make the choice to go and see about Rob. At least you went with her. Where are you?" Sam questioned.

Joe

"I just left Alton's house. I needed to talk to him about everything that was going on. May I come over… please?" Joe asked.

Sam

"Sure, I'll see you when you get here." I said. I can't believe I gave in so fast. But truth be told, my vagina has been yearning for some attention! Oh God, what am I thinking? Joe doesn't deserve me.

Joe

After talking with my brother, I was able to see that I'm just infatuated with Aubrey. I think I love Sam, and I know that if chosen, she would make a great wife. But there was absolutely *something* missing. I didn't know what that something was, but I wasn't gonna dwell on it and mess everything up either. Alton told me that I had the tendency to push women away from me that didn't fit in my mental 'box' that I created in my mind over the years. That makes sense to me, in the way he explained it.

He told me that I've always unconsciously compared my relationships to his, because while I'm on the outside looking in, I think what he and Shay have is perfect. He told me that just like other couples, they have their ups and downs. Shay even took him back after being unfaithful to her. To think that my brother would be unfaithful to this most 'perfect' woman in my eyes, further let me know that there was absolutely no hope for whatever woman would ultimately end up in my life. It made me even more nervous, dealing with Samantha because of the type of man I *could* be. Alton said he makes it his mission to prove to her daily, that she's the most important person in his life. It incensed me to no end that he would step out on her, but I'm grateful to him that he trusted me enough to share that with me.

After that conversation, I realized that I unrealistically assumed my big brother was perfect, which wasn't fair. I mean, he's always been a superhero to me, but he's actually very human. With that realization came the other side of it. The pressure that I unknowingly placed on him to be perfect. I appreciated that conversation he had with me, and it further made me realize that I needed to make up with Sam.

I picked up some flowers to show her that she's very special to me. As I parked and got out of my car, I saw that she was standing in the doorway waiting for me. I also noticed that she was wearing her black satin robe and it looked as if nothing else was under it. Her hair was freshly done and when I got close to her, she grabbed my hand and led me into the apartment. She smelled and looked so delicious. I handed her the flowers and she then kissed me.

"I'm so sorry for shutting you out babe. I didn't know how to process my feelings. Thank you for allowing me to see you."

Sam

"Just don't let it happen again, babe. All I ask is that you communicate with me. And if you need space, just tell me that. Thank you for the beautiful flowers. I've missed you so much."

Joe

"I missed you too babe." She hugged me so tight and I felt like this was exactly where I needed to be. She kissed me with such ferocity, that I felt the love she possessed for me.

Sam

"You wanna come show me how much you missed me, Joseph?" Sam asked him seductively.

Joe

When she asked me that, she opened her satin, floor length robe on one side and ran her fingers very seductively from her neck, to her right titty, across her torso to her center. I was already brick by the time she started touching herself in front of me. I went to her, traced my hands along the curve of her breast and then underneath her robe across her shoulder to remove it. She let it drop to the floor. I ran my fingers through her hair and grabbed a handful, just as she likes it. She moaned softly while removing my belt. Samantha then unbuttoned my pants, then she slid her hand in my boxers and caressed my hardness. She squatted down in front of me and took me into her warm mouth as she slid my pants off of me.

When she emerged, I gripped her hair, licked and sucked her neck while she nibbled on my ear. I smacked her soft ass and afterwards kneaded her skin. I ran my fingers across her pussy and noticed she was dripping wet. I removed my shirt and my shoes, then lifted her up as she wrapped her legs around me. I drove myself into her center and experienced immediate pleasure. Her creamy pussy was so tight, it gripped me back and I was in pure bliss. I placed her back against the wall while I drilled wantonly inside her walls. She wrapped her arms around my neck and arched her back against the wall in absolute pleasure as she climaxed for the first time. When I felt her pussy contracting from the inside, I plunged deeper to further the sensation.

I walked with our bodies still interlaced, over to the couch and lowered us down so she could ride me. Samantha steadied herself by placing her feet onto the couch on both sides of me. She knew that I loved when she rode my dick. She went to work, too. I kept my hands on her ass to guide her all the way down. Her juices flowed once I felt her cum again. She had me and the couch soaking wet.

After she came down from that bout of pleasure, I carried her over to the bed because I was not yet done, and she was slowing down. Luckily, I had energy for the both of us. That pussy was so good, and to know she had never given it to anyone else, made fucking her so much better. I placed her on her bed while she got in her favorite position. I wasn't complaining at all. I loved it when she was face down with that pretty pussy facing up at me.

I positioned myself behind her and she guided me inside. She threw that pussy back on me like it was no tomorrow. I held onto her waist and when I felt her backing off again, I knew she was about to cum. I thrusted in and out going as deep as I could to intensify her impending orgasm and all you could hear was our moans mixed with our sweaty bodies slapping against one another.

She said, "let me taste you baby," and pointed to her tongue. I told you she was my personal porn star. I wasn't able to remove myself from her warmth this time though and ended up releasing inside of her. It felt like all the stress from the last few days had flowed from my body and all of my stress seemed to start melting away. I had to apologize after I caught my breath.

"Baby, I'm so sorry, but I just couldn't help it. You felt so good; that thang was extra gushy today. I wanna live in that pussy!" We both laughed and finally collapsed from the pleasure, then cuddled with each other for a while. I apologized to her again and promised to always communicate. Eventually we both fell asleep in each other's arms.

Chapter 19

Alton

Sharing with my baby brother about my infidelity, knowing how much he thought I was the perfect man and also how much he adored my wife, was definitely one of the hardest things I had to do. A close second to losing my parents and raising him on my own while forfeiting my own young adult years. Now don't get me wrong, I have no regrets because my brother is easily one of the most important people in the world to me. He's always thought of me as his hero, not knowing I have my demons as well.

The only person that knows the full extent of those demons is my sweetheart. Through my substance abuse and alcoholism, Shay still took a chance on me and loved me right on through it. It was only right, I thought, since she'd always been there that marriage was what she deserved. I experienced a brief stint with an addiction to Ketamin pills for depression after my parents' accident. That euphoric and tranquil existence lasted for the better part of the year afterwards, until Shay presented me with an ultimatum.

Seven Years Ago

Shay

"Alton, I'm pregnant."

Alton

I was high out of my mind when she told me that, and really didn't know what to say to her other than, "you sure?"

Shay

"Yes, and I'm telling you, with or without you we will be alright. Considering your current state of mind with your depression and all, I think it may best that I leave and take Joey with me. He doesn't need to see you like this. You need counseling to learn how to deal with this, Alton. I can't continue to sit here and act like everything is ok with us."

Alton

She walked over to me and started snapping her fingers in front of my face as if I didn't hear what she just said.

Shay

"Hello? Alton, do you hear me? Are you listening to me? Look at you! High outta your got damn mind right now!" I sighed. I tried another approach as I sat near him and held his hand. "I know it's hard baby, but you have to figure this out!" Tears started flowing while I am trying to get through to the love of my life. I don't want to leave him, but I will not sit here while he kills himself slowly. "We have a family now! And Joey needs you! You are not the man that your parents raised you to be! And with this pregnancy, I will not let the stress of what's going on affect my baby... *your son,* Alton." Shay proclaimed with tears in her eyes and her resolve unshakeable.

Alton

I just sat there, speechless. I didn't know what to say. Did she just say she was having my son? Shay turned her back to me and started to walk to the back of the house, after I didn't respond to her for what seemed like hours. My mind was still foggy, but that instance, when she said, *'your son'*, I vowed to God that I would get myself together.

She left a little while later, with Joey in tow, and they stayed out for the night. I didn't call her, but I sent a text to her phone letting her know that I did, in fact, hear what she said to me.

<<<text message>>>

Baby, I was listening to you earlier and heard every word you said. I want you to know, that starting tomorrow, I will be making a conscious effort of getting back to the man you met and married. I was lost, losing both of my parents and being thrust into parenthood so early in my life was a shock.

But I'm a man, your man, and I vow just like I did on our wedding day, that I will give you the very best of me, to carry you and to be carried by you, to journey with you and to love each minute of our lives together. I vow to love you as you love me, through all hardship, darkness, and pain to reach our joys and our hopes together, always with honesty and faith.

With all of the love that God has blessed my heart with, it is yours, always and forever. I love you.

Alton

I went into recovery with a clear heart and a foggy mind. I can't say I haven't had my moments where I thought I wasn't gonna make it, but my resolve remained stronger than I imagined it would. I never touched Ketamine again. But there were other traps I fell into. Socially, I started to drink alcohol as a way of "relaxing" while out with friends. One thing I learned about, much later on, was as a recovering addict that it's easy to relapse. But not until I actually did.

One evening, I went out with my friends after work on a Friday evening. It was something we did once monthly, so it was no big deal with Shay. Besides, she had just had the baby and wanted her own bonding time with Ahmad since she recently returned to work. He was not yet four months old and it was exciting for us as a family to experience this new life, but, Shay and I didn't get too much alone time and I understood that. At least I thought I did.

Our sex life went from sensational, especially while she was pregnant, to absolutely nothing even past the mandatory six weeks. I didn't blame her for it, nor did I feel neglected. I was still trying to show my wife that she and this family were my priority. And it was all about Ahmad, for both her and I. Until it happened…

It was the middle of March and the air was a bit brisk, so I decided to dress warm. It was the night me and the fellas were linking up. We decided to hit up a restaurant in Adams Morgan for happy hour. My friends Carlos and Brandon met me there. We had been sitting there sippin' while catching up and eating some wings.

Brandon

"So, tell us about the baby man! Congrats again, but I still can't believe you got one of the finest women at school to marry you and have yo' baby too!" He joked.

Alton

We all busted up laughing. I knew my lady was all that. Even after having my son, she was sexier than ever. "Aye man, well you know I'm smooth with it! My lady loves everything about me, and I know you still salty because I got to her first! Told you I was gonna lock that one down. Get your own woman, dude!" We continued clowning with each other. I was so glad that I had these two in my life.

Carlos was the playboy of our group, he always was. He was of Puerto Rican descent and moved from New York to Maryland with his family when we were ten. I met Carlos first, in the fifth grade. He grew up with a single dad and two other brothers. His mom was in and out of their lives until Carlos' dad put his foot down and separated from her. Needless to say, Carlos didn't have too much respect for the ladies. I warned him that he would meet his match one day, but he always welcomed the challenge.

Carlos

"Aye Alton, you know Brandon tryna wife ol' girl he met a few months ago, right?" He said as he laughed.

Alton

Brandon looked so uncomfortable like he didn't want me to know. "What happened to Felicia though? I thought y'all were good?" I noticed Carlos was holding something back. "What? Am I missing something?"

Carlos

"Aye Al, B told that bitch bye!" He said as he continued to laugh even harder still.

Alton

"Huh?" I guess I just didn't get it.

Brandon

"Alton, don't pay this corny ass fool no mind! He's saying I said, bye, like 'bye Felicia' to her when we broke up. From the movie Friday. She wasn't the one man, and I finally figured that out. Way too materialistic."

Alton

I looked at Brandon, then Carlos who was crying laughing by this point and back to Brandon. We all laughed together then. Felicia was always materialistic. We warned him of that before he got serious with her. Better late than never though. But that was my boy, always giving the benefit of the doubt. Or like Carlos said, he was pussy whipped.

I met Brandon in middle school. He was always considered the nice guy by all the girls. He was the type of guy that would bring individual roses for the girls in our class on Valentines Day. But his pecan brown complexion with the thick glasses over his bug eyes couldn't compete with Carlos' wavy hair and DeBarge like looks. And since Brandon still hadn't hit his growth spurt at the time, he was like five foot three until the summer after ninth grade.

The girls always gave me and Carlos more play. We were almost six feet tall by eighth grade.

We remained the best of friends throughout high school and college. They were there for me when my parents passed. They even watched Joey for me when I had to work. I considered these guys my brothers, we couldn't get any closer. I truly appreciated our bond. Brandon worked on Saturdays, so he had to bail early. Then, one of Carlos' many women called him up, so you know he left to go check her out. By this time, it was quarter to eleven at night and I knew everyone was sleep at my house, so I decided to stay just a bit longer.

Waitress (Alexandria)

"Hey Al, you want anything else suga?"

Alton

"Naw Alex, I'm good for now. Thank you though."

Alex

"Oh, okay. I'm not used to seeing you here alone. Your friends coming back?" I made sure to get closer to him so that he could get a whiff of my new perfume. Al was so sexy to me.

Alton

"No, they already left. I'm just chilling for the time being. Why? You need my table for other guests?" Now, I was already tipsy by this point and Alexandria was *very* easy on the eyes. She was tall and slender, but curvy in all the right places. She was light skin, with long brown hair and her eyes were light brown with a hint of green. She was always nice to us, but we never carried on this much conversation before now. And whatever she was wearing, she smelled wonderful.

Alex

"No hun, I don't need the table. I was just making conversation. But I won't bother you. Let me know if you need anything else though. I'll be around." I was so embarrassed!

Alton

In hindsight, that should have been the end of our conversation that night. But obviously, it was not. I grabbed her hand before she could walk away. "Alex, I didn't mean it like that, sweetie." As I lightly caressed her fingers. "You know, I wouldn't mind you keeping me company if your boss isn't around. You're always a pleasure to speak to when we are in here. And to see as well." I made sure I looked her up and down as I said that. I just wanted to make her night. When she smiled that big pretty smile, I knew right then that I should've gotten up and took my ass home. But I didn't.

I stayed there talking with Alex until her shift was over. She had a few drinks, but I had stopped so I didn't have to pay for a ride. We walked outside, and once I saw that she was about to call a cab, I offered her a ride home.

Alex

"I live about thirty minutes from here, you sure it's alright? Don't you need to get home?"

Alton

"It's not problem, I can take you. And yeah, I'm good. It's on my way. I live in Clinton about ten or so minutes from your area. We got in my car and we continued our conversation as I drove. Her scent swirled in my nostrils, making my nature rise. I don't think she noticed, but her body was turned toward me as she spoke.

Alex

"Alton, I've always thought you were so handsome, but I never said anything because I knew you were taken. I not sure why I'm telling you now, maybe it's the alcohol speaking. Either way, you've always been such a gentleman to me, unlike that Hispanic guy you roll with. No matter how many women I see him with, he's always trying to flirt."

Alton

"That's Carlos for you, but he's harmless. He won't bite." I laughed because he did that with all the ladies.

Alex

"He won't bite, well that's good. But how about you?"

Alton

I looked over at her and noticed the lust radiating from her and then I started to think about what those pouty lips would feel like on mine. "Will I what? Bite?" I said as we stared at one another the traffic light that had already turned green. I didn't care. I just wanted to know what she was going to say next.

Alex

"Well yes," I started as I rubbed the side of his face. "Do you bite? I would very much like for you to show me." I unzipped my coat slowly and unbuttoned my work shirt thereafter. I started caressing the skin on my neck down into my lace bra and I could tell he liked what he saw. I grabbed his hand and as he touched me very softly, then the car behind us beeped their horn very aggressively. Alton withdrew his hand as he started to drive again. I fixed my clothing and we remained quiet until he pulled up to my apartment building. "Would you like to come up for a cup of coffee?"

Alton

Alex was so seductive. Those eyes drew me in completely and I wanted to explore her a bit more. "Yeah, a cup of coffee sounds nice." I parked my car and followed her to her second-floor apartment. Upon entering, she removed her coat and asked for mine. She then led me to the living room, while I waited for her to bring the coffee out. "Do you need some help?"

Alex

"I'm already done, handsome." I brought out the coffee pot, two mugs, sugar, cream and a couple of spoons. I poured the coffee in silence and we both fixed ours to our individual tastes. We avoided making eye contact until I decided to break the tension. "Alton, do you mind if I get a little more comfortable? I've been in my work clothes all day."

Alton

"Oh no problem, go ahead sweetie. I'll be here when you get back." I knew I should have been heading home. I shouldn't even have been here. I was setting myself up. But I didn't leave. We hadn't done anything wrong, yet. I enjoyed my coffee until she reemerged a while later. I could tell she took a quick shower because her hair was damp. She had on a pale pink knee-length jersey dress that hugged her petite frame. Her breasts were generous as they flowed freely underneath it, her waist small and the outline of her hips made my mouth water. Her scent was almost hypnotizing as she sat beside me and refilled her cup with more coffee. "Thank you for the coffee Alexandria. I think it's time for me to head out."

Alex

I placed my cup on the table as I got up before he did. I stood in front of him, and he sat against the back of the couch. I continued what I started in the car, as I trailed my hands from my neck down the front of my dress until I reached the hem. I slowly raised it until my bare sex was directly in his view.

"May I have your hand?" He gave me his hand and I allowed him to explore my folds until we couldn't take is any longer. He picked me up and carried me to my bedroom as our tongues danced and he made love to my body like I'd never experienced.

Alton

I didn't get home until almost four that next morning. Shay was asleep with the baby, so I took a shower in Joey's bathroom and fell asleep on the couch like I sometimes did. The affair with Alex and I lasted for a couple of years. Shay found out because once I began trying and distance myself from Alexandria, she started popping up at places I would be. Even when I was with my family. And that woman's intuition is not a joke. Shay found out where she worked and confronted her. Alexandria couldn't help but tell her everything. Shay wasn't nasty to her, she approached her on some grown woman shit. Alex was apologetic and even let her know that I was trying to break it off, but that she wasn't trying to let me. I knew nothing of their conversation, until Joey called me at work one afternoon, while I was still at work.

<<<ring, ring>>>

Teenaged Joe

"Hey bro, are we moving? I just came home and there's a moving truck here."

Alton

I was just as confused as he was. "No. Is the moving truck in front of our house? Where's Shay?"

Teenaged Joe

"Yeah, it's in our driveway and she's taking stuff out to the truck. Sis, Al wants to speak to you."

Alton

I heard Joey walking towards her to give her the phone. She told him that she would take it in the room.

Shay

"Boobah, I got it. You can hang up." She said to Joey.

Teenaged Joe

"Okay sis." The phone then disconnected on one end.

Alton

"Hey baby, what's going on? Joey told me you were taking stuff and putting it into a moving truck. Where are we going?"

Shay

"*We* aren't going anywhere. Ahmad and I, and Joey if he wants to, are moving out." She said very matter of factly.

Alton

"Babe, what's going on? Why are you moving? Talk to me."

Shay

"Talk to Alexandria. I advise you not to come to this house until I'm gone. I can't promise you that I won't shoot you where you stand. And I know you don't want your son's mother in jail.

I'll be out of here around five. You'll be receiving something from my lawyer via the mail carrier. Goodbye."

Alton

"But baby-". She hung up on me before I could reply. One of the conditions of our marriage was that she would be outta there if there was any infidelity on my end. So, I knew she was serious. At that time, she had been studying for the police academy and her aim was on point. I headed home anyway.

I got there shortly after she left, according to Joey. He decided to stay home, because he wanted to know why Shay was leaving. Of course, Shay being her loving self, told Joey she needed to be closer to the academy for her studies. Of course, I went with it.

Present Day (one day prior)

Alton

"So after a year of begging and pleading with Shay to come back, going to individual counseling for both my alcohol use, which I didn't think was out of control, and my infidelity, our family was whole once again."

Joe

"I can't believe that I never put that together. We still had dinners together, both of you were always at my games, you both saw me off to the prom and my graduation together. The alibi just seemed to fit. Damn." I sat there quiet for a moment as I took all of this information in. I was angry for Shay, but because of the love I had for my brother, it subsided quickly. In some ways, I felt like that vulnerable little boy again and I didn't know why. It just made me think of Sam and the relationships I had with women before her. Maybe it had something to do with genetics. Maybe me never being satisfied had something to do with that. I don't know.

Alton

"Little brother, I know that you weren't expecting anything like that from me, but it happened and I'm not proud of it. I just want to let you know that it's never happened since. I don't even look at other women. Well except for Rihanna and them Cardi videos." Joey laughed a bit with me, but I could tell he was hurt.

"I know you're a little confused about Samantha, and that's normal when you love someone. But communication is the best thing you all can do for one another. Be vulnerable with her. She's in love with you. Don't repeat my mistakes. This Aubrey girl is in your imagination. She may be fine and all that, but y'all are not connected in that way." I hope he listened, so he didn't risk losing his women like I almost did.

Chapter 20

Taisha

I felt like I was back in the game! Not only was Don paying my mortgage, he was paying me over seven gees to fuck him on a regular basis. I couldn't get over how good life was at the moment. But no matter how hard I tried I couldn't get Money out of my mind.

I was still madly in love with him, and all the money, gifts and all of the rest of that shit couldn't replace him. Good distraction, but nothing replaced having him as my man. All he ever asked me for was loyalty, respect and to never change. Essentially, that's exactly what I did the opposite of and I see that now. And being inside of this big ass house all alone, day in and day out, reminded me of just that.

<<<ring, ring>>>

Monroe

"Hello?" Monroe answered.

Taisha

"Hey baby, how are you?" I sexily replied.

Monroe

"Who is this?" He asked in an irritated tone.

Taisha

He clearly sounded annoyed. "It's me Tai. You were on my mind and I hadn't spoken to you in a few months, so I decided to call. How have you been?"

Monroe

"Tai, why are you really calling? Do you need some money or something? 'Cause I ain't got it." Monroe replied in a huff.

Taisha

"It really hurts my feelings that you would say that, but I understand why. No, I don't need any money from you. I was wondering if maybe we could get together and have some coffee one day. We've known each other for so long that I would think we could still be friends." I was on the verge of tears at this point.

Monroe

She sounded like she was about to start crying. Just because I didn't want to be with her any longer, didn't mean that I had to be so harsh. We used to be friends, somehow it just got lost in translation. And with everything going on with Aubrey, coffee wasn't such a bad idea. Just as friends though, nothing more. "Okay, if you're available on Monday, I'm free." Monroe said, hoping he didn't regret this.

Taisha

"Monday is perfect! I look forward to seeing you in a couple of days. We can go to that spot down on Independence Avenue like we used to." Taisha squealed. It was perfect! My schedule with Don is Tuesdays, Thursdays and Fridays, but only in the mornings because his wife comes in the afternoon on Fridays. Monroe and I used to go to that coffee place all the time when we were in college.

Monroe

"Alright bet." Monroe replied with uncertainty. I hung up with her and went back to reading about how to assist patients with recovery while I sat with Aubrey. Dr. Sawyer came and talked with us yesterday about her prognosis. Aubrey was expected to recover, but she wasn't sure how the head injury would affect her. She explained the possibilities which included mood changes, memory loss, difficulty speaking, incontinence, seizures, weakness and what she's currently experiencing, varying degrees of consciousness. Whatever she experienced when she woke up, I was going to be there for her. One hundred percent.

Taisha

I was too pumped about meeting up with Monroe. I figured if I could get him to remember that girl that he first met and fell in love with, this little fling with whoever the fuck 'Ms. Little Perfect' was with would be dead in the water. "I'm on a mission to get my man back! By any means necessary!" Taisha announced while admiring herself in the mirror.

James

Free, Tamia and I arrived at the resort at Virginia Beach and had been just relaxing in the room for a minute. Free had been unusually quiet over the last couple of days. She hadn't really been herself and I could understand that. I was hoping that by taking her away to the beach to just relax and inhale the sea air, that it would encourage her to open up to me with the change of scenery. I really wanted to take her to the Bahamas, but the baby was currently too young to fly. I can't imagine the trauma she experienced that day she was kidnapped by the lil nigga, but I tried to be as supportive as possible.

We walked down to the beach and sat on towels in the sand just out of reach of the waves lapping at us. Tamia was sleeping in my arms and Free was gazing out at the ocean. The weather was clear and the all you could hear were the waves crashing against the rocks and birds shrilling near us.

"Fresia, you know that I grew up here, right?" She looked at me quietly and shook her head no. "I know you think we're from Washington, DC, but no, I was born about forty-five minutes away from here in a place called Newport News. We named it "Bad Newz" growing up due to the crime and its gang activity. I had a really close bond with my mother's side of the family while growing up here.

"My grandmother was the matriarch of our family and became the strength for my mother and her siblings after my grandfather passed in 1982. Her name was Mabel, and she was born and raised here. She had my mom when she was sixteen and got married to my grandfather shortly thereafter. Everyone knew her and everyone respected her. Even the white people that lived here during that time respected and loved my granny.

"Spending time with my granny was something I relished. She wasn't your typical grandmother. Don't get me wrong, she was a sweetie and would do anything for anyone, but she was not to be played with. She had the best stories, and as I matured, I realized that she shared her most vulnerable moments with me that would essentially become doctrine on how I lived my life. The story that resonated with me most was when she found out a close family friend "had eyes" for my mother when she was a little girl. This "friend" grew up with my granny as a brother because her parents took him in when his mother could no longer provide for him. Granny said she took him everywhere with her. She was his big sister and wouldn't let anything bad happen to him.

"She said that when she had my mom and married my grandfather, things became different between her and Walter. It sounded to me that he held it against her for leaving him, but she wasn't too far. Right down the road from the house my grandmother grew up in. She still made time for him and had him over to her and my grandfather's house, but as he got older, he became a bit more distant. She recounted the disdain that had developed over time, for his birth parents and for her, but she decided to let him be.

"That was until he started to reappear once my mom became a teenager. Even though she still regarded Walter as family, she told me that she knew by this point he no longer did. He had become engrossed in the street life, but this unnatural obsession had developed and gotten stronger for my mom even though he was still considered her uncle.

"Well one day, Walter saw my mom walking home from school and saw a guy named Drew approaching her. He waited to see what happened, and just like he thought, Drew was trying to hit on her. My mom allowed him to walk her home, but he was trying to get in the house, and she wasn't letting him in. Once Walter saw that he was starting to become forceful, he went over and handled Drew.

"My mom was thankful and trusted that Walter was looking out for her because he was family. She didn't know him that well, but she knew of him as my granny's brother. He asked her to let him in the house to wait with her in case Drew came back. She did.

"My grandfather made it home first that day. He walked in on Walter trying to force himself on my mom. I understood from what my granny didn't say, but I knew my grandfather killed Walter.

"She let a few tears fall, after sharing that with me, and I didn't understand the lesson then. But I do now. It was the first time she had been betrayed by someone she once loved, but through her faith in God and in her husband, she overcame adversity. I could always count on my grandmother to keep it real with me, even though I was young. And what my grandfather was to her until his death, that's exactly the type of man and protector I vow to be to you and Tamia."

Free

I knew and felt what James was saying was true. But I also knew I had to work through my demons on my own. We sat there quiet for a while until Tamia started to stir from her sleep. "Jay, you want me to take her?"

James

"No sweetie, I got her." I said as I soothed Tamia back to sleep. Free still looked exhausted, but I felt there was something else underneath her expression. "You wanna talk about it honey? Is there anything I can do right now?"

Free

"I was just wondering, since we're so close to your hometown, if you still have family here?"

James

"I'm not sure. After the situation with Walter, the family disassociated themselves from my grandmother. She and my mom were on their own once grandpa died, but there could still be some people here."

Free

"Have you ever thought about contacting any of them?" Talking about family had me thinking about my mom. But it was always bittersweet, because of how my mom's life ended. And, it was all my fault and my birthday would never be the same again.

Eight Years Ago

It was two weeks prior to my seventeenth birthday and my mom had everything planned out so nicely according to what I asked for. She arranged for me and my two best friends to go to NYC. My birthday, May thirteenth, fell on a Saturday that year. My friends spent the night before at my house and we loaded up super early in the morning on my birthday in my uncle's SUV for my mom to drive us there.

We checked into the Four Seasons because we were going to stay the night. Trey Songz was in town, playing at the Barclays Center. We were too hype! Mom dropped us off and we were supposed to call her when the concert was over. So, we enjoyed ourselves to the FULLEST! Nothing could have made that night better! Or so I thought. We left the venue and walked up the street to a pizza spot my mom said she would pick us up at. We ate, sang songs from the concert and I called my mom and let her know we were almost done. We were wrapping everything up when a couple of masked men ran into the restaurant and proceeded to rob them.

Masked Man 1

"Everybody get on the ground and pull out all your money and your cell phones. *NOW*!" We all did what he said. My friends and I got underneath our table and threw all of our shit out into the walkway. The second guy walked over to the girl behind the cash register, while picking up our belongings.

Masked Man 2

"Open the register slowly, give me all of the money and you won't get hurt. It's as simple as that. Don't move too fast, just give up the money. It ain't yours anyway." At that moment, I see my mom pull up and my phone starts ringing. I start panicking and just praying she doesn't come in. After two missed calls, I saw her get out as the men were preparing to leave. She must have startled them, because one of them shot her and ran out to drive off in my uncle's truck that my mom left running.

It happened so fast I thought I was in a movie. I couldn't move, I couldn't scream, I just looked at her while she looked at me and saw the light disappear from her eyes. I don't remember getting up from that spot. I don't remember being ushered to the police station as they questioned us about the details concerning the robbers.

Present Day

I sobbed a bit at the thought of Tamia not having any extended family. Who would take care of her if something were to happen to James or me? His lifestyle wasn't exactly safe in any sense of the word. And mine, well, through all of this, I couldn't grasp the idea that my future would be a bright one. James held me and started telling me about his grandmother again. I enjoyed his stories, and frankly, it distracted me from my own sorrows.

James

"I remember coming home from school one day. I was seven years old at the time and my day at school was really nothing out of the ordinary. I do remember not being able to sleep the night before and feeling a little uneasy all day due to the lack of sleep. Once school let out, I didn't hang around with my friends on the playground or anything like I usually would have done. I just headed on my way. I always went to granny's house after school because my mom worked late shifts at the diner a few streets over.

"Once my granny's house came into view, I noticed there were police cars in the front yard. I walked up and was able to get by them and inside the house, but I must have caught them off guard when they finally noticed me. I navigated my way through the house without them stopping me. I ran through the house looking for granny. I found her in the bathroom lying on her back with one of her hands on top of her chest and the other above her head. There was so much blood on and around her. Granny's eyes were still wide open, and her skin was still warm to the touch as I tried to "help" her. In my young mind, I thought maybe she just needed me to do something, anything to help her get up. I couldn't reconcile the act of death at that time.

"It turns out, somebody had come in through the side door, sexually assaulted and beat my granny to death. The talk around town was that the guy my mom was dating at the time did it. His name was George and I ensured that I never forgot his face. I remembered that he suddenly left town a few days later, because I heard my mother talking to one of her girlfriend's about how her so-called boyfriend could abandon her so close to my granny's death. Word was that he went up to the nation's capital to start over with some family members that were already there. I vowed that one day, I would find him, and I would kill him.

“Years after granny’s death, my mom, step-dad and I relocated to Maryland when I was twelve years old. It made it easier for me to keep up with George. I was obsessed with this dude. I always knew where he was. He went to jail for about seven years, and by the time he was released, I was twenty.

“He had a little girl and his woman was pregnant with another kid on the day it all happened. They were at a mall and I had been following them pretty much the whole day. I was just waiting for him to be by himself. They went home, and I camped out in my car for a couple of hours that night. He left their house around ten pm, and I followed him to a drug store. He didn’t lock his car, so it was easy to slide into it while he was in the store. I ducked down in the backseat, waited ‘til he started driving and popped up behind him, surprising George.

“I had a .45, the first one I ever bought, and pointed it at his head and told him to drive to an abandoned building I had scoped out. Once he saw my eyes in that rear view, he knew who I was. He always called me Jaybird, he said it was because I was always whistling like a Blue Jay. He referred to me as Jaybird that night. I forced him to get out of the car and led him into the building. I made sure he never came out too. He took someone from me that was the most special to me… until I met you.

“I told you that story to tell you how I felt knowing that lil’ nigga took you away from me. I swore that day, just like I did ten years ago, that he would never get a chance to hurt anyone else again. You can trust and believe he will never hurt you again. Do you believe me baby? Please don’t give up on us. Don’t give up on me. We need you. I promise you that I will protect you for the rest of my life. I just need you to be present. Please say something baby.”

Free

I just wept while he continued to hold me and the baby on the beach. I think I really just needed this get away. I was doubting my worth, while James was doing everything in his power to build me up. The confidence I once had was currently missing in action. All of the decisions I've made in the past had me questioning my worth. When James told me about his grandmother, it made me think about my mother. Regardless of all the decisions I've made in my past, I know she wouldn't have judged me. Over time, I'm confident that I will be able to get back to the Free that James loves, and I'm going to be the best mother to Tamia that I can, for the rest of my life. "I'm here baby. I believe you and I know that I'll always be safe with you. Me and our daughter." I reassured James.

Chapter 21

Monroe

There's been very little progress with Aubrey's condition. The therapist comes in everyday to move her limbs. I take the night shift so that her mom can get some rest, but she still shows up through the night when she can't sleep. We've definitely gotten to know each other better, even more so since the trip to Mexico. My parents and sisters have been here to visit Aubrey as well. My mom and dad even had Aubrey's parents over at their home for dinner a few times. Definitely didn't want them to meet like this, but I shared with my family that I had been planning to propose to Aubrey even before all of this happened.

Aubrey had lost a little weight, but it was nothing we didn't expect to happen. Dr. Sawyer had been especially helpful with helping us understand everything and preparing us either way. She was hopeful, but was very adamant about being honest with us, and I appreciated that. For some reason I couldn't sleep tonight, and I fully expected for Mrs. Roberson to come up here.

"Mommy..."

I thought I heard Aubrey say something. I got up to see if I was hearing things. There was no movement for a little while, but I watched her intently. I held her hand and her fingers gripped mine. They had been doing that recently, but this time, it felt a little stronger. I opened my book and continued reading.

"Mommy..."

I heard it again. I knew I wasn't going crazy. I called the nurse into the room and let her know what was going on. She started checking her vitals and everything. I wanted to call Mrs. Roberson, but I didn't want to let her down with more of the same. The nurse told me that sometimes coma patients will speak, grunt, laugh and may even snore. She tested her motor functions by trying to tickle her feet and also looked at the movement, or lack thereof, by shining a direct light into her eyes.

Nurse

"She's looking better every day, but there's nothing I can report at the moment. I'm sorry. Would you like a blanket or an extra pillow?"

Monroe

"No but thank you so much."

Nurse

"No problem. Have a good night and don't hesitate call one if us if there is a concern."

Monroe

I continued checking on Aubrey through the night. I listened closely to see if she would utter anything else with that soft, sweet voice. To my dismay, there was nothing but deafening silence for the rest of the night. This was the first time that I began to consider the possibility that she never wakes up again. What if I never hear her voice again? That was closest I became to getting emotional in recent years. I just miss my girl, damn.

Marie

Robert was really injured when I took him home. I made him as comfortable as I could. He would ask me to kill him, but that just seemed too easy a fate for him. From the time I met him, I would have visions of the mayhem he has caused people around him in life. I knew his mother was dead from a few of the visions I had, but I never could see the exact cause of her death. I knew he had a sister, but she wouldn't talk to him. His sister's distance from him was definitely a reason for his behavior and while his relationships always fail. That was a void in Robert's life that frankly he doesn't know how to deal with. He's never opened up to me or anything, but because of my gifts, I understand him on a deeper level. I also knew that he had a male child, I just could not see his surroundings.

I've given him several potions to heal his injuries to his skin, his internal injuries and even his anus. I knew his penis wasn't going to grow back, but once I felt he was up to it, I had ideas about how he could continue to pleasure me. I postponed my move for now, but the place I'm moving into would have to be a conducive environment to help him get used to his wheelchair.

"Yem numer fic bord sumna. Yem numer fic bord sumna. Au hei dse yem numer. Au hei dse yem numer." I chanted.

This was an old incantation out of Grandmother's book. It was to cleanse his mind from all others, so he would focus only on me. I didn't want him to remember that he had any feelings for any other women. He also didn't need to concern himself with any children but ours. I was pregnant with twins that I was sure to be girls. I had been taking potions to strengthen my uterus and allow my body to be receptive to all the sperm that Robert had been releasing within me over the past few months.

We were going to be parents, and all he needed to focus on was us. If only I could make him love me, all would be perfect. Well almost. What was I to do about sex in the meantime though? I guess I'll have to figure something out.

Sam

Ever since Joe had been back, it was sex session after mind-blowing sex session. Something still felt off to me though. I couldn't be sure what it was, but he still seemed a bit distracted. He was working today, so I decided to stop by the clinic with some lunch for him.

"Hi Kristin, is Joe available? I want to surprise him with lunch!"

Kristin

"Hey there Sam, isn't that nice of you. He should be finishing up with a patient, lemme go see how much longer he needs. Just give me two shakes and I'll be right back."

Sam

Kristin was a bubbly, petite white woman that reminded me so much of my mother. She was always pleasant and professional, not like that wretched Marie that she replaced. I don't even know how they could employ Marie at a dental clinic when her teeth looked the way they did. Anyway, I decided to bake some ziti, and substituted the ground beef with ground turkey. It was pretty tasty, if I do say so myself.

I started experimenting with my wardrobe because Joe told me I didn't have to be so "proper" all the time. I associated his meaning of proper as boring, so I hired a stylist. I had on some light blue jeans that were considered stone washed, an emerald green chemise, a colorful blazer and nude pumps. My tan Chanel bag with the chain link strap tied the look together.

When Joe emerged from the back of the clinic, he had this curious look on his face. So, I decided to play along. "You like?" As I did a three hundred and sixty-degree turn.

Joe

"Yeah, I like very much. Turn around again, lemme see that ass baby." Damn, she always made me think about sexing her. It didn't matter where I was or what I was doing.

Sam

I blushed from embarrassment when I noticed that Kristin heard what he said. He came over to me, put his hands in my hair and whispered sexily in my ear.

Joe

"You know you're looking good enough to eat. And your ass looks so good in those jeans."

Sam

He nibbled my ear a bit and I swear the flood gates opened in my underwear. This man turned me on so much. "Thank you, baby. Can we stop making out in front of your receptionist in this lobby though?" He laughed a little bit as if my question brought him back to reality. "I did bring you something to eat though. Are you good on time to have lunch with me? I don't mind sitting in the break room." He just kept staring at me, and I knew that look. I just knew I wasn't getting out of here without sexing him, and I was happy to oblige.

Joe

"Okay, okay. Let's go and eat." Damn I wanted to put my dick in her right now. I loved that she took my suggestions seriously. If it was up to her, she would dress like Meghan Markle and the rest of them royal bitches in England. She could stand a little more ass, but if I keep hitting that the way I been doing it, maybe I can convince her to get one of those surgeries. "Mmmmmm baby, this smells and looks delicious. So, you been spending your day cooking for me? You supposed to be enjoying your day off."

Sam

"You know I can't enjoy my day off without you being part of it. Now eat up before your food gets cold." I removed my foot from one of my pumps and started rubbing his manhood through his scrub pants under the table. I wanted him just as much as he wanted me. His boss then walked in to get some coffee and I was busted. He acted like he didn't see, but I know he did. I was way too obvious.

"I'm going to sit with Aubrey and her mom today. They said she's shown progression. I think it may be good for you to stop by sometime this week as well to see her." His face became a bit sad for a moment, then he perked up and said he would. "You have about twenty-three minutes left on your lunch hour. You wanna do a little something?"

Joe

This girl makes me crazy! But I love it. She came up here looking fly as hell and all I could think of is fucking her with those heels on. "Come with me, I have a place." I took her to the back office storage area. This wasn't just your typical storage room. There were medicines, tools, solutions, as well as a twin bed for the doctors to sleep on in case they were on standby for an emergency situation.

I locked the door behind us as she pulled down her jeans and her panties. She bent over and I licked her pussy from the back until she came. Her shit was so wet, that I knew it was going to be over much sooner than these last twenty minutes. I dove into her wetness and pinched her nipples as I steadied myself with my other hand. "Got damn, baby, this shit is so good."

I knew I was on the brink of nutting when suddenly Aubrey's face entered my mind. I imagined being in her pussy with her ass clapping against my pelvis and her big beautiful titties swinging underneath her. "Ooooooohhhh shit," I whispered as I exploded deep within her still stroking that sweet pussy. I felt so guilty, because this wasn't the first time that I thought of Aubrey while fucking Samantha. At this point, I'm really not sure if this is just infatuation. I may in fact be in love with her.

Rob

The last few days have been very foggy, but I know where I am and that I'm back with the crazy bitch. How I got here, I have no idea. I've been sleeping most of the time, and I hurt everywhere. This is worse than death, why didn't those niggas just kill me? And here this bitch come. Smiling with that big ass space in her mouth, and lighting those stank ass candles and incense and shit. I fucking *hate* her ugly ass!

She did find a way to help me pee since they cut off my dick. I have no fuckin purpose now, I'm prolly not even considered a real man anymore. I can't even fuck bitches anymore. I wonder how... damn, what's her name again? I can see her face but can't remember her name. Pretty brown skin girl with long hair and an ass that was so damn phat. What is this bitch giving me?

"Please just kill me. I wanna DDDIIIEEE!"

Marie

"Oh no, no, no baby! You're mine. I told you that already. I would think by now you would have sense enough to thank me for saving your life. But as usual Robert, you're just being selfish and thinking about yourself. What about our babies? They need their father. And I'll need my husband."

Rob

"Husband? I ain't yo muthafuckin husband bitch! And babies? I ain't got no dick to make no babies. You'll never get pregnant by me bitch."

Marie

"Tsk, tsk..." I said as I caressed his face and then grabbed his jaw harshly. "Robert, Robert, Robert... your mouth is quite foul to be in the position that you are in. You are healing, but we can reverse everything that Monroe and James did to you, especially if you cannot be mindful of your manners. I no longer have to get pregnant, you silly boy." As I released his face and got closer to his ear. "I already am." His eyes got big and then he started to cry.

Rob

"Why are you torturing me? Why can't you just let me die? I don't wanna be with you! I don't want no babies with you! I want... I want..." I could see her face but couldn't remember the other woman's name either. She was light skin, short and had big titties and a phat ass. She was perfect. "I know I want someone else. It ain't your crazy ass though. Just let me fucking die, already!"

Marie

I slapped him as hard as I could on the side where his eye was swollen shut. I could tell it was very painful, because tears started pouring from his eyes then. "Now that I got your attention, let's be clear, I will not kill you. I've already told you that. Don't ask me that again. You can't do anything for yourself, so you ought to start being a bit more appreciative of me. Like I said, we are having twins and I'm sure they are little girls, so 'Daddy', you need to recover and learn to respect me as your new wife and your kids' mother. Are you ready to eat?" He shook his head yes, while tears were still streaming down his sad face.

Taisha

Finally, it's Monday! I'm getting dressed to go and meet Monroe for coffee. I missed him so much, and I wanted this meeting to go well. I didn't dress in my usual attention-grabbing clothes. To be honest, my body and my face would demand attention in a moo moo. I'm just that bad! There was never a shortage of men for me to choose from, but I've only ever wanted one. And I won't stop until I get him back. I know he still loves me; you can't just stop loving someone.

I decided on a high waisted black pencil skirt that stopped right above my knees, a white sleeveless button-down blouse, tied right where my skirt began. I sported a gold embroidered leather Gucci jacket that I would just hang on my shoulders and my new Gucci python sandals with sequins. Couldn't forget my red Gucci purse with the gold flecks throughout. I wanted my outfit to be simple, but classy for my man. He knew I was fly, but I had to show him what he was missing.

I got there super early, so I could pick the perfect table. When he walked in, he looked around and I waved my hand so he would see me. I tried not to look too excited, but I smiled modestly. When he got to the table I stood up and we embraced quickly as I kissed him on his cheek. He looked so damn good, per usual. And smelled even better.

I could tell he had just gotten a fresh haircut; his mocha brown skin was absolutely flawless per usual. I just wanted to run my hands through his curly hair like I used to. He had on some dark grey joggers which made his ass look absolutely scrumptious, a white fitted tee which displayed all of his muscles... whew! And the matching jacket for the pants. He looked so damn good, I felt my heartbeat in my pussy, and I was heating up on the spot.

Monroe

"Hey Tai, how have you been?" I'm trying to be friendly with her, she hasn't had the easiest life. "What have you been up to lately?"

Taisha

"Nothing much, just keeping my head above water, you know. How are you? You look a bit stressed. Are you doing okay?" He looked good, but something was going on with him. The last time he looked like this, his best friend was sick.

Monroe

"My lady is in a coma. She was in a bad car accident that almost took her life. Things are progressing with her slowly, but the waiting game is arduous."

Taisha

I tried my best not to look bored, but he just gave me the 'in' that I needed. "Sorry to hear that. What coffee would you like?" I said as I changed the subject. I draped my jacket over my chair and walk right in front of him so that he could get a better view. I knew he was looking at my ass, so I walked forward to the counter while putting some extra stank on it. If she's been in a coma for a while, that means he hasn't had any ass. "You want your usual or you up to trying something else?" Just like I thought, his eyes were right where I thought they would be.

Monroe

Damn, she was looking so good. That ass in that skirt. She knew exactly what she was doing, but I wasn't gonna fall for it. But my dick is saying entirely something else. "Lemme get that caramel macchiato with the extra shot of espresso." I said as I started walking up to the counter so that I could pay for the order.

Taisha

"Nah, I got it baby. I'm paying this time." I also wanted to show him that I wasn't trying to get anything from him. I wanted him to fall in love with me again, so that I could show him that I'm the woman he needs in his life. "Still want that old thang, huh? Them caramel macchiato's do be on point though." I played on my words to get him thinking about me.

Monroe

I know she was tryna be funny. I can play this game too. I scooted up behind her so that my dick was on her. I know she felt it too. And at this point, all I wanted to do was fuck the shit outta her, but then I thought about Aubrey and I backed away.

Taisha

Okay! Push up on me then. I made sure to press back on him until I got my change, and that dick was too hard. Mmmmmmm, I wanted to take him in the bathroom. I went and sat down while he grabbed the drinks. I watched his dick in them pants as he walked toward me. "So, what's new with you baby?"

Free

James was at the pool with the baby while I was relaxing. I set up the room, because we hadn't yet had our first time, and it was well past my six-week check-up. I just hoped I was mentally ready to satisfy him the way I wanted to. I wasn't going to dance for him today, but I did have something else in mind. I put on a long white negligee, that had lace down the sides. Although I was still a few pounds from my goal weight, I must say that I wore my pregnancy weight very well.

I lit lavender vanilla scented candles all around the room and also dimmed the lights. I was hoping Tamia would be knocked out from all the pool activity and from being in that sun. I had some room service delivered so that we could have a meal and then spend some quality time together, just the two of us. I wanted James to know that I truly appreciated him.

James

Tamia is such a good baby. She was knocked out and I'm tired as shit too. I missed my Queen though and couldn't wait to cuddle up with her tonight. I tried adjusting my dick at night when we were in the bed. I didn't want Free to think I was trying to rush her because of what she had been through with that fuck nigga. And I didn't want her thinking nothing about that situation whenever we were together.

I entered the room and it smelled like there was some food in here. I placed the baby in her bassinet and Free was standing by the dining table looking so sexy with a glass of wine in her hands. "Hold that thought baby. Let me jump in the shower real quick. Need to get this chlorine off of me." That was the quickest shower I have ever taken.

Free

"Hey baby, did you all have a great day at the pool?" I handed him the glass of wine and picked up a glass of juice for myself. "I would like to propose a toast to the man I love. You have shown me that no matter what, you have my back. You have shown me a love like no other. I'm so glad that I'll get to call you husband in a few short months. I love you so much, James. Thank you for being not only what I want, but also the man that I need."

James

"Damn baby, you make it easy for me to love you. I just appreciate you giving me another chance to be with you. I love you and Tamia with everything in me." With that I kissed her and then she took over completely. She had set the food on the table, but right now I was hungry for something else. I picked her up and took her to the bedroom that the baby wasn't in so we wouldn't wake her. It had been so long since I've been inside her. So, I was going to take my time tonight.

I laid her down gently on the king size bed and kissed her lips. I lifted her gown and started at her pretty feet. I then sucked the inside of her toned calves, moved my way up to her silky thighs. I noticed she was trembling. "Are you okay, my love?" She nodded her head yes. I made my way to her pretty pussy and swirled my tongue around her clitoris. I sucked and licked… licked and sucked, while she moaned. I felt her swell in my mouth and I knew she was about to erupt. I grabbed onto her hips so that she wouldn't be able to squirm away from me.

I removed her gown and slid on top of her while we resumed kissing. I entered into her velvety folds, slowly. She moaned softly in my ear as I kissed her neck. "Fresia, you are the most important woman in my life. I'm so grateful to God that you're going to be my wife. I love you."

Free

"Mmmmmmm baby, you feel so good. I love you too." I climaxed for the second time and he did too. It was good to make love to my man again. But it wasn't easy. Rob still haunted my dreams and I couldn't tell him about it. Once he fell asleep, I went and got my baby and changed her. I fed her until we fell asleep and I got to resume my worst nightmare once again.

Free *(Dreaming)*

"You know how I like it, bitch. Get on your knees and open up wide. Take all this dick down your throat, and you better not nick me with your teeth! If you do, I'm gonna fuck you up so badly, my daughter won't recognize you. Yeah bitch, suck that shit like your life depends on it." Rob demanded.

I did what Rob told me to do, just as I had done each night since my nightmares first began.

I woke up with a jolt. Tamia slept soundly in the crook of my arm. I gently placed put her down. Each night ended the same, with me standing over my daughter's crib with my heart beating so hard with fear, that it threatened to come through my chest. I just had to figure this out. I need to be okay.... I just couldn't tell James.

Monroe

Me and Tai ended up spending about two hours at that coffee shop. I forgot how funny she was and how much I used to enjoy her company when we were friends. Anything beat sitting in a gloomy hospital, but I realized I was actually enjoying myself with her and that I felt just a bit guilty about it. My phone rang and it was Mrs. Roberson.

<<<ring, ring>>>

"Hello Mrs. Roberson. Is everything alright?"

Dee Dee

"Monroe, she's awake! Hurry!"

Chapter 22

Sam

I arrived at my practice about seven this morning to inspect how the contractors are doing. I met up with my project manager, Keith, who assured me that construction was on schedule. My dad introduced us about five years ago because he said Keith would be great to help me with my prospectus. Keith was the most handsome man I had ever seen. He was newly divorced, but he and his ex-wife were my dad's patients. Things were slowly coming together, and I had Keith to thank for it.

"Keith, I can't tell you how much I appreciate the work you're putting in for me. You've truly been a blessing!"

Keith

"Samantha, I truly appreciate the opportunity. Things had been rough during the time of the divorce and having something to keep me busy was just what I needed. With all of that said, thank you." I said as I kissed the back of her hand, very gently.

Sam

He looked at me with those grey eyes and I just about melted. He was about six-one, and was mixed race just like me, but looked like he was Hispanic. His dark, wavy hair was always cut close, and he was very well dressed. He had a medium build and was about nine years my senior. You wouldn't know he was in his late thirties, because he gave men my age a run for their money. He kept himself in shape and always asked me if I wanted to join him at the gym because I always said I wanted more definition in my arms. I was always too shy to accept his invitation though.

We wrapped up our business and set the next inspection date. "Keith, would you like to join me for coffee? I was just about to head out. I promise, no talking shop." He accepted and we both strolled to this coffee shop not too far away. When we walked in, I thought I saw someone familiar, but I couldn't place him from this far without my glasses. I didn't pay any attention to the man again until he jetted out of the coffee shop. So, I did recognize him, it was Monroe. But what was he doing with that woman? I sat with Keith a little while longer before we said our goodbyes.

Keith

"We should do this again sometime. Maybe catch a movie and dinner?"

Sam

I couldn't believe he was asking me on a date. But I had to keep it professional for now. "Maybe that's not such a great idea. I'm dating someone and I'm not sure he would be too pleased with that."

Keith

"I understand. But it was worth a try, gorgeous. I guess I'll see you in about twelve days."

Sam

"Oh yes. It was really good to see you. And again, thanks for everything." We embraced before he departed, and his scent lingered encapsulating me. He made my mouth water. Whew, that man! For some reason, I decided to check out the woman that Monroe was with. She looked happy, and she was very attractive. I decided to bump into her on the way out.

<<<thud>>>

"Oh, excuse me Miss, I wasn't paying attention to where I was going. Hey, are you a model?" I knew she wasn't a model with all that booty and those hips. I was envious as hell. She seemed perfect.

Taisha

"No, I'm not a model. But thank you for the compliment." *I do wish you would watch where you were going, though.*

Sam

She was trying to leave the store when I just asked her what her name was. I know she was getting annoyed. "I think I know you from somewhere, and I could have sworn it was like on a magazine cover or something like that."

Taisha

Yes, bitches be hitting on me too. "No, I wish. But people have said that I resemble Jill Scott. I think she's absolutely beautiful. My name is Taisha Saunders. And you are?"

Sam

"My name is Sam. Well it was nice speaking with you Taisha. Have a wonderful day." I was looking her up as soon as I got home. I'm sure it was innocent enough, he met with her at a coffee shop. But you couldn't believe that these dudes were innocent though, Joe has been talking in his sleep lately. I try to listen to see what he's talking about, but he's a light sleeper. When I start moving, he gets quiet. I'll figure out what it is one day. Until then, I'd continue to be the good little woman he takes me for.

Joe

We had just gotten a new receptionist and she was definitely a step up from Marie's talking ass. Kristin was a very bubbly, very personable young lady. I definitely appreciated seeing her on a daily basis. "Good morning Kristin, how was your weekend?"

Kristin

"Oh, I had a great weekend Joe. I went to a sculpture class on Saturday and then I went to a hip-hop club that night with some friends. You should join us sometimes."

Joe

I couldn't tell whether she was being friendly or flirty, but I continued with the conversation. "Wow, a hip-hop club? Do you dance? Who are some of your favorite artists?"

Kristin

"I like Plies, Jeezy, and Cardi B. She's doing her thing and representing the ladies. Yeah, I love to dance, well I like to twerk. But it's been some time since I was able to enjoy myself like that. My girls are super cool. I just moved here from Tennessee and this area is way cooler."

Joe

"Oh word? I grew up in Lanham, Maryland. Nothing special about that place. I live in Bowie now. Tennessee is somewhere I've always wanted to visit because of Graceland."

Kristen

"Ahh, you're an Elvis fan?"

Joe

"Nah, not really." I laughed. "He was just another muthafucka that ripped off my culture and made it big. I wanna piss on the grounds!" We both had a big ass laugh about that.

Kristen

"Well maybe you can come home with me sometime."

Joe

So, she *is* flirting with me! She caressed my hand when she said it. "Well alright, Kristin, I'll talk to you later." As I quickly removed my hand from hers and started to walk away. "It's almost time for my first patient of the day." The thing about Kristin was that she was cool as shit. Not what I expected from a white girl. Kristin is thick, with a phat ole ass on her and them hips make my mouth water. Nice titties and a pouty little pretty ass mouth that I can picture my dick inside of. I'm not sure why I even thought about her like that, because Sam was sexing me almost every day and that gushy was amazing!

Speaking of Sam...

<<<ring, ring>>>

"Hello?"

Sam

"She's awake! Baby, Aubrey's awake! I'm on my way to the hospital. Meet me there!"

Joe

I ran into the boss's office to let him the good news about Aubrey. "Doctor Saul, Aubrey is out of her coma. Do you mind if I leave early today? I need to go and see about her if you don't mind." Joe said.

I was hoping he didn't say anything out of the way, I wasn't taking no for an answer. He said one of the other techs could take over for me since the workload was pretty light today. Doctor Saul said he would be up there to visit her after his last patient. Kristin tried to ask me where I was going but I just kept running until I got to my car. She had never met Aubrey, as she started working here a few days after the accident. I tried not to drive fast, I had to remember the reason why Aubrey was laid up. She wasn't going anywhere, so I drove the speed limit, and I was so happy that she woke up.

I got there in about nine minutes and found a good parking space. I ran into the hospital and up to her room. They knew who I was, so they didn't stop me at the desk. I slowed down right when I got to her room so that I could slow my breathing. I smoothed out my clothes and wiped the sweat off of my forehead. I entered the room and when she saw me, she smiled as tears welled up of her eyes.

Aubrey

"I'm so sorry, Joe. If it wasn't for me, we wouldn't have gone-"

Joe

"Shhhhh, baby girl it's ok. You're ok now. I'm ok and I'm here." We just embraced until she settled down. When I looked up, I finally realized that Aubrey's mom and stepdad were in the room and so was Samantha. I walked over to hug Mrs. Roberson, I shook Mr. Roberson's hand and then embraced my girl. I sat beside Aubrey's bed and we were just talking and catching up. She was still a little banged up, but she was a good sport. She didn't complain about anything. She just wanted to go home. I couldn't help but notice that Monroe was missing. But you know I didn't give a fuck.

Monroe

How did I end up in this fucking traffic? Had I taken the back roads, I would have been there by now. FUCK! My baby was probably wondering why I wasn't there, while I was over here smiling in Tai's face and shit. Tai had me distracted as fuck, and I won't deny that she seemed like the girl I met a long time ago, but I can't forget what she morphed into. I loved her at one time, yeah, but that love didn't compare to anything close to what I felt for Aubrey. She was going to be my wife. I felt that in my soul.

I arrived at the hospital and had to park far as fuck, of course. That was just my luck. I jogged lightly to the entrance and went down to the gift shop to pick up some tulips. They didn't have any, but they had those colorful roses that she liked. I was so excited to see my baby again. To feel her hug me back, to feel her kiss my lips. To start this new life with her that I envisioned. I got to her floor and the nurse that was always on duty when I was there at night gave me a thumbs up. I returned the gesture. I entered her room all smiles with the roses in my hand.

I walked over to her, while that bitch ass nigga Joe was mean muggin' me. I just smirked at him, I knew he wanted my girl while he stayed frontin' for his own. Samantha deserved so much better. Anyway, Aubrey was oblivious to my presence. She faced me curiously as I approached her.

"Hey baby, I missed you so much." I hugged her until I noticed she wasn't hugging me back.

Aubrey

"I'm sorry, but who are you?" She asked, genuinely confused.

Chapter 23

Aubrey

Who was this guy? I've never seen him before in my life! He's trying to kiss all on me, and I'm looking at him like, who are you? I looked at my mom and she was like, "hug him Aubrey". I'm like hell nah, who is this nigga? I remember that bitch ass nigga Rob, but I swear I'm on some ole other shit now. I wanted to continue choppin' it up with my friend, Joe, but in walks this nigga tryna kiss all over me and shit. Fuck outta here. "Excuse me, but who are you?"

Monroe

"It's me baby, Monroe. Come on baby, you know me! I want you to be my wife! You're wearing my ring. Baby I love you. Come on, what are you saying to me right now?" I was truly confused.

Aubrey

"I don't know you, though. Mommy, what's going on? Who is he?"

Dee Dee

"Baby, that's Monroe. Here, look. These are pictures of us in Mexico. He took us all there, remember baby? You love him. Look at the pictures."

Aubrey

I went through the pictures on my mom's phone and sure enough, there I was, there *we* were, smiling with this nigga all in the pictures. Like, I believed my mother, but for real for real, I don't know this pretty boy ass nigga. The last thing I remember is running away from Rob and that truck running into me. Why was I crying when I was driving? Why was running away from Rob's bitch ass? Why didn't I fight this muthafucka back? I know one thing for sure, I hated that nigga.

Here come this cute ass nurse and she got a nice lil onion on her. I wanted to touch that shit, too. Rob turned me all the way the fuck off from niggas, I guess. Bits and pieces coming back to me. I know he raped me a couple of times, but I just couldn't understand why I didn't fight his ass back? Why did I *let* him beat my ass? I swear to God, I'mma find that muthafucka and murk his ass. Trust.

"Hey, Ms. Nurse, what's your name? Will you be here all night?" Why is everybody looking at me all strange and shit. "You don't have to be shy. Can you tell me when I can go home though?" The nurse looked at my mom, and she was trying to talk to me, I guess to distract me. But the lil bitch was fine as fuck. All I wanted to do was talk to her.

Dee Dee

"Aubrey, baby, ok. Are you hungry? Let me see if you have a fever baby." I placed my hand on Aubrey's forehead. First, she didn't remember Monroe, and now it seems as if she's trying to flirt with the nurse? My baby has never swung in that direction, this behavior has to be a side effect from the coma.

Aubrey

"Ma, I'm good. I'm good. It's too many people in here. Aye Mike, can you take my moms to my house. I just need some time alone. Joe, thanks for stopping by." Then I looked to my right, and this simp ass nigga still standing here with these colorful ass, funny looking ass flowers. If anything, I like tulips, but I ain't even a flower type of person no more. "Uh, Monroe is it? I mean, thank you for stopping by, but I'm gonna need some time alone please." Then I looked at everybody. "Uh, hello? Can you all come back later please?" Once I said that, everyone started leaving.

My mother explained to me what happened to me. She said that Joe told her all about the night Rob called me because our receptionist Marie was holding him hostage in her apartment and that I went to rescue him. As much as he used to beat my ass, you would think I would know better. After she told me that, I started remembering how he wouldn't let me go and how he beat my ass in that apartment. I didn't tell my mom though. She didn't need to know about any of that other shit. None of this made sense though. Why would she have been holding him hostage when I was in a relationship with him? But I guess I wasn't. I was in a so-called relationship with the pretty boy. The nurse came back to my room and I asked her when I would be able to take a shower.

Nurse

"We can provide you with soapy water, then when you're finished, clean water to wipe you down with.

Aubrey

"I kinda need some help." As I held up my arm with the cast.

Nurse

"Oh, it's no problem Ms. Collins. I can arrange that for you."

Aubrey

"Will *you* be the one doing it?" She looked at me strangely and I explained myself before she could figure out my true motives. "It's just that I was told you were the one that has been taking care of me. And my mom trusts you." Her face relaxed and she smiled warmly.

Nurse

"No problem, Ms. Collins. I work the late shift and leave about three in the morning. Your boyfriend is usually here from eleven at night to sit with you until your mom comes in the morning. Would you like your sponge bath before he gets here?"

Aubrey

"Sure. Thank you, but what is your name?"

Nurse

"Oh, I'm sorry, my name is Sierra. I'll be back in an hour or so."

Aubrey

"Ok Sierra." I had my eyes on her sexy ass until she left the room. I almost rolled my eyes when she mentioned my *boyfriend.* I don't even know dude. But if he was going to come back up tonight, I had to let him know that I was not interested in no previous situation that may have been between us. And I took that ring off my finger too. Just then, Dr. Sawyer entered my hospital room.

Dr. Sawyer

"Hello Ms. Collins, how are you feeling?"

Aubrey

"I'm doing well, a little sore, but nothing I can't handle."

Dr. Sawyer

"Okay, that's good to hear. I wanted to examine you really quickly if you don't mind."

Aubrey

I agreed. My mom told me that the doctor was very nice and took great care of me when I was in the coma. If my moms trusted her, I would too. "It's not a problem. Would you also know when I will be able to remove these casts? I'm itching like crazy under here."

Dr. Sawyer

"Can you move your foot for me? And then I would like to see you point your toes up to the ceiling and then back down towards the floor."

Aubrey

I did as the doctor requested. It was surprisingly very easy to perform the movements. "Is that it, Doc?"

Dr. Sawyer

Okay, next, I would like you to rotate your foot as if you're trying to make a circle. Very good. We may be able to remove this cast in the next two weeks with more exercising. I want you to practice writing your name in cursive in the air with your foot. This will strengthen those muscles that have been lying dormant. Now, for your hand, I'd like you to do the same."

Aubrey

By this time, I was sweating. That foot rotation was harder than I thought, and I guess I was just going to follow the doctor's orders for the next couple of weeks. Now my arm was a totally different story. I could move my fingers, but my wrist was still in the early process of healing. She told me my arm cast would most likely be on there for a little longer. She did a few more tests, looked at my eyes and told me the bruise on my face didn't look like it came from the accident. She also wanted to talk to me about my memory because my mom told her that I didn't remember my "boyfriend". I wish they stopped calling him that. "Yeah, I don't remember him, Doc. He's not my boyfriend. I don't know him. I'm starting to remember parts of the accident and the day before. If he was really my boyfriend, why wouldn't I remember him too? It just doesn't make sense."

Dr. Sawyer

"The temporal lobe is what controls your memory. It's also the location of where you sustained the majority of the damage. I explained to your mom that it can take from days all the way to years for your memories to come back and unfortunately, in some cases not at all. We need to stimulate your memories by bringing people around you as well as talking about things that you can't remember. Please don't shut Mr. King out of your life just yet. From what everyone says, you two had a very special connection. It just takes patience, even if you just maintain a friendship."

Aubrey

Yeah whatever, I'm sure he thought when I woke up things were going to be different, but I'm good on all of that. Rob ruined me, and I can't wait to find his bitch ass, so I can return the favor.

Dr. Sawyer

"One more thing, Ms. Collins that I wanted to discuss with you. You are in the early stages of a pregnancy. I did not disclose this information to anyone else, because you are not a minor and there was a chance that the pregnancy wouldn't sustain your injuries. In your current state, I cannot grant an abortion. But you still have time to consider your options."

Aubrey

"Pregnant?" This was not what I wanted to hear. And I vowed last year when I went through my first abortion with Rob, that I would never do it again. "How far along am I?"

Dr. Sawyer

"You are fourteen weeks along."

Aubrey

"Dammit!" Tears immediately sprung to my eyes, because I wanted the next time to be special. How the fuck was I supposed to do this? I need my mom. I'll tell her tomorrow. "Doc, if you don't mind, could we resume tomorrow? I just need some time alone to think."

Dr. Sawyer

"Not a problem at all. If you need anything, please don't hesitate to page me, my card is on the bedside table."

Aubrey

"Thank you." I continued to cry in silence. But I refused to let this situation take me over. I was going to think through this and recover from it the best way I knew how. I won't bother my mom tonight, but I need her advice and most of all, her support.

Monroe

This had to be the absolute worst outcome from this situation. I'm at my house drinking vodka and cranberry, getting drunk while sitting in the dark. I thought about going back to the hospital like I do most nights to sit with Aubrey. What if she never recovers from this memory loss? What if she decides she never wants to be with me? I hadn't even considered this being a possible outcome at all. I have to figure out what to do. Mrs. Roberson was very encouraging, but that's not what I need right now. I need my lady. My phone began to ring, and I got excited because I thought it was Aubrey. "Hello Aubrey?"

Taisha

"This is Tai, are you okay? I was just calling to check on you since I know your *friend* is in the hospital."

Monroe

"She's awake, but she doesn't remember who I am. The doctor said this happens sometimes, and I want to be hopeful. But this is just wrong."

Taisha

He slurred his speech and sounded like he wanted to cry. "Money, are you drinking? This is not how you handle issues. I'm coming over right now."

Monroe

"NO, Tai, you don't have-", click. She hung up. We were just friends, right? She knew how to talk me down off the ledge. I haven't drank this much in a long time. Oh well, lemme fix myself another drink. I stumbled as I made my way to the kitchen, but I didn't fall. It was kinda funny to me at the time, but then I almost felt like crying until my doorbell rung.

I answered the door and Taisha had her hair pulled up into a sexy ponytail, like I used to ask her to wear for me. She also wore a one-piece red body suit with white stripes down the side with some white shell toe Adidas. That suit was hugging every curve on her body and her pussy print was on display as well. The zipper was halfway undone which caused her voluptuous titties were to be on display. I could feel my dick rising. I wasn't gonna fall victim to her tonight, but got damn she was looking so good!

Chapter 24

Joe

That nigga face was on the ground when Aubrey rejected his punk ass in front of all of us! I could have done a cartwheel down the muthafuckin' hallway! I missed her ass, but she was different. I knew that there was a possibility with her coming out of it and us having to adjust ourselves for Aubrey's sake. I expected to have to be more patient, remind her of some things, run a few errands from time to time and sit and visit with her. But now that Monroe is outta the picture, I got my girl back! I won't have to share her time with anyone other than my lady after Aubrey's parents go back home.

Does Aubrey like girls now though? I hope not, I need that sexy, brown sugar with that phat ass and titties to be feminine. I don't need her covering up that beautiful body with clothes like I wear. I also don't wanna be competing with her when we're around bitches. And no more lip gloss on them plump lips? Nah, fuck that shit! I don't want her ass with Pretty Ricky, but I still want her and her beautiful ass back to normal. What the fuck?

Sam

"Babe, are you here?" I had just gotten home from work and we were both still so excited about the fact that Aubrey was awake. But not remembering Monroe? That was so sad. And was she hitting on the nurse? I didn't know what was going on.

Joe

"Yeah sweetie, I'm here. You want me to cook something or you want takeout?" I knew she wouldn't want me to cook. But that didn't mean I wasn't gonna offer. A little reverse psychology, it made my lady feel appreciated.

Sam

I laughed a little because he knew doggone well I didn't want him to cook. "Let's go ahead and order out tonight." My phone rang and it was Keith.

<<<ring, ring>>>

"Hey Keith, did you get my email?"

Keith

Although Samantha was a few years younger than me, she had absolutely grown into her beauty. Her dad and I met through my ex-wife when I had assisted him with the add-on to his home. He then referred me to his daughter when she decided to open her practice. "Hello gorgeous, yes I got the email and wanted to further discuss the changes. How was your day?"

Sam

I stepped onto my patio so I could have some privacy. "Hey Keith, my day was good. Just got home. What about the changes did you want to discuss?" I was so curious about why he was calling me, as I had spelled out everything in the email that I had previously sent.

Keith

"Well that's why I was calling. Would it be possible for us to meet this week? I think I have some ideas that you may like. I think your changes would suffice, but I also know that a little variety is the spice of life, or so they say." I flirted just a bit to see how she would respond to me.

Sam

That deep bedroom voice was gonna get me in trouble. I was going to have to either take a shower immediately or change my panties. His voice, his style and his swag were just amazing. "Sure, I would love that." I cleared my throat nervously. I hope he couldn't tell I was blushing.

Keith

"Ok, well how's tomorrow? Would you be able to stop by my house? We can discuss the ideas I have, and I can have my chef whip something up for lunch."

Sam

"Yes, of course, I'd love to." Why was I blushing? At least he couldn't see me.

Keith

"I'll text you the address. See you around ten am?"

Sam

"I'll see you then." We hung up and Joe caught me daydreaming.

Joe

"Babe, I ordered Chinese, hope you don't mind. I want to head back to the hospital to sit with Aubrey before it gets too late."

Sam

"You've been there every day this week. I'm sure she'll be fine if you don't go tonight." This is crazy. They didn't see each other this much before the accident. I mean, what's really going on?

Joe

"She's expecting me, we spoke earlier. She's bored babe, I won't be gone long."

Sam

"Mmmmhmmm." We haven't had sex since she woke up six days ago. Not even a pinch on my booty. I have been masturbating with my shower head since. "Well, don't worry about it. I'll just see you tomorrow."

Joe

Well damn. I'm just trying to spend time with *our* friend since she's been in a coma for a few weeks. "Babe, she's trying to figure out why she lost her memories. But I'll call you tomorrow after work."

Sam

"Goodnight, Joseph."

Free *(dreaming)*

"Get on your knees bitch and suck the nut outta this dick with no hands." Rob said to me as he held the sides of my head while ravaging my throat. "Ahh yeah, suck that shit baby. Ooooh shit baby, that mouth is fire! Shit!" He continues to pump in out of my mouth repeatedly and then slaps my face. "Watch your teeth bitch, open that throat up for me baby. Yesssss." Tears were spilling out of my eyes due to the sting of his slap.

"Alright turn around and toot that ass up for daddy, I wanna feel you on this dick. Lemme see that pretty ass in the air baby." He ordered.

I did as he told me and let him have his way with my ass until he was ready to ejaculate. He tapped me and I turned around and opened my mouth and stuck my tongue out so he could release in my mouth.

"OOOOOOHHHHHHHHH, sssssssssss fuck baby!! Suck that dick baby like I taught you. Yesssssss baby, I ain't gonna never leave you." Rob said in ecstasy.

Free

That is always about the time that I wake up in a cold sweat. I feel as if I'm going crazy! I see his stupid fucking face every night in my dreams. Reality was so perfect, yet my dreams were always nightmares. We're back at my house and we've already listed it for sale upon our return from our mini get away. James had already bought out his lease at his place upon my insistence and lived with me so that we would be able to save that extra bit of money. Now I was regretting the fact that it was my idea.

I got up and the baby was laying quietly in her crib with her eyes wide open. "Hi pretty baby, did you miss mommy?" She smiled so brightly it was almost enough to forget why I was so sweaty. I went into the guest bathroom and wiped my breasts down so she wouldn't be sucking sweat from my skin. I also took that time to slow my heartbeat, as it still felt like it would burst through my chest.

I picked her up and fed her in the rocking chair while humming quietly. She always looked me right in my eyes as I fed her, and it was the most special bonding time that I never imagined experiencing. She was so perfect, but I noticed that she wheezed sometimes while breathing. I burped her and she started getting a bit fussy but wasn't making any sound. I noticed her skin turning blue and her eyes watered. "Mi Mi, what's wrong baby? JAMES!!! JAMES, get up please!" I tried soothing her, but nothing was working.

James

"Baby, what's wrong?"

Free

"We need to take the baby to the hospital. She's turning blue. She's choking!" I screamed. I tried to clear her airway but couldn't find anything impeding her airway. Then I stuck my finger in her throat to see if I could make her throw up. "Baby, hurry!" I got a blanket to keep her warm while I held her in my arms. Her breathing was very shallow, but she was still breathing. I got in the backseat of the car and James jumped in the driver's seat. I put the seat belt around me and the baby and while James pulled off, he called the hospital to let them know what was going on and that we were on our way. We drove to Southern Maryland Hospital Center in Clinton, Maryland. He stopped at the emergency room entrance and he ran inside with my baby.

James

We arrived at the emergency room in record time and I took the baby from Fresia and ran in the entrance. "I need some help! My daughter isn't breathing right. Please! I need help NOW!" I felt so helpless as they took my baby and rushed her into the room to be examined. She was still taking short gulps of air and Fresia was absolutely hysterical. I held her as we looked on from the hallway while they hooked our daughter up to all these machines and applied the oxygen mask to her little face. Her color still wasn't improving, and I felt myself starting to panic, until I looked into Free's face. My fiancé was on the verge of passing out at this point.

"Baby, you need to calm your breathing. Look into my eyes. Free, LOOK at me!" I yelled. "Breathe in and out, in and out. That's it, baby, calm down so we can both be here for her when she comes out of this. Because she *will* come out of this." She hugged me so tight and buried her face into my chest as she cried. I rubbed her back until I felt she had settled down. I got her some water and prayed silently. "God, please let Tamia pull through this. Fresia won't make it without her, and I won't either. I know I haven't been what you wanted for my life, but I've never asked you for anything. PLEASE Lord, please! Come through for me this one time, I need you. Amen."

Chapter 25

Monroe

I was in and out of it. How did I make it to my room when the last thing I remember was being on the couch? Must've been having a nightmare. I dreamt that Aubrey woke from her coma and didn't remember me. I could tell I was still drunk, but my baby was lying right next to me. Her skin felt so soft and her perfume was different, yet familiar. I started caressing her cheek while she slept and started to run my fingers through her long beautiful hair. My finger got stuck in a fuckin' weave track. Who the fuck was this in my bed?

The sliver of light coming through my curtains let me know that I had fucked up already. How and why was Tai in my fucking bed? I tried to sit up, but my head was spinning already so I had to lay back down and try again. Once she felt me stir, she put her leg on me and breathed lightly while she continued to sleep. I really hope I didn't fuck her. I was able to ease her leg off of me without waking her. I sat up slowly this time and went into the kitchen to get some water.

I saw how much vodka that was left in the bottle. It was more than halfway gone! I stopped drinking when my best friend, Gary, got sick. He had developed sclerosis of the liver, which killed him slowly. Gary had started drinking in high school, and all throughout his twenties, he popped pills, drank liquor or whatever could get him high. He died at the age of thirty-one, about two years ago. I always called him my big brother, but now he was gone. James was the only other person I let get close to me and he never tries to compete with Gee's memory. Taisha was there for me during that time, I almost lost myself and my own life. And tonight, was the closest I'd gotten to that feeling since. I appreciated her concern, but I hope I didn't fuck her. Aubrey was still the only woman I wanted.

Dee Dee

Aubrey was different. She talked different. Her mannerisms were different. And she still couldn't recall Monroe. Aubrey and Monroe had major chemistry. It was different from what she shared with that thang, Rob. But she was harboring bitterness towards him in the worst way. "Baby, you wanna get out of the room today? Let's go to the pavilion and smell the flowers and look at the water outside."

Aubrey

I was depressed. I was having an identity crisis and was pregnant by a man that I wasn't feeling. From what everyone keeps telling me, I was so in love with him. Why is it that I couldn't forget that fuck nigga Rob, but I can't remember Monroe, who was supposed to be such a great dude? He's been up here a few times when he thinks I'm sleep. He tells me how he feels about me and I keep my eyes closed. He kisses my hand and then puts his forehead down on it where he kissed me for a minute, as if he's praying. It's really making me feel some type of way, but I still don't remember him! "Mommy, I just don't feel up to it, but I know you won't leave me alone, so let's just go." I snapped.

She helped me into my wheelchair, made sure I was comfortable and then we were on our way. The pavilion was beautiful. It was serene and my mom knew just what I needed, as always. I was getting my leg cast off tomorrow, so I was happy about that. But in the meantime, I was twelve weeks along and my belly has already started to harden. I hadn't said anything to my mom about anything, I just felt that she would say something to Monroe.

Dee Dee

I just wanted my baby back. It had been a little over two weeks since she's been awake. I encouraged Mike to go back to Miami while I got Aubrey situated. After confirming that she was going to be able to move around with the knee scooter tomorrow, I was taking her home to her house. I've already gotten it ready, with the assistance of Monroe, of course. He hired a physical therapist that would make home visits and ensured that she would have groceries delivered on a weekly basis. He also installed a ramp in the front of her house and in the back so that she could come and go any time she pleased. Although she still didn't remember him, he still was around. He gave her space, but he was never too far away. That was true love and I love him for it.

Any chance I could, I ensured I spoke about something she had previously discussed with me to try and spark her memories. It hadn't worked quite yet, but I remained hopeful. She started gaining a little weight back and if it wasn't under these circumstances, I would have thought she was pregnant. But with the trauma her body has been through, I don't believe her injuries would support a healthy pregnancy. I would just keep encouraging her to be positive, and make sure that she was calm.

Aubrey

The only thing I keep thinking is if I decided to go through with the pregnancy, how much the medicines used to keep me alive would affect my baby. I'm scared to ask Dr. Sawyer the question. I know she will run down each and every little thing that she knows could affect it. I could still love my baby if he wasn't perfect, right?

Taisha

So, I've been checking on Monroe every chance I get, as a *friend.* I explained to him that the night he was drinking, I came over to check on him and he 'insisted' that I stay because he didn't want me to leave. Of course, that was a lie, but he didn't need to know that. I made sure I wore the sexiest shit that would seem casual to him, when we were together. I knew he was borderline depressed, but I planned on keeping him distracted every chance I got. After that first night staying over, I did try to get some. I pulled out his dick during one of the times he passed out. I put him in my mouth, and I was trying my damndest to stimulate him. It didn't work for shit. When he finally noticed I was there, I made sure that I removed my bra and that my titties were close enough to his face when he awoke.

He just eased out of his bed, placed the covers on me and spent the night on the couch. He had like four other rooms in this big ass house and decided to sleep on the couch. What was that about? But when I came over, I ensured that I pushed my booty up on him when I "fell asleep" during whatever movie we decided to watch. One night, instead of waking me, he carried me upstairs and I made sure to nestle my face in his neck. Instead of taking me to his room, he took me to one of the guest rooms. I was so disappointed. And to add insult to injury, that bitch that couldn't remember him was all up in my face. There were pictures of her ass all over this place. Uggghhh!

<<<ring, ring>>>

"You have a collect call from..." I accepted the call.

Big Don

"Aye baby, what you doing? I'm missing you?"

Taisha

I rolled my eyes. "Oh, nothing baby, just thinking about you." I lied.

Don

"Oh really... cuz word on the street, is that you're back with Money."

Taisha

Word on the street? What the hell? These niggas talk more than the bitches dancing at Sugar's. "Donnie, Money and I are just friends. He'll tell you himself. But what's up baby? You called to talk to me about Money? Or you called me to talk about how I put it down yesterday?" I replied seductively. Can't mess up my cash flow. "I can't wait to see you on Saturday baby. Any special requests? I got some new shit that I wanna try on you baby."

Big Don

"Sounds good lil mama. Wear all black and wanna see you dressed up like a stripper. I'm talking the heels, the costume, you know how you do. Bring that glitter shit that you put on your skin and wear your hair short for me."

Taisha

Damn!!! Now I gotta go get my hair redone. I just got these damn bundles!

Free *(dreaming)*

"Ride that shit baby... oooohh shit! Turn around on this dick and let me see that ass clap." Rob delighted as he tortured me.

I turned around and did as he asked while he kept slapping my ass as hard as he could, it seemed. I just knew he was going to leave bruises on me again.

"Get on all fours like you on the stage and lemme see you pop that pussy for a real nigga." Rob directed.

I did as he said, he liked when I put my sex real close to his face as if he was examining it. It was weird. I was out of breath, but as long as my baby was over there in her baby seat in the corner, I was doing whatever I had to, to keep her safe.

"Lay on your back and lemme get on top of you, baby." He requested.

I hated when he was on top of me, because he wanted my ankles by my ears. And while his curve felt amazing to me in any other position, it was a bit too much for me to take missionary. I always felt like he was tilting my uterus or something. But I did it anyway.

"Damn Free, this pussy has my name written all over it. Have you been taking your birth control like I asked baby?" He asked out of breath.

I nodded yes and just wished he would just finish already. He was enjoying himself too much.

"I'm so deep baby, this shit is unreal." He whispered as he tried kissing my lips.

He thrusted in and out, back and forth into me with all his might. He didn't care anything about my pleasure. It was all about him and what he liked. "This pussy was made for me baby, I'm bout to nut all up in you baby. You ready for this hot shit baby?"

I nodded while trying to breath. He kissed me all over the side of my face. I was thoroughly disgusted.

"MMMmmmmm Free, this... pussy... is... fire... OOOOOOoooooohhhhh!" He said as his eyes rolled into the back of his head in total pleasure. "We can't have no more babies though."

Free

And then I woke up sweating from my nightmare, just like before. Oh God, please make it stop! I don't know how much longer I was going to be able to deal with this.

"Tamia!" I cried. James was still holding me. He was awake and looked concerned. "What, what's wrong with my baby?" I started crying again. I just realized we were still in the hospital with Tamia.

James

"Baby, she regained her color, and she is resting. The doctor wants to speak to us, but I wanted to let you sleep. Breathe baby. Remember, in and out, breathe in and out, slowly. Control your breathing baby. Then we can go see Tamia."

Something is going on with Free, and I need to figure this out. She's lost so much weight in a short period of time. I know she was getting ready for the wedding, but I feel like it's something else going on. She's also not sleeping, but she hasn't spoken to me about it. We're going to ensure the baby is fine for now and then I need to figure out what she needs.

We walked into Mi Mi's sterile room together. "Stay strong for our daughter, baby. She needs our strength right now." Fresia stood at the door for a minute to process the sight before her. The baby hooked up to all of those tubes and machines beeping and whirring around her almost broke me down. Once she was sure she gathered herself, she walked over to Mi Mi and caressed her little cheek. Although she still had the monitors connected to her, she seemed comfortable while she slept. The doctor came in and he had the look on his face that doctors had when they wanted you to think the best, when the prognosis was the worst.

Dr. Thompson

Hello Mr. and Mrs. Casey, your daughter is a fighter. Her breathing was constricted due to a congenital heart disease called Ventricular Septal Defect or VSD, otherwise known as a hole in the heart. She has a hole in the wall between the lower chambers of the heart. Sometimes these conditions can repair themselves. We'll monitor her for a few days, until the test results come back. Do you have any questions for me?

Free

I wiped my tear stained face before I opened my mouth to ask any questions. “If it doesn’t repair itself, will she need to have surgery? Will she be able to eat? Can I hold her? Will this cause any problems when she’s older?” I was totally frightened.

Dr. Thompson

“Yes, she would need surgery to repair the opening if it doesn’t close by itself, before the lining of the heart becomes a permanent part of her heart. Yes, she can eat and yes, you’ll be able to hold her. Breastfeeding is certainly a good idea. Theoretically, yes, it could cause problems for her when she’s older, which is what caused the shortness of breath. There is a very high success rate for these surgeries. I assure you that she will receive our absolute best care. We still have a few days to find out. Please, don’t hesitate to let me know if you have any further questions.”

James

“Thank you, Doctor, we’ll contact you if we have more questions.” I said as I shook his hand. Free was happy to be able to hold Tamia. She was still a bit sedated, but she was no longer blue. “Baby, she’s gonna be alright. I feel it in my soul.”

Free

“I know baby, I feel it too.” And I believe I genuinely smiled for the first time in weeks.

Chapter 26

Sam

Since Joe was *busy* last night, I took the time to lay out my clothing and ensure that I was freshly shaven. *Everywhere.* I had this amazing burgundy pantsuit that I was wearing to Keith's. I was going to pair it with a pale pink lace and satin chemise. The shoes, a pair of burgundy and rose gold colored Saint Laurent strappy sandals. My hair was sleek, cut into layers and framed my face. I had learned how to apply a little bit of makeup and went with a natural look, but my glow was on point with the new Anastasia Sun Dipped Glow Kit that my stylist recommended.

I met Keith at the address he texted to me the day prior. When I got there, I entered through an arched security gate that was absolutely beautiful. I pulled up to a circular driveway, and Keith met me at the beautiful double glass door entrance to his home. Upon entry, it looked like a mini mansion, with gold crown moldings, tray ceilings in the main rooms and the kitchen's recessed lighting made the home look imperial. I could tell, the details were well planned out for this structure. This is what I would call a home with "good bones". It was a very nice estate, that I imagined a big happy family living in.

Keith was wearing off white linen pants with a classic white linen button down shirt that was open at the collar. He looked so relaxed and so sexy. I didn't realize I was staring at him, until he waved his hand in front of my face with this big smile on his face.

Keith

"Hello..." I said as I waved my hand in front of Samantha's face. She seemed mesmerized by my home, which I knew she would be. Most people were, but it meant more to me because I knew she had a great eye when it came to the little details. She was absolutely beautiful and dare I say sexy, and it was nice to see her coming into her own. "Glad you found the place okay. I hope you're hungry."

Sam

I was so embarrassed. I was just staring at this man like a schoolgirl with a crush! Hopefully, he thought it was his home that stopped me in my tracks. It was absolutely stunning! "Yes, my GPS is very handy at times. And it didn't take me around the world to get here." He didn't have any shoes on and all I could think was that his feet were perfect too. Damn, he is so fine!

Keith

"Can I take your jacket, gorgeous?" We embraced briefly, and it seemed like she was bit nervous about being here. "Let's go into the parlor and get a bit more comfortable." She looked nervous for some reason, and it was at that point that I realized she was just as into me as I was into her, regardless of her so-called *relationship* status with whomever. I asked her again, "Would you like for me to take your jacket? I want you to be comfortable as we navigate through these plans." Plus, I wanted to see more of her body. She was very sexy, but it seemed as if she dressed for business. I wanted her in the mood for nothing but pleasure.

Sam

"Um, sure, thank you." I felt like I was starting to perspire, and I needed to figure out how to relax in front of this man that I've known for a few years. Divorce really looked good on him. Oh my God! What am I saying? That is awful to even think about someone. But he was the reason that I was always so wet these days. And since I wasn't getting any attention from Joe... let me calm down. This is business. "You have a very beautiful home."

Keith

"Thank you, Samantha, come on, let me give you a tour. I built this house after my divorce."

Sam

"I meant to tell you how very sorry I was to hear about that." It was genuine, I hated to hear of couples separating. I would be devastated if it was my parents.

Keith

"Oh no, don't be. But I appreciate you. That marriage should have been dissolved years ago. I believe we got married for the wrong reasons. Karen was pregnant in college, but after we got married, we lost our daughter. A rare genetic disease. We had never gotten pregnant after that, and there was really never any real chemistry between us. We were just great business partners. And that's why we've been able to maintain a great friendship. She told me to tell you hello, by the way."

Sam

I'm not sure how to feel about the last statement, but she was always nice to me. I don't know how she would feel about the way I was eyeing her ex-husband though. "Oh, well I'm glad to hear that you all don't have any bad blood between you." We continued on the tour, just chatting and laughing with one another. There were seven bedrooms, five and a half bathrooms, a living area, a den, a parlor, and entertainment room with theater style seats. The master bedroom was very large and also the only one on the east side of the house. His bed looked very inviting, the master bath had a jacuzzi tub that looked like it could fit four grown adults, and the shower had two shower heads on both ends with a marble bench inside.

I imagined sexing Keith all over that bedroom and in that shower. Riding him into oblivion, I wonder what his face looked like during his climax. I felt my nipples get hard through my chemise. I wasn't wearing a bra because the back dipped low, and because my breasts were very perky. I could see us on the side of that jacuzzi tub in front of that beautiful bay window, with him gripping my hips as he drove himself in and out of my walls.

I felt his hand on my lower back and it was nothing but electricity as he brought me out of my fantasy. He continued to guide me through the kitchen, I even thought about riding him on top of the elaborate and remarkable marble island. I just wanted to feel him inside of me.

But then there was Joe. Joe was who I considered my first, so that automatically made him special to me. But outside of the bedroom, what I thought was chemistry between us just fizzled out. He's fine with being a dental technician. I've asked him about his goals for the future, and outside of having a family like his brother's, there is no real ambition there.

Keith on the other hand... he's just got it going on in every way. He's absolutely gorgeous, he's driven, he always has something interesting to talk with me about and he's accomplished. I know that if he wanted to, he could retire and his money would still make money. I also know that money is not his goal, he just loves what he does. I've learned quite a bit from him, and I think I was ready to explore a bit more.

"This back yard is amazing!" I love the set up. There was a built-in grill, with a stove and a sink. The pool was gorgeous, with a slide and a waterfall that I imagined Keith and I swimming naked in any chance we got. I wanted to christen each every room on this property. What am I thinking about? He is not my man! Let me get it together before he notices me zoning out. Since I've been working on my practice, I've also been recording things that my home must have. "I may have to hire you build my home as well. I think I want a property just like this. You've spared no expense." I looked to my right and saw the chef setting up the outside eating area for us. I was glad, because I was starting to get hungry.

Keith

"Well this home is definitely a bit big for just one person, you could always just move in here with me." It was wishful thinking, but I was joking and was glad that she laughed along with me. "Let's sit and eat, and afterward we'll talk business. Can I interest you in some wine? My chef suggests one of these, I've sampled both and they are both delicious." I said as I pulled her chair out for her.

Sam

"I'll take a glass of whatever you suggest. Everything looks delicious. I appreciate the invite to your home. This is the nicest setting I've been to in a long while." 'And I want to ride your face', is something that I also wanted to add. *Calm down girl*, I thought to myself.

Marie

I applied for a job at a local boutique near my apartment. I was working on purchasing a small home that I found not too far away from where we currently lived. I wanted Robert to be able to come and go as he pleased once I felt comfortable that he didn't remember the two other bitches he always wanted to keep in contact with. I mean, I guess if I were a man, they would do. But neither one of them was me.

He had almost fully healed with the exception of his ruined foot, and my belly was now showing. My doctor confirmed that it was two babies, and I felt like they were little girls. It was still too early to tell though. That was supposed to be my legacy, according to Mother's dreams long ago, but that didn't mean that it would happen that way. I was supplying hopeless individuals with readings concerning their futures in the back of the boutique. I don't think most people took me seriously, but they should have. I was telling them nothing but the truth.

"You will have trouble in the very near future with your boyfriend. You would be better off without him. You will never have a child with this man, but the sooner you leave him alone, you'll be happy again."

"She is sleeping with one of your family members and your daughter is not yours."

"Your mother has relapsed and is currently living in an abandoned home near a school. The school is surrounding by trees and it houses grade school aged children."

These were some of the readings I provided to my customers daily. But I already knew before they showed up, that they wouldn't believe me. It is what it is. Easiest money I've ever earned and because I was with child, my gift was stronger. It didn't even take any real effort.

I headed home and I was excited to see Robert. I was horny as ever, but he didn't have a penis, so there was that. Anyway, once I got home, I realized that if I didn't make him get up and do things for himself, he would always expect me to do everything. So, I didn't change his piss bags, I didn't escort him to the restroom, and I didn't make his plates anymore. I just went into my room after making my plate and ate my food and went to sleep.

Rob

"So, you just gonna let me lay here in my shit? I'm hungry as fuck and you ain't gonna feed me now?" I was used to her cleaning up behind me. What the fuck was the difference now? Maybe if I offered to suck her pussy, I wouldn't have this problem. But fuck that. I wasn't even attracted to her ugly ass for all that. AND it wasn't offering me any pleasure. I could pour this piss bag all over this floor and it wouldn't make me no never mind. Fuck it. That's just what the fuck I did, too.

"MARIE! MARIE!"

Marie

"What do you want?" I asked as I held my breath, it absolutely was unbearable in his room."

Rob

"You gonna clean this up or what? I been smelling my own shit for a whole day now."

Marie

"Actually, no. You can sit up, put your own self in your wheelchair and all of that. So, you can also clean up behind yourself. I'm trying to encourage you to become more independent. We have babies that will be born in less than six months and I will need your assistance. I can't depend on you for support if I'm doing everything for you."

Rob

"Why don't you come over here and sit on my face baby. Let me make you feel good." She looked uncertain for a minute, but eventually she brought that ass here. I had to gain her trust if she was going to give me access to this apartment. I still can't come and go as I please, but I will be able to someday. I'm gonna get outta here and get my revenge on them niggas Money and James, and every fucking body they loved. Maybe I'll suggest using a strap on for her pleasure? It didn't take much for her to feel appreciated.

Marie

"On second thought baby, can we please go in my room? My sense of smell is very delicate."

Joe

When I returned to work, I filled Kristin in on some of the details surrounding Aubrey's accident. Not everything though, because she didn't need to know all the details. She listened intently and asked me if I wanted her to help me get back on track. I declined, but we just kept talking into the evening hours. What the hell did that mean, anyway?

Kristen

"Do you like Crown Royal, Joe? I have some and since everyone is gone, why don't we indulge?" I really wanted Joe to fuck me. Ever since I saw him and Sam in the break room, I've wanted his dick in my mouth. I've been sending him plenty of hints, but he hasn't been taking the bait.

Joe

"Oh word? You got some Crown? Fuck you into shawty?" I'm curious to know what she got going on. Them lips looking real good right now and she wore a skirt over that phat ole ass today. Kristin gotta know what she's doing to me. I ain't had no pussy in a minute. Sam has been all the way *unavailable*. Hasn't even been at home that much lately, but I understand. She's getting her practice on track. She and her father's friend, Keith, have been working overtime. I've been trying to be good, but Kristin looks so fucking good. I just wanna bite that ass.

Kristin

"I always have some Crown on Fridays. The question is, do you want some?" I asked as I turned my back, and especially my ass to him. I already knew that the black guys couldn't resist a white girl with a phat ass. And that was me. I wanted that big black dick he was holding on to. But I didn't want to come off as a tramp. If he was with his girl, I knew he didn't like scandalous women, which is exactly what I was. I wanted all of that hot seed released into my mouth, mmmmmm... But the choice had to be his. And when he did make that choice, I was gonna fuck the shit outta him. Sam sure didn't know what she was doing from what I saw. I bent over slightly as I acted like I was looking for something and was awaiting his reaction. I know that by now, he realized that I didn't have any panties on.

Chapter 27

Taisha

Don was a bit too rough yesterday when I went to see him. I had walked past his wife too when I was leaving out. He was getting careless with his arranged visits. I showed up in all black as he requested, but his demeanor seemed to be a bit bothered. I had worked on one routine a week for him to a new song, but why did it seem like this visit was a punishment? I just knew my ass was going to be bruised for a few days from him slapping it hard as fuck like he was. I knew better than to complain though, I'd been through worse in the club.

When I got there, he made me deep throat his dick, as if I hadn't been doing it before. I could hardly catch my breath, so my eyeliner and mascara were running while he punished my throat. Luckily for me, I had a gag reflex that could rival any of the gay guys. It still didn't keep my eyes from tearing up though. However, I didn't complain. I let him do what he wanted to me, but he was damn sure paying me for it.

This time, he decided to enter my asshole. I didn't bring lubricant for that, so we just had to make do. Don started out gently, but he got way too excited and held my waist when he was fucking my ass until he came. This was the first time. He wanted to do it again, and like I said, I'm not gonna fuck up my money. So, he was able to dig up in there again. At the end of that, he told me that the guards had honored a request to let a friend of his in the room. I had to pleasure his ass too. It didn't take him long to nut, but it was just the fact that Don didn't let me know that before I got here and it irritated the fuck outta me. Like he was pimpin' me out or something. After I let his "friend" get some, Don wanted some head, so I obliged. I sucked the soul outta that dick because I didn't plan to return. I wanted him to know just what he was missing out on for disrespecting me and not honoring our agreement. When he was done, I spit that shit out on the floor at Don's feet and walked outta that prison.

Monroe

It was evening time and I was missing Aubrey something terrible. It had been almost four weeks since she had woken up and seven weeks since the accident. I craved this woman. She was no longer in the hospital, so I could no longer visit her whenever I wanted to when I knew she was sleeping. I knew she would be taken care of though, because I arranged it. I made sure to deal with her mom when she needed anything, because I didn't want Aubrey to despise me even more.

I was leaving my warehouse after receiving a shipment and just wanting to be totally alone. I was feeling super depressed and Taisha was wearing on me. She came over every single day, with something to eat and a movie to watch. She was truly a great friend, because I would have been thinking of nothing more than what I was missing out on with Aubrey.

Taisha

It was the Labor Day weekend and Monroe just wanted to stay in the house. He still hadn't given up that good dick, but I was determined to get it tonight. I decided to wear a very short skirt that showed my ass cheeks if I bent over in the slightest and a halter top since it was so hot out. I also wore some heeled sandals to go with my outfit. I rung the bell and I heard him moving around prior to opening the door. I ensured that my titties were on display before entering his house. No bra, no panties.

Monroe

"Who is it?" I was painting one of my guest bedrooms a shade of purple that I was sure that Aubrey would like, once she remembered me, if she ever remembered me. It was Tai, I was used to her being over here daily, so it wasn't like a surprise or anything. I opened the door and she hugged me so tight as if I hadn't seen her the day before. She entered with this halter top on that showcased all of her titties. She also had on this short ass skirt that I couldn't wait to see from behind once she passed me.

Damn, that ass looked so good to me that my dick was saluting her in my sweatpants. I didn't even try to hide it. I didn't care at this point; she had already known that I was depressed because of the way Aubrey wasn't responding to me.

Taisha

I saw his dick pointing straight at me in those sweatpants but ignored it. I didn't want him to be embarrassed from how he responded to the way my body looked today. I brought in the groceries I bought earlier so that we could grill together tonight. "So, I wanted to know if you minded if I took you somewhere just to get a change of scenery with everything that is going on with you and Aubrey for Labor Day?" I was faking. I cared *nothing* about that bitch.

Monroe

During the six years that we had been together, Taisha had never taken me anywhere. I was curious about where she wanted to take me. She had been so understanding about my situation with Aubrey, that I completely trusted her. I agreed to go with her to Atlantic City, but I had to see about Aubrey prior to leaving. She said she didn't have a problem with it.

Taisha

He always wants to talk about the dyke bitch, Aubrey. She likes girls now; I think it would be safe to say that she no longer wanted his dick. I mean, here I was working so hard for it. I wanted that dick. I didn't understand why he just didn't want to give it to me. I know Don wanted to. But I was ignoring that ass, because I was going to act like "he hurt my feelings". He was just allowing me more time to focus on the man I truly wanted, and that was of course, my baby Money.

Monroe

When I got to Aubrey's house, I saw that she was in the kitchen doing something. I rang the doorbell once and she opened the door and walked away once she saw who I was. Her face looked a little fuller, so I was happy that she was healthy. "Hey Aubrey, I just wanted to stop by and check on you before I stepped out of town for a couple of days. You're looking well. Do you need anything? How is the chef treating you?"

Aubrey

"I'm alright, Monroe. I gave the chef off for the holiday weekend to spend with his family. I don't think he should be at my beck and call just because I cannot cook for myself at the moment. I hope you enjoy yourself over the holiday weekend." I sat down on the couch so that he couldn't see my rounded out almost five-month along belly. I was supposed to find out what I was having last month, but I decided against it. Dr. Sawyer tested my baby for EVERYTHING. No Down syndrome, no special needs, just a strong ass baby! I was actually getting excited. I felt it in my soul I was having a boy. "There's no need for you to stay with me." I noticed he didn't make any moves whatsoever.

Monroe

"It's okay, I don't mind staying here and cooking for you if need be. That was very nice of you to let the chef enjoy his family this weekend. Of course, you know, there's no place I'd rather be." She was just so beautiful to me, and I just missed her so much. "Have you eaten today, Beautiful?"

Aubrey

I wished he didn't call me that. I sure didn't feel beautiful at the moment. "Monroe, why do you keep coming around? I mean, you just seem like a glutton for punishment." I saw his reaction to my question and it almost got to me. But I looked away, and I was able to maintain my composure.

Monroe

"I keep coming around because I love you, Aubrey. And I know you love me. I just need for you to remember. There's no other woman in this world that has ever loved me like you. And I'm not giving up on you." I meant every word too.

Aubrey

I was fed up with this. "Just give up already! I don't know you! I'm sorry! But I just don't. What do you want from me?" At this point, I was just hopeless. I wanted him to have a life of his own with no resentment toward me in the future. I didn't want him to stay because he felt he had to; I have a medical condition that would keep him around me.

I mean, what if I never remembered him. What if he stuck around for the rest of his life and because of the way Rob made me feel, and I never let him touch me again. I didn't want that kind of responsibility. I couldn't be responsible for yet another human being and it not be my choice! I already had to have a baby. What else was I gonna have to do that I didn't want to handle? I couldn't even take care of my damn self! His feelings would just have to be hurt. Better now than later.

Monroe

I felt defeated at this point. I thought I was ready to go to the ends of the earth for Aubrey. I just hung my head in defeat. Here she was telling me that once again she didn't know me. I felt hopeless. I was just going to let her go. I love her more than I love myself, but there is nothing I can do if she wants me to leave her alone. "Aubrey, I love you. But if you don't want me, there is nothing that I can do about that. I just wanted to ensure you had everything. Everything that I could provide, to ensure your recovery was smooth. I still want to marry you. You are the first thing I think of in the morning, and the last before I go to bed at night. I want you to know, your rejection is the worst thing that could happen to me. But I will not force myself on you. I wish you the very best that life has to offer. I love you with everything that I have." With that, I got up, kissed her on her forehead and walked out of the door. It wasn't until I got to my car, that I realized I was crying. I drove around until I could get my mind right. I was sure Taisha was at my house just awaiting my return.

Sam

Keith and I ironed out the details of the business proposal and as it turns out, he had a much better idea for the lobby of my practice. I'm glad that he called me back about it now that I was able to see it. We ate the meal the chef prepared for us and enjoyed each other's company for the remainder of the day. The bottles of wine his chef recommended were top notch. And Keith was such a jokester! He kept me laughing! I was having such a great time and then I realized that I was so intoxicated.

He was nice enough to allow me to stay in one of his guest rooms. I was dozing in and out of sleep when I started wishing that I could get my fill of Keith this evening. I was so turned on! For some reason, I started to think about Joe and my mind was filled with all the great sex we always had. I'm so thankful that I didn't buss it wide open for Keith because based off of how I was feeling tonight, it was a very real possibility. I knew that we were both pretty gone off of that wine. And he was flirting pretty heavy too. And I enjoyed it.

Keith

"Sam, do you need more covers? Are you comfortable?" I just wanted to check on her prior to lying down in my bed for the night. I was pretty drunk, if I was being honest. I brought some covers and extra pillows to the west wing to ensure she was comfortable.

Sam

"No baby, I just need you inside of me." I wanted Joe to come and give me that dick that he'd been withholding from me for so long. "Ooooh baby, please just kiss it for me. PLEASE baby."

Keith

"Sam, I'm not sure you know what you're saying, gorgeous. I'm gonna be in my room if you need me. I'll place the extra covers and pillows right here on the loveseat in the corner." Just then, she opened her legs and pinched her nipples through her chemise. I just watched her from the doorway as she started to remove her pants, while bending over to show me her seductively tasteful nude lace thong. She got back on the bed, laid on her back and placed one hand into her panties while she caressed her sweet spot. My dick grew in my linen pants as she continued to rub herself. I turned to go to my room, when she called me back into the room. Her voice was raspy and sexy at the same time. Her words had sex dripping from every syllable. It was almost hypnotizing.

Sam

"Don't leave, baby. Come touch it for me. Please..." I wanted Joe inside me in the worst way.

Keith

"Are you sure Sam? I don't want to rush anything. Anything at all."

Sam

"Mmmmm baby, I want to feel you inside of me. Please." She repeated to Keith.

Keith

I started toward the bed, as I removed my shirt and when I approached her, she took my hand and pulled me on top of her. She kissed me deliberately, and I placed my hand into her panties to massage her softly. She was so wet that it made my manhood jump. I decided to remove her panties and kiss the inside of her thighs. She purred and placed her fingers into her mouth. I hungrily planted my face into her center and massaged her deliberately with my tongue. She cried out softly, turning me on even more. Samantha wrapped her legs around my neck while I pleasured her.

Sam

"Oh baby, you are making me feel so good. Please don't stop baby, *PLEASE* don't stop. Ooooooohhhhhhhhhh…" It had been so long since Joe made any time for me. I so looked forward to this love making session after all of this time.

Keith

I inserted two of my fingers inside of her as I continued licking and sucking on her center. I pushed her legs back once she released her grip and thrusted my tongue in and out of her. Immediately thereafter, I felt her core start to tremble. I locked my hands down on her thighs so I could continue the assault with my tongue and pleasured her ferociously. I wanted her to cum so hard and luckily, I was able to capture her juices inside of my mouth. She squirted and moaned so loud while I suckled on her nectar. I knew she was in Heaven and that was all I wanted for to continue to feel.

Sam

"Fuck me baby, please." I was still trembling as I had never cum that hard before. This experience was so majestic, that I never wanted it to end.

Keith

I answered her call with my thickness. I entered her and she gasped loudly like she didn't expect my width or my length. She was so very tight and it was like she was filled completely by my thickness on the inside. I was in absolute bliss, as was she. I guided her left leg onto my right shoulder as I kissed it and continued to plunge into her sweetness. I felt as if I was about to release, so I changed position and entered her from the side as she threw it back on me, to my delight.

I kissed her neck and back as she continued to throw her ass back onto my length like she was trying to take my soul from me. She then sat on top of me and rode me until I was at the point of no return within her. It was absolute pleasure that I hadn't felt in years. Once we were done, I fell asleep inside of her in complete bliss.

Chapter 28

Sam

I couldn't understand why the light was so bright this morning, but I refused to open my eyes. I felt Joe lying beside me, and he must have missed me because he gave it to me the best that I had ever received it last night. I'm sure he was trying to make up for lost time, but how did I get home? I really hope I didn't embarrass myself at Keith's house last night. At least we got some work done.

I put the cover over my head and was about to fall back to sleep when I realized that I didn't feel Joe's locs anywhere near me. We always had such a time trying to sleep together with all that hair of his all over the place. He must have wrapped them up last night. I moved closer to him and he pulled me into him which was right where I wanted to be. I put my leg on top of his and upon doing that, I felt him put his thumb on my clit and apply just the right amount of pressure. I could already feel him getting aroused because his penis was right up against my other leg. He slipped two of his other fingers inside of me as he kept that pleasurable sensation going with his thumb. This is what I missed, being awakened this way.

I kept my face buried in the covers because neither of us had gotten up to brush our teeth as of yet. We didn't let that stop us from enjoying one another though. After I was satisfied that I was wet enough for him to enter me, I turned over and pushed my booty into him so that he could enter me from the side. He took his time and did just that and filled up my walls completely with his length and width. Is it possible that since Joe and I hadn't made love in weeks that it could feel this different? I mean, I wasn't complaining because this was more amazing than ever, but damn! I was in such bliss at the moment. Could he have grown?

"Mmmmmmmm.... sssssssssss.... mmmmmmmmmm...."

We continued to rock back and forth in perfect tune with each other's bodies when I felt my first orgasm creeping up on me. It started roaring through my body with such ferocity that I don't think I was quite ready for this morning. "Uuunnnhhhhhh, ooooohhhhhh, yessss baby, don't stop mmmmmhhhhhmmm sssssssssssss..."

Joe just went deeper as he rode my wave until it ended. He kept pleasuring my body so completely that tears spilled down my face. I couldn't believe how wonderful I was feeling in this moment. Just then, I felt an even more intense orgasm coming over me and this time, he got on top of me while I continued laying in that same position. He put his arm underneath my leg while lifting it slightly and worked me so good that I just continued crying those beautiful tears and moaning louder than I ever remember doing before.

I felt him move in and out of me with such a generous pace that I just knew he was trying to make up for lost time. I remembered that my eyes were still closed during this most amazing session and I just wanted to see his face and look into his eyes. I felt him speed up just a bit, so I knew he was about release and I loved seeing his face while he did it. As he released his seed inside of me, the third wave came over me again. I then realized that best sex of my life, this morning and last night, had been with Keith. I was still at his home, making love to him for the second time and in that instance I'd realized what I had done.

Taisha

It was Sunday morning and Monroe was on his way over because I wanted to fix a little breakfast before leaving town. He had agreed to go with me to Atlantic City for a couple of days and we were leaving right after breakfast. I waited for him at his house last night, but he didn't return after visiting with Aubrey. I felt some kind of way, until he called this morning confirming that he still was up to going on this trip.

I hadn't gotten dressed yet, so I decided to wear my crop top that barely covered the bottom of my breasts, my belly chain and my heather gray spandex shorts that accentuated these dangerous curves and the gap between my legs. I didn't bother to put on a bra on or underwear because I was in my home and the goal was still to get Monroe to want to fuck me.

I still had the short bob that Don had asked me to get done prior to the last time going to see him. And since that last time seeing him almost a week ago, I hadn't answered my phone when he called. And I wasn't planning to go see him this week or any other time for that matter. I did notice that he deposited ten thousand dollars in my account this morning. He must have been feeling guilty about the way he disrespected me on Saturday. I'll gladly take all that extra money, but I was not going back. All because he was in his feelings because someone told him that Money and I were back together.

I heard Monroe pull up as I pulled my croissants and bacon from the oven. I fixed exactly what I remembered was his favorite. I had the grits, fried eggs with a little cheese on top, some sausage links and bacon that only he would eat, and of course the buttery croissants. I cut up some fruit for me to enjoy with my granola and yogurt. I had to keep this body right. I went and opened the door for him, and we embraced as he entered. I had to get on my toes to do so and it just felt so good to hug him, even though he was still only placing one arm around me as a friend, I guess. I closed the door and was sure to walk in front of him so that he could salivate at the jiggle of my perfect ass to the kitchen.

"I made some food so that we wouldn't be hungry on the road. I hope you don't mind." I had to get on my stool to grab a couple of plates and bowls from the top shelf and I knew he would get the full view of my perfect breasts underneath my crop top. I poked out my ass just a little to entice him with that as well. I was working every angle, trust me. And I think I was starting to wear him down. Once I got down, I noticed him looking at me and I knew my nipples were pointing right at him once I placed his plate in front of him. "Are you okay hun? What's on your mind?" I asked as I walked over to him and made sure my face showed concern.

Monroe

My dick is trying to bust through my pants right now at the sight of Tai. I just had the full view of those phat ass titties underneath that little ass shirt she had on. And her ass just make a nigga wanna live in that pussy. I don't know how much longer I can hold back. I do know that I'm in a very vulnerable place right now, and I haven't been with anyone sexually since before Aubrey's car accident.

"Nothing is wrong, I'm just thankful that you're my friend. I know we've been through a lot together and separately, but I just really appreciate you for not allowing me to end up in the same space I was in when Gee passed."

She came over to me and hugged me and told me she would always be there for me and kissed me on my neck. I hugged her back and felt her kiss me again on my jaw. She moved her way up to my lips and kissed me gently. I felt my hands move from her back to now cupping and then gripping that ass. I knew I was in trouble now. We now were tongue kissing and she was sucking on my bottom lip, which absolutely drove me crazy. I was grabbing and squeezing all over her body when she broke the embrace and grabbed me by the hand to lead me out of the kitchen and up the stairs.

James

Free and I pretty much stayed at the hospital and Tamia seemed like she was back to her happy self. She kept trying to remove her breathing tube from her nose, but we just put it back whenever she took it off. I was watching Free to ensure she was eating. Now that the doctor let us know that the hole in Tamia's heart shrunk by twenty three percent, he was confident that it would resolve itself. Free was much better now that we knew Tamia could make a full recovery and most likely not have to undergo surgery. She was breastfeeding Tamia right now and I realized that she was born to be a mother. The baby was her greatest joy and I was glad to be part of this transition. Still, there was something off about her and it had been since the kidnapping.

She was now rocking the baby to sleep, so I thought I would talk to her about how I was feeling. “Fresia, we need to talk about something. I think you’re still having difficulty with what happened to you. Your sleep isn’t restful, I notice you wake up at all hours of the night sweating and crying in your sleep. I think it’s time that you spoke with someone about your feelings, now that we know Mi Mi is going to be okay.” She looked at me as if she was trying to absorb what I just said.

Free

I know he’s right, but how is telling someone that I allowed this man to treat me like a whore and I liked it, going to make me feel better about myself? How can I convince a therapist that this man, that I let treat me this way for so long, is now haunting my dreams? I believe I deserve everything that’s happening to me. I mean, now that my baby is okay, I feel like nothing can bring me down. Not even a few nightmares. It’s not even real anymore!

“I’m alright baby. I think I can handle it, especially with you by my side.” How could I ever tell him that I see Rob’s face when James and I are making love? And it’s always right at the moment of my orgasm. Just like when he made me sex him. Why did my body still like it? James would never be able to process that information without thinking that I still want him, so I could never admit it aloud. I was going to get through this, it was just taking a little longer than I thought. What I struggled with, was do I still want Rob? Am I having nightmares about him because I unconsciously still want him? God help me.

Joe

I hadn't heard from Sam in a couple of days, so I decided to stop by her apartment this morning with some food and some flowers. I know that she felt some kind of way about me always being at the hospital but now that Aubrey was back home, she said she had to work on some things to get herself back into the habit of doing for herself. I took that as my cue to give her some time, but I would continue to call her everyday though.

<<<ding, dong... ding, dong>>>

There was no answer. I thought maybe she was in the shower, so I used my spare key to open the door and enter. I placed the food on the counter and walked into her bedroom to surprise her. She wasn't there. So, I went into her other bedroom, upstairs where Aubrey used to stay, and she wasn't there either. Where could she be this early in the morning? She liked to sleep in on Sundays, so it didn't make much sense. I looked outside and that was when I noticed her car wasn't there. Well, maybe she was running an errand. I'll just sit here until she comes in.

Sam

Keith didn't notice how startled I was because at the time I noticed I was lying underneath him, and he had made me cum for the third time. I was totally speechless, because I didn't remember much of the last half of the evening, yet he ended up in my bed. Well the bed he let me sleep in, in his home.

Keith

"Good morning, gorgeous. I hope you slept well; I know I did. I'm going to ask Betty to go ahead and get some breakfast started for us." She looked as if that morning dick took her words away. I hope that she wasn't embarrassed that we enjoyed one another. Her body was super sensitive, and it was my pleasure to ensure she was taken care of. I want her all to myself. I'm not sure how serious she is about this guy she was "dating", but I would take care of that if need be.

On my way downstairs, I got a phone from the prison. The only person I allowed to call me from prison was my brother Donnie.

Automated Prison Operator

"You have a phone call from 'Donald Weathers', an inmate at a federal correctional facility. If you wish to block this call, press 'nine' now. If you wish to accept this call, press 'zero' now."

I accepted the phone call and was hoping he wasn't calling with any bad news, because Sundays weren't our usual days to chat.

"Don, what's up bruh? You need anything down there? Are the guards treating you right?" My last question was code for are they allowing my product to pass through those gates.

Don

"Yeah bruh, everything is good. Look, I know this isn't our usual day, but I need for you to send one of the goons by Taisha's house to see why she isn't answering my calls." I was doing my best to remain calm. I know she was angry with me, and I was experiencing withdrawals. I had to have that pussy again. These other bitches wasn't cutting it.

Keith

He sounded like he wanted to cry or something. What the hell did he want with Money's girl? "You talkin about Money's girl? What would you need with her?" I hope he aint into no foul shit that is gonna have Money coming after him. I'd hate to have to kill him, I really liked Money.

Don

"Money's *old* girl. She's one of mine now and I need to talk to her."

Keith

"Don, I'm not even gonna ask about it. It sounds like some foul ass, disloyal shit if you ask me though. Gimme her number and her address." I hated this side of his ass. Only because this nigga was my brother was I gonna handle this shit for him.

Don

"I appreciate that *little* brother. I just need this favor from you as soon as possible. And make sure your goon knows not to touch her in anyway. She's mine." I said authoritatively.

Keith

That's how I knew his ass was gone. The last bitch he claimed was Renee. Well Renee decided she didn't want to fuck with Don anymore and stopped going to see him. Renee was found in the dumpster, bloody and bruised up with her pussy lips and tongue cut off. She decided she wanted to be with her child's father. But Don didn't care, nor was he willing to share. There is no reneging on what he thinks belongs to him. It ain't right, but you don't fuck with Don. I just hope this Taisha doesn't end up being another Renee.

Chapter 29

Aubrey

I found out that I was having a little boy, by accident. The nurse didn't get the memo that I didn't want to know. The bitch was new. And just like I knew it wouldn't, this news still didn't get me excited about my pregnancy. I went home and my physical therapist was standing there in in front of my house waiting for me.

"Hi Jordan, I'm sorry I'm a bit late. I just came from my doctor's appointment." I still felt defeated. I still wasn't sure about what I was going to do. I was no closer to regaining my memory and it had been so long since the accident. Monroe no longer stopped by, but I knew he kept in contact with my mom. I convinced her to go back home to be with her husband, but I knew she would be right back next weekend to check in on me. My mom was my best friend and I loved her so much. She just didn't understand that I needed to be alone.

This baby growing inside of me was a constant reminder that there was a part of my life that I knew absolutely nothing about. That was absolutely depressing. I was frightened this baby would come out looking like a man I didn't know and maybe I wouldn't love him either. I just broke down crying, I was so helpless. Suddenly, I felt Jordan hugging me. She rubbed my back as she tried to soothe me. She just rocked me back and forth as she told me it would be alright.

Jordan

"Whatever is troubling you, please don't allow it take you over. You're a beautiful woman, who just got over the biggest hurdle of your life. And now you're about to be a mommy. You are here for a reason Ms. Collins. Believe that."

Aubrey

She was so sincere. "Please call me Aubrey." I looked into her face for the first time and saw how striking she was. She had caramel brown skin, a dark-haired beauty from the Dominican Republic with piercing green eyes. She had been strengthening my leg in therapy since I had been discharged from the hospital. She was slender, with fierce curves and a nice ass. She caressed my face gently while wiping the tears away. I appreciated the gesture, and it was nice to hear her words of encouragement.

Jordan

"May I?" she asked Aubrey.

Aubrey

She was asking to feel my tummy and I nodded yes. She was trying to see if the baby would kick her hand, but I've only felt flutters so far. He wasn't really kicking me to where I could feel him with my hand yet. After rubbing my belly, I felt her hand move up to my left breast. She looked at me to see if I would allow her to do it. I didn't object as she started to caress my nipple through my shirt. I felt my pussy throbbing as I realized exactly what was going on.

She had me lie back on the therapy table that had been adjusted to accommodate my progressing pregnancy. She helped me remove my shirt before doing so, so that now I was just in my sports bra and basketball shorts. I was a bit nervous, but the way she looked at me made me relax. She started me off with a simple stretch for my healing leg prior to assisting me with the therapy session. Every time I would show her progress with my movements, she would kiss me somewhere on my body.

The first kiss was behind my kneecap, the next, on my outer thigh. She kissed my belly, my hand, my shoulder and then my neck. Once she finished the therapy session, she assisted me with removing my shorts. She rubbed my sex through my underwear, and I closed my eyes at the pleasurable sensation. She again started to knead my nipple between her fingers softly, as she continued rubbing on my pussy. She stopped suddenly and I opened my eyes to see her staring at me.

Jordan

"You are so beautiful, Aubrey. I want to continue to make you feel good, but I need you to say it."

Aubrey

"What do you want me to say to you Jordan?" I was genuinely confused. I thought that she already knew that I was okay with her pleasing me. I was in such a pleasure zone and I felt like throwing a tantrum at her abrupt torment.

Jordan

"Tell me that you want me to." She prodded.

Aubrey

She started touching me again, but this time, she ran her fingers up and down my body, and when she got to my private areas, she would skip over them. This was agony! I wanted her to touch me like she was doing before. My breathing sped up as she continued to tease me. "I want you to." I whispered.

Jordan

"You want me to what, Aubrey?" She questioned me with lust in her eyes.

Aubrey

She kept running those magical fingers along the length of my body. Up and down…. Up and down… "Please... I want you to... make me feel good. Please, Jordan." With that, I felt her lick along my inner thigh, as she hooked her fingers into my panties. She slowly removed them as she looked me directly into my eyes. She gently spread my legs as she climbed on the table and lowered her mouth to my vagina. She softly licked my lower lips as I gasped at the intense pleasure. She allowed her tongue to do a bit more probing inside of my treasure. She found what she was looking for and I lifted my torso a bit off of the table to guide her to where I wanted her to go.

She had me moaning and couldn't believe this was happening with this beautiful woman. There was nothing else on my mind, other than Jordan having her mouth on me. Until... I started to feel a bit dizzy and suddenly was having flashes of a man performing this same act on me in the past. I'm sure this was a memory that was trying to resurface, but I didn't need that right now. I just wanted to concentrate on Jordan's indescribable onslaught of satisfaction with her hot mouth.

I felt her stop and immediately, my eyes flew open at the unexpectedness. She got off of the table and unzipped my sports bra which made my breasts spill out. She touched the left one with her hand and brought her mouth down on the right one. Her touch awakened all of my nerve endings at once and the pleasure was insurmountable. I can't describe how I never wanted this feeling to stop. She squeezed my breasts gently and sucked and licked my nipples at the same time. I felt like I would cum just from that alone. She moved from my right nipple to the left one, and the feeling was even greater still. I felt my body start to tremble as the first orgasm ripped through me.

Jordan then inserted her fingers into my sex as my juices flowed and started to massage my g-spot. She did this over and over, until the tremble started to take hold of me again. It was even more powerful than the last and she wouldn't let up on my g-spot as I squirted until I was done. Once that was over, she resumed her position and lapped up my juices as she stared at me with those beautiful ass eyes.

She lapped at my clitoris with such determination while being gentle at the same time. She caressed my breasts and was careful not to put any of her weight on me or my growing belly. Once I felt that tremble starting to overtake me once more, I arched my back while Jordan continued to lock in on her target. Again, my juices flowed, and she allowed all of it into her mouth while still pleasing me.

At this point, I was exhausted, and my eyes started to get heavy. I heard her packing her things, while moving about in my living room. Once she was done, she took my hand and assisted me off of the table. She led me into my bedroom and supported me into the bed and tucked me in. She placed a glass of water onto my nightstand and kissed me gently on my lips before leaving my room. I smelled my essence all over her face and mouth and kissed her back. She left without saying a word to me. I believe I was sleep before she closed the door behind her. It was the first time I had slept soundly since being home from the hospital.

Joe

Sam didn't return home by the time I left around four pm. I was angry, but I would get over it. I went home, and on my way, I saw a woman that resembled Kristen very closely trying to get away from a man with some tired ass braids that I had never seen before. Once I saw him slap her face, I pulled over, exited my car and placed myself in between the two of them.

"Is there a problem here? Why are you putting your hands on this woman?" I asked as I approached him menacingly.

Dude

"Aye man, what you need to do is mind your muthafuckin' business. This ain't got shit to do with you, period. This between me and my bitch." He snarled.

Kristin

"Joe, please. Please go." She cried.

Joe

He tried to charge at her as she ran away from him trying to get behind me and he lost his footing. I'm sure he felt embarrassed and that's why he charged at me next. I punched the shit outta him and he was dazed for a minute.

Kristin

"Joe, please. Can you take me home, please?" I opened the passenger door and let her get in first before walking around to get in myself. He was staring a hole into me, but I silently dared him to do something. Don't no female deserve to be treated like that. And how the hell you doing all this fuck shit on the street so everyone can see you. Niggas these days are so fuckin stupid.

"You alright Kris? Is there anything that I can do?"

Kristin

I was so embarrassed. I broke up with him months ago. Why the fuck was he here? I bet my stupid ass mama told him where to find me. Taz probably gave her some drugs or money. She don't give a damn about me. I'm so scared right now. "I appreciate you for taking me home. But honestly, I'm good." We arrived at my apartment complex. "Would you mind walking me inside please?

Joe

"Yeah, I'll walk you in. It's no problem." I saw that she was really scared so it wasn't a problem. I parked my car and walked behind Kristin as we went to her building. Her ass is super phat and those hips look so good to me. I hadn't gotten my dick wet in some time.

Kristin

"Joe, would you mind staying, just for a little while? I'm not feeling safe at all. I thought that once I got here, I would be okay." He agreed. "Would you like something to eat? Something to drink?" It was getting late and we both had to work tomorrow, so I decided to cook because he was being so nice to me. "Do you like spaghetti? It's something quick." I asked as I handed him the glass of water.

Joe

"Whatever you fix, I appreciate it. Thank you." I couldn't take my eyes off of her. She removed her jacket and had this little tank top on with no bra. She passed me the remote. She got dinner started and took a shower before we ate. She came out in this little short set. She's killing me, her butt was coming out of the bottom of them shorts and I couldn't stop staring at her. I decided to ask her about ole dude to distract me from her body.

"So, who was that, Kristen? Why was he attacking you in that manner?

Kristin

"We met in high school and we were together on and off from the time I was fifteen, up until a few months before I came here. I used to hide from my family how he would beat my ass. I would leave, and he would sweet talk my mom into letting him in our house even if I told her not to. Once he figured out that my mom was getting high, he would bring her a little something when he came over. She wouldn't bother us. She didn't care that he was forcing me to sex him.

"When I turned eighteen, he convinced me to live with him. After I moved in, I found out that he had not one, but two girls pregnant. And one was fifteen years old. The older one moved in shortly after. It was a totally toxic environment. He would get high and want to fuck. Needless to say, if I didn't want to, he got violent. Neither of the girls ever helped me or came to my aid and honestly, I don't even know how Taz convinced me to stay. He had my mind so twisted up and always told me that no one would want an ugly little white girl with nothing or no one, so I just stayed. He made me go to work and I would come home late at night and they would either be laid up sleep in my bed or fucking. I would just wait until they were done to see if Candace was going to go get in her bed or I would just lay on the couch. When I got paid, the money was used for the house. I never was able to do anything for myself.

"After three years of living in that situation, and four more kids 'on the side' later, I left with no money to my name and just the clothes on my back. I came here for a new start and it had been good until today." We talked just a bit more and then Joe said he would see me tomorrow, and that if I needed anything to give him a call. "I really appreciate you, Joe. See you tomorrow."

Joe

"Good night, Kris. See you tomorrow and lock this door behind me." I left and while heading home, I saw that Sam was calling. Good, because I needed to get some pussy after being around Kristin's fine ass.

Chapter 30

Joe

<<<ring, ring>>>

"Hey Samantha, how are you?"

Sam

"Hey, I'm good. I saw from the flowers and the food that you were here today. What's going on? How's Aubrey?" I know I was being petty, but I didn't care.

Joe

I chuckled a little at her last question because I guess she was trying to be funny. "Yeah, I stopped by to see you, but you were out. Where have you been?"

Sam

"Oh, um, I was handling some things with Keith." More like I was getting handled by Keith. Ooh, my pussy jumped just at the very thought of it.

Joe

"Oh, ok. I thought you went yesterday."

Sam

"Yes, I did, we are getting close to finalizing some things. I'm about to turn in, but I wanted to call and say hello."

Joe

"Hey, can I come over? We have been pretty distant all week and... I miss you."

Sam

"Not tonight, I'm wiped out and want to get an early start tomorrow. Rain check?"

Joe

Damn, she rarely ever told me no in the past. Especially since we hadn't fucked in almost two, no, it's been almost three weeks. Fuck is wrong with her that I hadn't gotten none of that fire ass pussy this long? I'm surprised she's not trying to get some dick. "Alright, I'll see you later. Goodnight baby." Damn, she just hung up. I'm gonna really have to make this shit up to her because I feel like she's tired of my ass.

Sam

I know I should feel guilty about spending time with Keith and about what happened, but I don't. Once I got over the shock of it being him and not Joe inside of me, I realized that I'm just a very sexual person and I can't be waiting on any man that would rather spend time with another woman. Speaking of which, I needed to check in on Aubrey.

Before I went home, Keith and I had breakfast after he handled some business with his brother. We did finalize a few more plans and also made a date to see each other again soon. We had this amazing chemistry and an undeniably great sexual relationship. He kissed my lips softly and walked me to my car. I couldn't wait to have him inside of me again, but for now I had to get back to real life.

Taisha

I led Money up the stairs and into my bedroom. We started kissing on the bed and I started removing my clothing until the only thing I had on was my belly chain. I went down on him and just as I started getting sloppy with it, my phone started ringing. I decided to just ignore it because I thought it may have been Don again. Money was on the verge of orgasm when my doorbell rang. I wasn't stopping until I took care of him though. I knew it had been some time. The doorbell rang again after I finished, and I tried ignoring that too, but Money told me it might be important.

I put on my robe, rinsed and wiped my mouth, then went to the door to answer it. I recognized the guy as Bennie, who Money knows as well. I stepped outside so that Money wouldn't hear what we discussed. Couldn't have been nobody but Don's ass sending him here. "What's up Benny? Why are you at my home?"

Benny

"Big Don sent me to find out why you're not taking his calls." He said as he looked over at Money's car and then back to me. I guess you could put two and two together with that picture.

Taisha

"Don knows why I'm not answering his calls, B. Now if you will excuse me." And I proceeded to open the front door. Benny grabbed the doorknob and shut it back. "What are you doing, B? Why is this your business?" I was confused at his forcefulness. He was acting like I was his bitch or something.

Benny

I hated to be rough with women, but this one is trying my patience. Now she knows that whatever big Don wants, that is exactly what he gets. "Tai, you know I was sent here to give you a message. You have until tomorrow to either answer his calls or to visit him. Please don't make me come back here. It's not going to be pretty. Ask Money about Renee. And don't worry, Don doesn't need to know about him being here."

Taisha

He said that as he looked back at Money's car again. He walked away and I knew Benny was serious. He's worked alongside Money on numerous occasions, and I knew that Money didn't allow just anyone in his presence.

I entered the house and Money was coming down the stairs at the same time. At this point, I was shook. I couldn't go out of town now, I had to go see Don. "Umm, Money, that was my girlfriend coming to pick up something she left here before." He came over to me and opened my robe while kissing on my neck. It was what I wanted more than anything else, but I didn't want to lose my life. I didn't need to ask Money about Renee, I remember when they found her in that dumpster. I just wasn't aware of the details on how she got there. But I could make an educated guess.

He started to lick my nipple and his dick was straining against his pants. I wasn't in the right frame of mind currently, to sex him. "Hey sweetie, I'm not feeling so good all of a sudden and I think I just need to lie down. Get you something to eat while you're here and I'll call you a little bit later. I'm sorry, I won't be able to go on the trip."

Monroe

Something is going on with Tai, but I'm not going to press her. She'll tell me when she is ready. I made me a plate and took it with me. I was starving. Since I wasn't gonna be eating pussy, this was the next best thing for now. But I felt lighter after she took care of me after so much time. She wasn't Aubrey, but she knew what I liked.

Marie

My babies were growing so much. Robert seemed to be coming around. He still couldn't remember Aubrey or Free very clearly, but I knew he tried to. He was getting better every day, and now that he knew he had to do things on his own, all was going well. He also pleasured me all the time, and usually he asked to do it for me. He asked me to purchase a strap-on device of my choice a few weeks ago. I would have never guessed that Robert would entertain such a thing. But just like his natural appendage, he worked this one and pleasured me just the same. It appeared he was sincerely trying to be a part of this family with the twins and I. It felt like we were finally becoming a family and I even trusted him to cook for me at times.

"Good morning baby, you wanna get out of the house today?"

Rob

"Yeah babe, lemme throw something on real quick. Come here though, let me feel my babies." I was playing the role and she was trusting me more and more with each passing day. I kissed her belly and rubbed her on that phat ass. Pregnancy looked good on her. Titties was fat, ass was even better than before. I'm gonna kill them niggas for taking my dick. I played with her pussy and her titties for a few minutes before getting dressed, so that I could convince her to let me get out a little more often.

Once we left, we went shopping for the babies, got some food, and headed back to the apartment. Because she was getting bigger, she always had to go to the bathroom. I would take that time to use her phone and transfer a little bit of money at a time from her account to my own, so that when I left, I could maneuver just a bit better. I also got James and Money's phone numbers and any other information I could gather. She came back to the car and I held her hand for a while as she drove back to the house. So far, my plan was working out very well. I just had to be careful not to end up in the closet again.

Keith

I sent Benny over to speak with Taisha on Don's behalf. I would really hate for something bad to happen to her, but she knows Don don't play. Don fucked around and got caught up over some pussy… *again*. He's never been able to say no to pussy. He was even fucking little girls in high school when he was in his thirties. I've always told him that shit was going to be his downfall.

He had a bad wife too, and seven kids. Three of which were actually from his wife. Stacia was from Bolivia. You wouldn't even know she was pushing fifty years old. I met her first when I went to make one of my runs, about eighteen years ago. I had just got on from my mentor and this was the second time I had made the trip. I took Don with me because I had fucked up and told him about the women down there. And every time I saw him, he would ask me about taking him with me on my next run.

I introduced him to this game, and he had no problem taking orders from his little brother because he knew I was going to be successful due to my strict work ethic. And I believe the way I didn't hesitate to use my weapon had something to do with it as well, I thought to myself as I chuckled. Had I known that he wouldn't have changed his ways, I never would have brought him in. He eventually took over my organization while I became the plug. I just maintained the supply now. He got knocked when he fucked a seventeen-year old in one of the warehouses that stored our product, of all places. Her father got wind of his daughter hanging with a grown ass man and called the police.

They were already watching this nigga and he just handed his own ass to them on a platter. The next time Don had the little girl at the warehouse, the father followed them and gave the police the details. He was caught literally with his pants down as this little girl was head bobbing on his dick. There was a shipment that had not yet been divided amongst the crew, and they found all of it. It was one of the smaller shipments, but still was worth one point three million dollars that I had to assume responsibility for. Money was the natural choice to take over. Since he considered my brother a mentor, I was confident he would be an associate who could handle the day to day operations for me. Besides, Money was smarter than Don and took the business seriously.

Don was charged and convicted of drug trafficking and with distribution of controlled substances, sex crimes, sexual assault, sexual deviancy, and other sex charges dealing with a minor. The list of charges was extensive, and his sentence was for fifty-seven years with no possibility of parole. I had friends in high places, so he was afforded certain conveniences that his peers would not receive. Jessup doesn't even allow conjugal visits, but they have set up a personal location just for him because we kept their pockets loaded.

Anyway, I ensured his wife was taken care of. I also made sure the women that went to visit him knew the rules and consequences or breaking the rules and his children were not allowed to follow in the "family business". This current issue, with Taisha was not the first, nor was it going to be the last with a female. But my brother is who stepped up once my father left our mother. Kept me in school, ensured that I didn't fall into the same shit he had. So, I was going to be there for him, no matter what, while he was inside. I believe that's the real reason that I never really made time for myself since my divorce. That was about to change though.

<<<ring, ring>>>

"Hello Samantha, I don't believe that I can wait until Tuesday to see you. Can I interest you in a night of dancing? Or even a ferry ride accompanied by a nice meal?"

Sam

This man has to know I want to jump his bones again. A night of dancing? A ferry ride? *Please…* But I'll play his little game. "Oh, hey Keith, of course, I would love to. Just let me know the time and place and I'm there."

Keith

"How about I come and pick you up tonight after you get off of work. Bring your work clothes with you... you know. Just in case."

Sam

"Hmmm, I don't need any time to think about that. I'll be ready by seven, handsome."

Joe

"Ready for what? And with who?"

Chapter 31

Three months later

Monroe

Mr. and Mrs. Roberson were due back in town this morning and I, of course volunteered to pick them up. It had been about three months since I last spoke to Aubrey. I chose not to infringe upon her privacy, no matter how much I longed for her presence in my life. Her mom used to try and reassure me all the time, but not recently. She does keep in contact with me from time to time just to see how I'm doing.

Their flight was due in, in about twenty-four minutes. This time they were going to stay for about a month. I wondered what the extensive stay was all about, but I didn't bother to ask. I pulled up to the Baltimore-Washington International airport and parked in the short-term parking lot. I walked into the airport and sat at the baggage claim assigned to their flight. I brought a couple of auto orders with me to go over so that I could validate them to make use of my time.

<<<ring, ring>>>

Taisha keeps calling my phone, which I no longer answer. Shortly after I considered almost having some sort of relationship with her, I found out that she was fucking Big Don. I have no ill feelings toward Don, as I know his weaknesses. But she knows that was not a smart move, for herself. She made a deal with the devil and will forever 'belong' to him now.

Mrs. Roberson and her husband were walking towards me at the baggage claim. Now I don't know what to think about this extended stay, but I know something is up. I'm on the lookout for anything strange. Aubrey's arm and leg healed months ago. I'm wracking my brain trying to think of anything that could be going on that I don't know about.

“Mr. and Mrs. Roberson, it’s very good to see you both here today.” I said as I looked at Aubrey’s mom. She just smiled at me. I’m sure if there was anything going on, someone would alert me sooner or later. I took them over to Aubrey’s house and when we pulled up, I saw the curtain pull back. Aubrey knew I was outside, but she didn’t want to see me. I helped the couple take their bags inside the house, but I didn’t see Aubrey. I told them to tell her I said hello and then I was on my way.

Aubrey

I went and sat in my bedroom when Monroe helped Mike and my mom in the house. I would be nine months next week, but according to the docs my due date may be off by two to three weeks due to his size.

“Mom, I could have come and gotten you from the airport. Why do you keep including him into our lives?”

Dee Dee

“Baby I want to keep the lines of communication open with Monroe because sooner or later you’re going to have to tell him he has a son. I would like to be able to facilitate some type of relationship between the parents of my grandson.” I said as I rubbed her belly. “I just think that you’re being selfish by not sharing the information with him now, instead of later.”

Aubrey

“Mom, I know how you feel, but have you ever stopped to think about what I’m feeling? Do you think it’s easy having a whole part of my life unavailable to me? Yet I have a living reminder of that fact, growing inside of me. You have no idea how that feels.” I said as tears ran down my face. This wasn’t easy for me in the least.

Mike

"Alright, Dee, enough of this talk and let her rest. Aubrey, I understand your pain, but you have to realize that your mom just wants the best for you. Denise, this isn't easy for her. And while you have the best intentions, let's allow Breezy to make her decisions with no regrets."

Aubrey

Mike was always the voice of reason amongst us stubborn women. I went to my room and fiddled around with a few things. I had hung all of Monroe's belongings in my closet and I went to them from time to time to inhale his scent. I had a few memories that came back to me, but other than seeing his smiling face at places we must have frequented, it wasn't really much. Seeing his love making faces has sprung up from time to time when I experienced my own orgasms with Jordan. But other than that, there was nothing.

My baby boy was kicking up a storm today, maybe he felt his daddy's presence. I couldn't be sure. I was experiencing the Braxton-Hicks contractions, but it wasn't too bad. I was ready to see him, but I didn't know if I was ready. I'm just glad that I am blessed with parents that are always willing to support me at any given time. The baby's due date, for now, is December seventeenth. Monroe's birthday is December ninth. We'll see when baby boy will make his debut though.

Free

My nightmares occurred much less frequently than they used to, and I was thankful that my husband was so patient with me. We decided on a destination wedding, and Monroe and my girlfriend, Crystyle from Sugar's, were our Best Man and Maid of Honor. We went to Cabo and had a beautiful little ceremony with a waterfall as our backdrop. Our pictures were absolutely perfect, and I was genuinely happy. Tamia was good and juicy at five months old in those pictures and loved being in the water. The hole in her heart repaired itself, thank God. Crystyle was trying her best to get Monroe to pay her some attention, but he knew she was cool with Taisha.

James and I moved into our new home not too far from where we were living in Waldorf. It was a beautiful home and Tamia's room was so pretty. It was purple and gray with an elephant theme. "James, can you come here for a second babe?" I needed him to hang up this curtain in our bedroom. He came in wearing my graduation cap. "James what are you doing?" I asked as I laughed. He knew I couldn't graduate until April of next year.

James

"Baby, the school called and said they miscalculated your credits. They said in two weeks, when you're done with your current class, you will have fulfilled all your requirements for graduation! You did it, baby! I'm so very happy for you. You stayed the course, despite all that has happened this year." I embraced my wife and I was truly in awe of her.

Free

"What?" Free exclaimed animatedly. "No baby... you're kidding?" I jumped up and down for joy! "We need to celebrate!" James said he would make it happen. This is great news! I kissed him so passionately and decided to start the celebration right here in our bedroom.

"Take me to our chair so I can show you just how much I appreciate your support. I know it's been a lot with the baby, my schooling and the wedding, but it's because of you that I was able to reach my first goal. Now let me reach my second..." I chuckled and he obliged with delight.

James

I picked her up and carried her over to the chaise in our room, per her request. Free pushed me down and then unbuckled my pants. She overwhelmed my senses as she placed me in her mouth. “Oh baby...” I whispered excitedly. I thought this was a celebration for her, but I’m definitely not complaining!

Taisha

I was currently at my midweek conjugal visit with Don. Ever since I resumed my visits with him, I have been completely turned off. There were no more sexy costumes or routines. I didn’t even bring my radio with me half the time. I started getting high before visits and he hated that heroin smell on me. But I didn’t care. I was maintaining my end of the deal by showing up each week and on schedule. Don got the same three positions and I did not participate. I did not appreciate my life being threatened.

Don

“I know what you’re trying to do Taisha. But you asked for this. If you want me to start really being disrespectful, keep throwing this amateur ass tantrum. Now you better give it to me how I like it, starting right the fuck now.” Tai looked at me and with tears sliding down her face, started riding this dick just how I like. “And turn around and pop that pussy on the dick for me. I see enough sad shit on a daily basis, so fix your face. This is about the fantasy for me. Make that another thing not to do when you come up here. I want see that sexy shit, not this boring ass shit you been wearing lately. And when we’re done, I have a friend for you. You ain’t gotta go all out for him but let him nut on your face. He likes that.”

Taisha

I have to figure a way outta this shit and quickly. This just cannot be my life. I knew what I was doing when I got home though. One of my old customers from the club asked me to stop by and I knew he had what I needed to forget about all of this shit temporarily. And because of Don reaching out to Money a little while ago about what we were doing in here, he no longer wants anything to do with me. He almost came around, but I had to go on and fuck that up. Just when I thought he could love me again.

Sam

"Oooh baby, right there... right there!" I couldn't get enough of this man and what he did to my body! Keith was stroking me so good, if I had to pay for it, he would get all of my money! We had been spending time together the past couple of months to the dismay of Joe. Ever since that night he caught me on the phone making plans with Keith, it's just been what it is.

Two months earlier

Joe

"Ready for what? And with who?" What the fuck? Samantha must have me fucked up! She over here on the phone in my muthafuckin' house making plans with some other nigga? Nah, I ain't having that shit.

Sam

"Look Joe, we haven't been on the same page with each other for quite some time now. I just stopped by to tell you in person that I can't see you anymore." I then grabbed my purse and my jacket and was walking to the door when he stopped me.

Joe

"Samantha, I don't understand? I thought what we had was good! Can you tell me what the problem is? I know I fucked up and left you hanging before, but all of that is dead now. I promise. Let's just get back to us." As I placed my arms around her. Until I noticed she wasn't hugging me back.

Sam

"Joseph, I am smarter than you think I am. For sure. You don't think I pay attention to the words you don't say to me? For as long as we were together, I always felt like there was something missing between us. I was searching for it and searching for it, until I started hearing what you would say in your sleep. You moan for Aubrey and still yearn for her in a way that I refuse to try and compete with. I was always second choice, but I'm better than that. I deserve better. And thank you for awakening my sexual prowess. It's proven to be something that I enjoy exercising quite often."

Joe

"So, you fucking that nigga too? That's MY pussy Samantha. You hear me?" I noticed I had her pinned up against the wall and her face told it all. I was acting like Rob's bitch ass. I let her go while apologizing profusely, and she walked out of my life.

Present Day

Sam

One thing I will not tolerate is a man putting his hands on me. I don't care what the circumstances are. Keith has proven to be my perfect fit. Well for now anyway. I even stay over his house most of the time. He always says that he was serious about me moving in. I'm not ready for all of that yet. He's gotten me so addicted *and* spoiled. I never knew that I enjoyed being spoiled, there's never been another man to make me feel this way. He continuously has something new for me when I come over. Jewelry, designer shoes and clothes, or even having his personal chef fix a delectable meal that he believes I would enjoy. And then, Keith tops everything off with that A1 dick. I just might be in love! I knew I wasn't dealing with Joe's shit anymore and it's turning out to be the best decision of my life.

Joe

It's been a couple of months since Samantha left me and I must say that when I sat down and actually thought about it, everything she said was true. I knew I still wanted Aubrey, but I settled for Sam because she was the next best thing. I still thought that I could settle down with her though, she was damn near perfect. I just can't believe I'll never sample that pussy again. My stamp was recorded all through that gushy. I can't believe the next man is benefiting from what I taught. I fucked that money up but fuck her if she can't see that I was trying.

I hadn't seen Aubrey in a few months, but I knew her parents were here. I talk to her from time to time, and I can tell that a lot of things have changed for her. She even stopped working at the clinic. I didn't know what to make of that, but she's alright from what I know. I'm sure I'll see her soon, until then I would continue to fantasize about how she used to be and jack my dick to the memory.

"Hey Kristin, wanna do lunch?"

Kristin

I'm not sure why Joe hasn't given up that dick yet. I know he likes the way I look. Taz went back to Tennessee, I guess. I haven't seen nor heard from him since that day. "Sure, wanna go back to my place? I fixed a nice Mexican dish last night that I know I won't be able finish on my own." I was leaning over the counter away from him so that he would have a nice view of my ass in this skirt. I was acting like I was faxing while I was talking to him. "Do you like Mexican food?" I stood back up and faced him with my average sized breasts on display in my v-neck blouse.

Joe

"Yeah, I like Mexican. And since you don't live too far from here, I'm down." Kristin has been throwing little hints at me since she's been here. But it seems like she stepped it up once Sam and I were no longer together. I was trying not to bring drama to work, but I may just have to take one for the team. That ass looks scrumptious. I had to get in that. “Let’s go sexy.”

Chapter 32

Taisha

Mannnnn... I'm feeling so good right now. One of my old tricks from the club, Travis, invited me over because he said he had some of that "new new". "Aye, Trav, what is this called again?"

Travis

"This that black tar mami, new shit. *'Bombita'.* Heroin... give me your other arm so we can have some fun mami. *Dame ese coño, bebé.* Gimme da pussy."

Taisha

I gave him my other arm so that he could inject the good shit into me again. Ooohhh, it worked instantaneously. I feel someone tugging at my jeans and my panties as I lie back on the desk. Then I feel someone enter my pussy. I'm so wet and everything just feels amazing. I see stars and rainbows and... is that a unicorn? I'm wildin'... but I feel so good!

Travis

"*Sssssss, este coño esta tan bueno bebé.* This pussy is soooo good. You can make me a lot of money. You wanna do that for papi? Lift your leg up, yeah right there, baby. Open dem legs for papi, just a little more baby. *Voy a acabar, abre tu boquita.* I'm about to cum, open your mouth for me baby."

Taisha

I felt someone pumping their dick in and out of my mouth until they released their seed down my throat. I didn't care though, I swallowed all of it. I imagined it being my love, Money. I would let him do that to me anytime he wanted. I loved pleasing him.

Travis

"You gotta go, mami. My wife is on the way. Call me tomorrow, I have some plans for you."

Joe

"Damn baby, you creamin' all over this dick." Kristin was insatiable. I thought Sam was my freak, but Kris took it to a whole other level. The way she would twerk that phat ole ass for me and gobble this dick up on demand. Currently, I was hittin' that shit from the back, and the way she was throwing it back, I knew I wouldn't last much longer. That climax snuck up on me, I started to moan. She forcefully guided me back on the bed without letting me pull out with this ninja like move and rode the rest of that nut up outta me, reverse cowgirl style. I see why niggas go crazy over them white bitches. Every day at work, she made sure to take me in the storage room so she could suck the soul outta me.

After she was done fuckin me, she went into my kitchen and fried some chicken, made some nasty ass potato salad with way too much mayonnaise and some green bean casserole. The chicken was good though, it wasn't my mama's, but good. I ain't even gonna front. I wasn't going nowhere.

Aubrey

These contractions seem like they are getting a little worse, but it only happens a few times a day. I don't dare tell my mom. I would've been admitted to the hospital three times by now. "Oooh mommy, what you cookin'?" I asked as I looked over her shoulder. I knew she hated that.

Dee Dee

"Now Bree, you can clearly see that these are rib-eyes. I got the green beans going with my turkey necks and I'm making you some mashed potatoes with the lumps in it like you like it. Now get out of here before I whoop your butt." I teased as she laughed.

Aubrey

We laughed at that one together because we both knew she was a softy. I went back to my room to get ready to take a bath when I noticed that there was fluid slowly exiting my body, indicating that my water was breaking. This shit is nasty. I didn't tell mommy right away because I wanted to eat that good meal before we headed to the hospital. I'm glad that happened before my shower because I would have been mad as hell! And I realized it didn't all come out in one big gush, as it trickled out for another ten minutes. When I felt it was done, then I got in the shower.

I checked my planner and sure enough, Monroe's birthday was tomorrow. "Baby boy, you just wanted to make your daddy feel special huh." I saw some other information in here that I still didn't understand, but who was I gonna ask about it? Not Monroe.

I got out, put some black leggings on and a pad in my underwear in the event that I had more leakage. "Ma, is the food ready yet?" I yelled downstairs from my room. She told me it was. I put on my purple Prince t-shirt because it was the most comfortable shirt I had. I put my socks on after I lotioned my feet and slid my feet into my Gucci slides. I knew I didn't match but I was going to have a baby today.

I went downstairs and placed my hospital bag and my coat on the couch. The goal was to be able to enjoy this meal without my mother rushing me to get to the hospital. Mike caught me on the way though, so I was caught.

Mike

"What's all of that for, Breezy?" He was the only one who called me that, especially when he knew I was up to no good.

Aubrey

I put my fingers to my lips like, shhhh and laughed quietly. “I just wanna eat that good food before we go to the hospital. PLEASE Mike, I’m not even contracting yet. No pain yet. I promise.”

Mike

“I don’t know about this one babe.”

Aubrey

“I swear, I’ll tell her as soon as I take my last bite. Honest to God, please just let me eat this food!” I pleaded.

Mike

“Greedy ass self. We’re leaving in twenty minutes. I’m not playing with you.”

Aubrey

I knew he was serious. But I walked into the kitchen like I had just won a prize. I was so glad that my braids were still fresh. I didn’t want my son coming out like, “Mommy you ugly” or nothing like that! ‘My son’…. I think I like the sound of that.

Marie

“Yessss, Robert. Ooooohhh baby, I’m there, I’m there! Ooooohhhhh!!” Robert was only getting better at this. I no longer had to make him perform oral sex on me. Intercourse was so amazing! He was even more comfortable putting on a strap for me and fucking me like that. I bought another one that closely resembled his curve and he made me cum every time. “Fuck me baby, please.”

Rob

Anything I could do to put her ass to sleep, I did. All she wanted to do was eat, fuck, sleep, eat some more, fuck some more and then go back to sleep. "Of course, baby. Turn around and toot that ass up for me." Anything so I wouldn't have to look at her grill. You would think that she would have gotten that gap fixed by now. That ass was so right, too fucking bad I couldn't dig them guts out myself. She was moaning so loud as I thrusted with this fake ass dick in and out of her soaking wet pussy. That shit looked so good to me. The way her ass bounced off of me as this thing entered her. She did a pretty good job getting one that looked like my real dick.

My plan was already in play. I now had a hard boot on my bad foot, and I could put my weight on it now. I was doing push-ups and sit ups to get strong every day. Marie was about seven months now, and she was so huge now. We confirmed that it was a girl and a boy, and I was excited about that because my son would be able to carry on my legacy. Them niggas thought I was going to die alone, with nothing left behind in this world, but I showed them.

Marie came twice and was ready to tap out. I made her give me that pussy for another ten minutes just so I could have some time to put my plan into action. I needed her to be knocked the fuck out for a good minute. It wasn't like I was coming back here or anything, but I knew I would most likely be caught or die. But I was ready. These niggas were gonna find out who they was fuckin' with.

Marie

"Oooh baby, I can't take anymore." My legs were trembling as I was about to cum for the third time. I had to lay down on my side, and Robert just kept drilling my pussy. It felt so good, but I was ready to go to sleep. I let that last orgasm rip through me and when it subsided, he kissed me passionately, washed the strap on and placed it in its case. "Baby, can you bring me some chips?" But before I even got to eat one, I was knocked out.

Monroe

"Hey Mike, what's up man?" Aubrey's parents had been here for a few weeks. "I was going to call you to invite you and your wife out. And Aubrey, if she wanted to come." I got quiet for a second. "My club is throwing me a birthday celebration tomorrow night and I would really like to see you all there. For my thirtieth."

Mike

"Hey Monroe. Umm, I was wondering if you could meet me at the hospital tonight? I need to speak with you about something. Nothing bad, but I just want you to meet me there."

Monroe

"Mike, is everybody ok? Is Aubrey doing alright? What's going on?" By this point, I was already in my car, but I forgot to ask what hospital. "Which hospital is it?"

Mike

"Southern Maryland. I'll be in the lobby waiting for you."

Monroe

"Alright, bet. I'm on my way." I dialed James' number to place him on standby, I might need his assistance.

<<<ring, ring>>>

Free

"Hi Money, how are you? James is in the shower. Is it an emergency?"

Monroe

"Hey Free? How are you and my beautiful God daughter?" Free gushed over how well Tamia was progressing since being hospitalized and released. "Nothing to worry yourself about though. Can you just have him call me as soon as he gets out please?"

I kept driving; it was about forty minutes away. I wasn't too worried because Mike didn't seem to be. I just wasn't sure about what to think. He didn't even tell me if it was Mrs. Roberson or Aubrey.

<<<ring, ring>>>

"James, I need you to meet me at Southern Maryland. I'm not sure what's going on, but Mike called. I may need you tonight. Put the goons on alert."

James

"Gotchu, boss. On my way." I got dressed and messaged Stevie, Goldie and Benny and told them to strap up and wait for my call. I told Free that I would let her know what was going on as soon as I found out. I kissed her and the baby before I headed out. Hopefully it wasn't too bad, I was tired as fuck from being up late last night.

Rob

I camped out in front of James' house waiting for all the lights to go off. Suddenly, I see him coming out of the house with the phone up to his ear, getting into his car. I ducked out of sight so that he couldn't see me. I started my car followed behind him at a far enough distance so he wouldn't notice me.

I arrived at Southern Maryland hospital as I saw James enter the building. I went in the side entrance and that's where I saw them both, James and Money, with another man I didn't know. They were so involved in their conversation, that they didn't notice me approach with my gun in my hand. I was so angry I saw red. I started lighting that whole muthafuckin lobby up until my clip was empty and someone from hospital security tackled me to the ground.

Stay tuned for Volume 3, Never Be Anotha: Redemption, coming in Winter 2020. Please enjoy the preview of the first two chapters of the next installment.

Coming Soon…

Never Be Anotha: Redemption, Book 3 – Winter 2020

<u>NEVER BE ANOTHA:</u> <u>*REDEMPTION*</u>

Book 3

Troii Devereaux

Chapter 1

Sam

Keith opened me up to a whole new world of sexual exhibition. Not that he knew that. I waited almost twenty-seven years to lose my virginity, officially, and now I just cannot get enough of it. I wanna "fuck" all the time. Keith likes when I say "fuck", he said it sounds sexy coming out of my pretty little mouth. So, I obliged him and said it quite a bit. I always wanted him inside of me. "You ready babe?" We were on the way to a nightclub called Silk's. Tonight was R&B night, and I was in the mood for some good music and some great food.

Keith

"Damn baby... you look so sexy. Not sure I'll be able to keep my eyes, or my hands, off of you all night." Was I imagining shit, or was my mouth watering at the sight of her?

Sam

I was wearing a black lace belted dress that hugged my modest curves. It had a nude lining under it, which made it look like I had nothing on underneath. The shoulder straps were thin, and my

Giuseppe Zanotti black sandals were four inches high with black lace on the satin material across my toe area.

"And I don't want you to keep your eyes or your hands off of me. So don't you dare try." I went over to him, grabbed him by his tie and kissed his lips. "But we've gotta go if we want to get to the club at a decent time."

Once we arrived, Keith pulled up to the front door where valet was stationed. He exited the driver's side to open my car door. He then took my hand and escorted me into the club. It was live up in there. Nice ambiance, lights weren't too dim, but weren't overly bright. Beautiful people everywhere. Sexy voluptuous ladies and fine ass men, who I'm sure had big bank as well as big dicks of all shapes and sizes. Keith seemed to know quite a few people there. How did a guy who owned a project management company know *these* people? Some looked like bankers, others looked like gangsters. But one man in particular that Keith was talking to, caught my eye.

Keith

"Samantha, I'd like you to meet an associate of mine, Jerrick Houston. He owns a few businesses and specializes in sales. Jerrick, this is my lady, Sam."

Sam

"Nice to meet you, Jerrick." As I took his hand in mine.

Keith's friend, Jerrick

"Likewise. My friends call me Benny. Jerrick is my father's name." Damn she was fine. I was hoping she wasn't here with anyone, but she just had to be fucking Don's brother. Damn. I guess that's out.

Sam

"Okay, Bennie. Would you like to be my friend?" I said as I licked my red stained lips. By this time, Keith was talking with someone else, so I'm sure he didn't hear my question. Benny was a tall, slender baby-faced man. But behind that innocence, I felt it in my bones that he was hardcore. He was chocolate, had a low cut, and dark brown eyes with curly lashes. He was beautiful, and he was swagged out to the max.

Benny

"Yeah, I wouldn't mind a friend that looks like you." As I licked my lips in return. This couldn't be his lady, the way she just winked her pussy at me. I guess we'll see though. "I'm sure I'll see you around, Sam. Have a good night."

Sam

"Yes, yes you will." I planned on seeing him again very soon.

Aubrey

"Why won't this baby come out already? Mommy, tell them to take him out NOW!" My contractions started as soon as I walked into the hospital. I wasn't prepared for this pain. At this point, fuck this birth plan. "Give me the epidural. I want it, please. Give me the epidural. Mommy, please! Make them give it to me!" I started to cry, I was in so much pain.

Dee Dee

"Baby, it's already too late for the epidural. You're at eight centimeters, you have to just let the birthing process flow." I said as I patted her face with a cold damp rag to cool her off. I felt so bad for my baby, but she originally told them that she didn't want the meds. She wanted to have the baby naturally. "Nurse, is there anything you can give her? She's been at eight centimeters for almost three hours."

Nurse

"I'm sorry ma'am, it's already too late. The doctor will be in shortly to assess the situation. My apologies." She said so nonchalantly.

Aubrey

"Mommy, can you pass me some more ice chips please?" After she gave me some ice, the nurse walked back in to ask my mother if she could speak with her privately. I didn't have the strength to panic. They walked out into the hallway after my mom ensured I was okay.

Dee Dee

"Is there something wrong with my baby? Tell me! What's wrong with my baby?" I knew I wasn't allowing her to speak, but why was she taking so long to get to the point? At that point, I heard Aubrey scream out in pain yet again.

Aubrey

I felt another contraction coming on and I gripped the sides of the little bed that I was in. "Nnnnnnnnnngggggggggggaaaaahhhhhhhh!!" I was sweating so much and I was so thirsty. "Mommy, ice chips, please!" I screeched.

Dee Dee

"One second nurse. Here Aubrey. I'm not going anywhere baby, I'm just gonna step into the hallway really fast. I'll be right back." I stepped out into the hallway in front of Aubrey's room, but she wanted me to come into a room across the hall. I followed her,

"What is this about? I have to get back to my daughter." I said as I folded my arms across my chest.

Nurse

"Ma'am, there has been an incident. A gunman came into the hospital and started shooting blindly. No one died, but your husband was among the people shot. He's being wheeled into surgery with a shattered clavicle as we speak, but he's expected to make a full recovery."

Dee Dee

I just realized he still hadn't returned from meeting Monroe in the lobby. "Why weren't there any alarms going off? Are we safe in this unit of the hospital? What floor is my husband on? When can I see him? What happened to the gunman?" What am I going to tell Aubrey?

Nurse

"The gunman is no longer here. He was taken away, maybe apprehended. Your husband is going to be placed in recovery on the fourth floor once he is out of surgery. That's all the information that I have, but I will ensure that you're updated. I'm so sorry."

Dee Dee

When I went back into Aubrey's room, I knew she was going to ask about what the nurse and I spoke about. I never lied to Aubrey before, but in her condition, she was under enough stress. "Mike slipped and fell. He hurt his shoulder so he's being seen for that. He's fine and should be out soon."

Aubrey

"Well damn, Mike is supposed to be here to cut his grandson's cord." That was the part of my birth plan that I still was interested in, unfortunately.

Monroe

"I'm here to cut my son's cord." I said as I walked into her hospital room. I had just finished getting my arm bandaged. That nigga Rob can't shoot for shit, but he'll get dealt with. This time for good.

Aubrey

"What are you doing here, Monroe?" I turned my attention to my mother. "Mom? Did you call him? Why would you do that knowing how I feel right now?" I felt betrayed and I started to cry.

Monroe

"Mike called me. Which is what you should have done. Why would you deliberately keep this from me Aubrey? I've done nothing but respect your wishes, I would have continued to do so. This is something that I should have been able to experience as well. He's my son... and my first child." I said I wouldn't get angry, but I couldn't help it. She was acting like I hurt her or something.

Aubrey

"I cannot discuss this right now with you, Monroe." He started to object, but at that very moment, another contraction felt like it was searing through me. "Ahhhhhhhhhhh, gggaaaaaahhhh! NURSE! Please check me again, it feels like I have to push right now."

Monroe

I went over to the side table and wet a cloth and placed it on her forehead. The nurse seemed to be moving way too slow for me. "Nurse, please call the doctor, she said she's experiencing pressure that feels different from the pain she was already having." Her mom gave her more ice chips and was rubbing ice along her neck and chest. When the doctor entered the room, he washed his hands and sat between Aubrey's legs.

Doctor

"She's crowning, let's get this show on the road, shall we? Now, Ms. Collins, I'm going to need for you to push only when I tell you to. It is very important that you do not push any other time. Understood?"

Monroe

Aubrey shook her head yes. It was eleven forty-nine pm, so maybe my son would share my birthday with me. Aubrey probably didn't know that, but my son did. That's my little champ already. I couldn't wait to see him.

Doctor

"Grandma, dad, I'll need your help for this next phase. She's going to need to focus on her breathing and we'll probably need to help with pushing her knees as far back as she can. Ok Aubrey, I see that your next contraction is about to start, you'll need to start pushing on the count of three. One, two, three… push!"

Monroe

"Come on Aubrey, you got this. Push, baby!" My son seemed like he wasn't budging at first, but you better believe, that as soon as that clock struck twelve, his head was out! After the doctor was doing whatever it was that he was doing down there, it only took a few more minutes for the baby to be out completely. "Aubrey you did so well baby." I kissed her on her forehead, and I felt her hand touch my face. I expected her to slap me, but in that moment, I think she was grateful that I was there.

Dee Dee

"Look at my grand baby! He's so beautiful! Baby you did great!" I looked back and she was hugging Monroe with tears streaming down her face. It was absolutely beautiful! And guess who had their camera ready! I captured the moment of their first kiss, their first embrace since her accident. And the first few moments as parents to this beautiful little boy.

Doctor

"Dad, are you ready to cut the cord?"

Monroe

At the moment, I didn't want to break away from my embrace with Aubrey, but it was time to meet our son. "Yes sir, I am." They placed my son onto Aubrey's chest while I cut the cord. Mrs. Roberson was just snapping away with her camera. We were just all so overcome with joy! My son weighed eight pounds, eleven ounces and he was twenty-two inches long. He is huge! And he looks just like me. It's crazy, Aubrey carried my little man and he looks just like me. After I cut the cord, they weighed him and cleaned him off.

Aubrey

"Happy birthday, Monroe. I love you."

Chapter 2

Free

I dropped Tamia off with Crystyle, so that I could go to the hospital. James was injured in a shooting at Southern Maryland and that was all the information they would give me over the phone as his next of kin. I raced there; I didn't care about police pulling me over. It was almost midnight and I needed to get to my husband. This year couldn't end fast enough. With the kidnapping, the baby's health scare and now this? It was time for 2017 to get the fuck on!

I parked my car, grabbed my purse and ran to the information desk. "Hello, my husband was shot here tonight. James Casey, I'm his wife, Fresia Casey. Can you tell me his status? Is he okay? Can I see him please?" I was so worried, and this bitch was the least bit accommodating.

Receptionist

"Ma'am, may I see your identification please?" She asked Free.

Free

I handed her my driver's license and she handed it back. She ruffled through some files until she came across the one she was looking for. She told me the floor he was on and pointed to the elevators. I took it up to the fourth floor where I came to another desk and realized that I was probably going to have to repeat the same procedure again. So, I gave them my driver's license to start with, told them my name and who I was there to see.

Receptionist #2

"Yes ma'am, your husband is in recovery and is a little sedated. He was shot in his right side flank, but the doctors were able to stitch him back up. You're welcome to go and sit with him, he's in room four twelve.

Free

"Thank you." I walked quickly until I got his room. He looked like he was sleeping, so I just sat beside him and held his hand. He opened his eyes once he felt my hand on his and I hugged him. "Hi baby. I was so scared. Are you alright? What happened?" Tears poured down my face.

James

I didn't dare to bring up that nigga's name to my wife. She was finally able to get rid of her nightmares and live normally again. "Hey my love, I'm ok. It was just a random fool from what I understand that just started shooting in the lobby. No one died though. They're just monitoring me for now, since a bullet grazed me on the side. They had to stitch me up, but I'll be okay. I should be going home shortly. Sorry I couldn't call you myself. I left my phone in the car, for obvious reasons." We never have our phones on us when we're handling business, and that's why thought I was here. "Money's old girl, Aubrey, was in labor with their baby. That was what we found out from her step-dad when we got here."

Free

Hmmm, I wonder why she didn't tell him before. I know she lost her memory, but did she think it was someone else's baby? I know she's not like that, or at least not while she was in college. "That's a good reason to be at a hospital, but I wonder why some crazy person would just start shooting up the place. Anyway, do you think it would be a good idea for me to apologize to her again while she's here? I really want to make amends with her, even if she doesn't want to resume a friendship."

James

"Baby I think that's a great idea. Especially since Money and I are so tight. Why don't we head down there together once I'm released? Or maybe we can come back during the day once she's had some rest. I'm hoping she had the baby by now, because we got here around eight o'clock."

Free

"Sounds like a plan, but for now, you need to get some rest too. Did you need anything? You thirsty? Hungry?" He declined, but he squeezed my hand and then drifted off to sleep again. I decided to find me something to munch on. I knew there had to be a vending machine around here somewhere. I ran into Mrs. Dee Dee and she looked at me as if she recognized me, but didn't, which is understandable since she hadn't seen me in a long time.

"Hello Mrs. Dee Dee, it me… Fresia." Once I said that, she came to me and hugged me. I was so relieved that there was no bad blood between us. I knew that she knew about what happened between me and Aubrey over Rob.

Dee Dee

"Free, you are looking good girl! I see you with the snap back. Aubrey told me you were pregnant the last time she saw you. And please don't be embarrassed. Life is too short for all of that and I've damn sure made my share of mistakes. I just hope after tonight, they put his ass under the jail."

Free

"Put who under the jail, Mrs. Dee Dee?" I'm confused at this point because I knew she was referring to Rob. But what did he have to do without tonight? I didn't get it. James didn't come out and say it, but I believed Rob was dead.

Dee Dee

"Robert's crazy ass. Why he would come in here shooting everywhere like that is beyond me. My husband just got out of surgery behind that mess. He's alright, Monroe is too. How's your husband? He's on this floor as well, right?" Free looked as if she saw a ghost, and I looked in the direction she was staring in as well. "Free, are you alright honey? Come on, let's sit down sweetie. Can I get some help over here?" I yelled to whatever hospital staff was near me.

Free

I can't believe James would deliberately lie to my face that way. He told me they took care of his ass months ago. How was that true when he came in here and shot at them? What the fuck? "I'm alright, but did you say that Rob was here? And shot them tonight? I thought he was dead! Are you sure it was him? How did he find them here?" I feel like I've lost my security blanket. I now know that I can't trust my own damn husband. "I gotta get out of here. I'm sorry Mrs. Dee Dee." She kept asking me if I was alright and wanted me to sit down and speak with her, but I had to get out of there. I ran back to my car with all my might so that I could go get my baby and figure out my next move.

Taisha

"You like that daddy? You like the way that pussy looks, huh?" I bent over in front of my newest customer and clapped my ass as he inserted as many fingers as he could up inside of me. He was stroking his dick as I danced for him, and hopefully I could make him nut even faster now that he's already gotten started.

Trick

"Alright little mama, turn around and get on your knees. I want you to suck this dick."

Taisha

"Okay now, do you need a run-down of my rates? To get your dick sucked, it's one hundred and fifty dollars. For me to top you off, it's two-fifty. So what do you want me to do for you baby?" I slurred.

Trick

"I want just like last time, top that shit off baby."

Taisha

I did just as he instructed. But how did I not remember doing this for him before? I deep throated his dick, letting it continually hit my tonsils while I kept it real wet for him. My mouth and my hand were in perfect sync with one another.

Trick

"No hands ma, ooohhhh, you about to make me cum all down your throat. Spit on it, bitch, make it real nasty for me."

Taisha

I ignored him, if I stopped to do all that, it would prolong his nut. I removed my hand, let my head go all the way to the base of his dick and kept repeating that motion. I'm so glad I have no gag reflex. About a minute later, I felt his warmth threatening to suffocate me as it coated my throat. I jacked his dick off to get the remainder out as I spit that shit out beside him. I grabbed my towel and wiped my hand and mouth off once I was done. Then I held out my hand.

Trick

"Come on Tai, how about I give you some of that good shit instead?" He asked, trying to play me.

Taisha

He then removed some heroin from his pocket and was trying to give it to me. "If that's what you wanna do, at least give me the equivalent of two-fifty. This ain't even a hundred dollars' worth. He shook his head while laughing and gave me the drugs and two hundred dollars cash. I was cool with that. He pulled his pants back up and left while I went and got ready for my next one.

Travis

"Mami, where's the money? You ready to please my next friend? You looking real good today mami. *Tu Culo esta bien gordo.* That ass is phat baby. *Tengo que meterme dentro de ti.* I gotta get in them guts tonight."

Taisha

"I got a hundred dollars for you baby. And yeah, I can't wait for you to fuck me again." I lied. Travis' dick only felt good when I was high because I ain't know no better. But I didn't mind. As long as he kept me high. And he let me keep half of the money I made. I knew he was dogging me out but fuck this life. I still belonged to Don, so I just didn't care anymore.

Travis

"Sí, sí... check it mami, Curt from the club is here. He told me that he was looking forward to seeing you. I want you to do him right, he's gonna pay five hundred *dólares* for the '*especial*'. He said you know what that is?"

Taisha

"Yeah, I remember what the fat nigga likes. Lemme just wash the last nigga off my face; he was sloppy. But stay close. Curt may try something on some get back shit. And I need a hit papi. Can you do that for me, *por favor* papi?" He agreed and went and got his kit. I brushed my teeth and washed my face. Once he came back, I tied myself off and he located the big vein for me and injected it for me. I could never find the big vein myself, so I loved him for that shit. "Ah yes papi! Mmmmmmm, this is soooo damn good. Mmmmmm."

Travis

"Mami, no nodding off. I need you to perform for this money. This fat ass negro looks like he cum *en un minuto!*"

Taisha

Travis laughed, but that nigga Curt was sitting on a schlong! And he wanted way too much all the time. I'm just glad they prearranged the amount. I went into the room where I would fuck him. I started putting oil all over myself like I remembered. He walked in the room and he looked different for some reason. "Hey Curt, what's popping daddy?"

Curt

"Bbbbb-bitch I ain't been the same ssss-since you pulled that ssss-shit the last time. But when I heard you was tricking ffff-for money I knew I was gonna come out here to ssss-see your ass. You fell off a lot huh? I can tell ffff-from the track marks that Travis added you to his ssss-stable. Come on over here and get this party ssss-started, bbbb-bitch. You know what I like."

Taisha

I knew he was only trying to make me feel bad about what I was doing, but I was way past that point months ago. I was halfway hoping he brought a gun in here and just blew my brains out to get me back.

Instead of fucking my pussy, because he said it was too "dirty" now, he pushed my head down on his dick while he wrapped my ponytail around his fat ass hands and fucked my throat, hard. It took him a while to nut and once he did, he held my head in place. I couldn't breathe, I couldn't move, and I was trying my best to get away from him.

Curt

"You bbbb-bite me bitch, and I'm gonna blow your muthafuckin head off. Take that nnnn-nut and swallow all of it. Don't let not a dddd-drop come out your filthy ass mouth, hoe."

Taisha

Yep, I brought this shit on myself. I almost passed out, until I felt him take his hand outta my hair. I then proceeded to choke as the tears fell from my eyes. I tried catching my breath as I gagged and coughed until my airway was clear enough to breathe deeply.

Curt

"I'll ssss-see you next week hoe. Make sure you rrrr-ready for me."

Taisha

And he threw the money at me while I was still trying to catch my breath on the floor.

ABOUT THE AUTHOR

Troii Devereaux was born and raised in Washington, DC. Her passion for fiction writing flourished in middle school, when her eighth-grade teacher encouraged her to read one of her creative writing assignments to her homeroom class, and the other eighth grade classes as well.

After a 20-year military career, Troii decided to make her passion for writing a full-time endeavor. When she is not working on a new book, she spends time with her husband, family and friends. Her hobbies are reading, writing, traveling and continuing to find inspiration for novel ideas to share with her fan base.

Previous releases:

Never Be Anotha: Resentment, Book 1 (May 2019)